POT LUCK

POT LUCK
A Western Quintet

Bennett Foster

SAGEBRUSH
Large Print Westerns

First published in Great Britain by ISIS Publishing Ltd
First published in the United States by Five Star

Published in Large Print 2008 by ISIS Publishing Ltd.,
7 Centremead, Osney Mead, Oxford OX2 0ES
United Kingdom
by arrangement with
Golden West Literary Agency

British Library Cataloguing in Publication Data
Foster, Bennett
    Pot luck. – Large print ed. –
    (Sagebrush western series)
    1. Western stories
    2. Large type books
    I. Title
    813.5'2 [FS]

ISBN 978–0–7531–8005–1 (hb)

Printed and bound in Great Britain by
T. J. International Ltd., Padstow, Cornwall

Table of Contents

The Man Who Broke the Bank at Gila City

Bennett Foster wrote seven stories about the denizens of Gila City, including the best-dressed gambler Bob Roberts and Old Man Duggan, a self-proclaimed Indian fighter as well as the town drunk. Six of these stories were collected in *Gila City* (Five Star Westerns, 2003). "The Man Who Broke the Bank at Gila City" was the seventh and last of these stories, originally appearing in *New Western* (7/48).

CHAPTER
ONE

Trouble comes from little things. The sun may be brightly shining, the soft wind blowing, the larks singing, and all well with the world; then a little cloud about the size of a man's hat appears and the rain falls straight down. In Gila City trouble was precipitated when Mrs. Luella Mae Fitzhenry black-balled the Widow Fennessy as a member of the literary society. Subsequent events made hell look like a burned-out Roman candle.

"The widdy," Old Man Duggan later said, "bowed her neck an' went to pawin' an' bellerin'. She throwed dust over both shoulders an' she had a horn drooped for trouble." Dandy Bob Roberts, as usual, had no comment, although he played a major part in the affair.

The Fitzhenrys — Luella Mae and Sholto — made a much-heralded arrival in Gila City. They came from Phoenix, where Sholto had run a bank, rented a house on the hill where lived Gila City's elite, and Sholto Fitzhenry, gray-haired, impressive and portly, visited the merchants, the mine owners, and others of wealth.

Luella Mae, working the other side of the street, as it were, forgathered with the wives of said merchants, mine owners, and others. From these endeavors arose two institutions. The men, with Fitzhenry as leader and promoter, subscribed stock, secured a charter, and organized a bank. The women, meeting with Luella Mae, formed the Gila City Literary Society.

Two prosperous citizens, the Widow Violet Fennessy and Dandy Bob Roberts, were excluded from the organizations. In the instance of the bank, the fly in the ointment was Old Man Duggan.

"I don't think," Jim Frazee, the postmaster, said, "we ought to ask Missus Fennessy or Dandy Bob Roberts to take stock. The widow's goin' to marry Duggan, an' Dandy Bob is Duggan's partner. If we take them in, we got to take Duggan, too, an' I don't want that lyin' old sot around any bank I'm connected with." To this statement the stockholders concurred.

It was otherwise with the ladies. Violet Fennessy's name was proposed by Mrs. Watson, the assayer's wife. "She owns the Limerick Girl Mine," said Mrs. Watson, "and she's wealthy. She could help out on the finance committee."

Luella Mae fixed Mrs. Watson with a clammy eye. "Really, my dear," she drawled, "I don't believe we should lower the tone of our little group, do you? I haven't met Missus Fennessy socially, of course, but we all know she has *that woman* living with her." At this point the meeting took time out for thirty minutes of scandal.

To understand Mrs. Fitzhenry's reference it is necessary to go back to an earlier date. Violet Fennessy did indeed have a house guest and it was quite logical for the ladies to refer to her as "*that woman*". Her name was Alice Moore and she came to the widow under unusual circumstances.

Gila City was not without reverence for the arts. Bill Fay operated the Gila City Opera House and internationally known *artistes* were sometimes imported from distant points to display their gifts. As a rule, however, Gila City audiences preferred less ethereal and fleshier talent, something like "Delehenty's Variety Show, Girls! Girls! Girls!" and it was from this very aggregation that the widow collected her guest.

The play came up shortly after midnight when members of the troupe were returning from the theater to the New York Hotel. Their way led past the widow's cottage, and, immediately in front of the cottage, Delehenty and his principal male comic undertook to settle an argument of long standing.

Eight shots were fired, one of which placed a period to Delehenty's career, a second broke the widow's parlor window, and a third accidentally found lodgment in Alice Moore, doing her no good. Dandy Bob Roberts, Old Man Duggan, and Violet Fennessy had been to the show and the men had taken the widow home. They were in her parlor when the altercation took place. Duggan dodged behind the widow when the shots were fired, while Dandy Bob went boiling out the door. Poor light and a stolen horse saved the comic, and Bob returned, holstering his gun, to find the widow and Duggan bending over the girl.

"That 'un's dead," Duggan announced with a casual nod toward Delehenty. "This one ain't, though. I guess I'd better take her in." He stooped to lift the girl.

5

"Ye will not!" the widow announced, noting the charms a disordered dress displayed. "Ye'd like nawthin' better. I'll take her in meself. Hold the light, Duggan. Bob, run for the doctor."

Duggan took the lamp, Dandy Bob departed, and the widow bent and lifted. When Dandy Bob returned with Dr. Speers, the widow had Alice in bed and was crooning over her.

"I'll not have it!" she declared when Doc Speers suggested that the girl be moved to the hotel. "Trust her to thim actors? No, indeed! I'll keep her here. Now, pretty, you lie still whilst the doctor fixes ye. Be easy, Doc. If ye hurt her, I'll have yer hide."

The widow's heart was as big as her shoulders were broad, and Alice Moore had won it in brief moments. So, while Delehenty's troop dispersed and went its way, the *ingénue* of said troupe remained at Violet Fennessy's cottage, gravely ill at first, and then gradually recuperating. To that cottage the men of Gila City beat a path.

The girl was beautiful. Wan from her illness, she held court in the widow's parlor, resting on the lounge. Her black hair, spread upon a snowy pillow, framed her pale, heart-shaped face. Her voice was sweet with a husky lowness, her eyes were blue as Irish skies, her lips, aided a little, perhaps, from her make-up box, were full and red.

Doc Speers called daily, long after his services were no longer necessary; Jim Frazee, the postmaster, delivered mail in person; Sol Finebaum came up from his store with a box of candy that he said the widow had bought but forgotten; Grady, who owned the Mint Saloon, brought wine for the convalescent; Watson, the assayer, came with a report on the Limerick Girl's ore.

All the single bucks and most of the married men came, but of all who called at Violet Fennessy's, Joe Glennen, editor of the *Gila City Herald*, was the most frequent and persistent.

"Sure," said the widow fondly, "it reminds me of whin I was a gurl meself, it does so. I was always the wan to have the men buzzin' around like bees. Ain't she the pretty thing now?" The widow smiled at Alice Moore. "Duggan, if ye so much as look at her, I'll give ye the back of me hand."

So Alice Moore, her past unknown and her future unpredictable, remained with Violet Fennessy while the bank was organized and the Literary Society formed.

When the widow learned of this later, and of her own failure to be included in the membership, her eyes clouded and her brow furrowed. When she discovered the purported cause, the widow clenched her big red fists.

"So," she snarled, "they say *that* about her, do they? I'll have ye know Alice is a decent gurl, she is. I'm goin' to keep her here. Sure, I've money enough for us both an' as for that high-toned Jezebel from Phoenix . . ." What the widow said about Luella Mae scorched the neatly starched and ironed curtains of the parlor. "I'll show her," the widow concluded. "Just give me time to think."

For a day or two she cogitated, and then summoned Dandy Bob. "Bob," the widow announced, "I'm goin' to give a party. Ye'll haul out what I need from Tucson, the next trip ye make. An' I want every man an' his wife in town to come. I want ye to see that they come."

Dandy Bob Roberts, tall and dark and saturnine cynical, felt that he was, in a way, responsible for Violet Fennessy. It was he who had discovered the lost vein in the Limerick Girl, he who had kept the mine safe for the widow when men had sought to steal it. Not that Bob had done these things from goodness of heart or greatness of spirit. In each instance Dandy Bob Roberts was trying to feather his own nest, but he felt responsible, nevertheless.

Moreover, he was at the moment engaged in a very lucrative business deal involving the Limerick Girl Mine. Through timidity on the part of certain individuals during a recent Apache outbreak, good straight shooting, and a lot of luck, Dandy Bob Roberts and Duggan had come into possession of a freighting outfit. Their wagons hauled ore from the Limerick Girl to the stamp mill in Gila City, and the widow could, if she wished, end this contract.

"Duggan," said Dandy Bob, "is goin' to Tucson tomorrow. We're goin' to haul the safe for the new bank. Give him your list. I don't know about the party, but I'll look around."

So next morning, armed with a shopping list and admonished by both his partner and his affianced, Old Man Duggan pulled out for Tucson, and, while he was gone, Dandy Bob Roberts made some overtures and some inquiries.

"Don't give your party," he reported back to Violet Fennessy. "They won't come. The men would like to, but their wives won't let 'em."

"Ye could make 'em," suggested the widow. "Bob, if ye put the pressure on, they'd —"

Bob waved a weary hand. "They're more afraid of their wives than they are of me," he said. "As long as Alice is here —" He stopped short, interrupted by a gasp. Alice Moore was at the door of the kitchen where Bob and the widow talked. Her face was more pallid than it should have been, and her blue eyes were wide.

"Now look what ye done!" the widow chided. "Ye've upset the child. Here, darlin', come back to bed now. Ye've no business bein' on yer feet."

The widow led her charge away, and Dandy Bob Roberts, alone in the kitchen, thoughtfully ate a chunk of gingerbread. Like every other male in Gila City, Bob Roberts was in love with Alice Moore. Also, Bob felt that he had been slighted when he was not invited to buy stock in the bank.

Reaching out for another piece of gingerbread, Dandy Bob Roberts sat down to think things out. It would be fine to help the widow and Alice; it would be good to take a fall out of the high and mighty Sholto Fitzhenry and show Gila City that Bob Roberts was necessary to a bank or any other enterprise. And — Bob's eyes narrowed — banks contained money. Maybe there was a way to get a little of it.

CHAPTER
TWO

Old Man Duggan's trip to Tucson was backed by a definite reason. Bob Roberts was negotiating for the purchase of the Star Livery barn and feed yard and he wanted Duggan out of the way. The old man lied, he talked, he bragged in the wrong places, and he got drunk. Bob, knowing thoroughly the havoc Duggan could cause, heaved a sigh of relief when the old man departed.

To secure the money, it was necessary that Bob mortgage both his own outfit and also the one he was acquiring. Deeds were drawn and mortgages made. Bob was lost in a maze of legal verbiage in which the words, "for and in consideration of one dollar and other good and valuable considerations", occurred again and again. From this maze he emerged, possessor of all Gila City's livery and hauling equipment and with the knowledge that he couldn't keep it unless he paid the new bank eight percent on a considerable amount of money.

Duggan, *en route* to Tucson, did not wonder why he had been sent. Duggan was accustomed to being ridden with a tight rein. When the bridle was pulled off, far be it from Duggan to ask why.

To do the old man justice, he did not take too great advantage of his freedom. Duggan's weakness was not cards or women, but liquor. He kept this in abeyance, drinking no more than a quart a day to stimulate his imagination.

While the teamsters, roustabouts, and warehouse men toiled to reinforce the wagon box and load the massive safe, Duggan kept out of the sun and bragged on Gila City. He found, naturally, that saloons gave the best shelter and offered the most willing listeners. In his way, Duggan performed the function of the modern Chamber of Commerce.

"Bank?" said Duggan to his audience. "Sure, we got a bank. An' lemme tell you, that safe ain't nowhere big enough. Sure, it's the biggest in the territory, but it's too damned little." He paused, hiccoughed. "That safe," he resumed, "is just to hold the small change. We dug a mine shaft a hundred feet deep an' put in a steel door to hold the real money. Why, say . . ."

At this point two of Duggan's listeners withdrew. One was the male comic of Delehenty's Variety Show and the other was a rock-faced man with powder pits liberally besprinkling his countenance. "Do you suppose that old coot's telling the truth?" the pitted man demanded.

Kerr Joslin, the comic, shook his head. "I was in Gila City, remember?" he answered. "That's where I downed Delehenty, damn him, and my wife's still there. That old fool's lyin', Spike."

Spike licked his lips and looked at the safe, standing on cribwork and ready to be put on the wagon. "If he was tellin' the truth," said Spike, "we could take every dime of it. Take a little nitro and I can open that old box as easy as I'd take the lid off a can of sardines."

"You could?" Joslin's eyebrows shot upward.

"Sure." Scornfully.

Joslin rolled and lighted a cigarette and squinted through the smoke. "I don't think," he said slowly, "anybody in Gila City would know me if I made up a little. Let's go down there, Spike. That damned wife of mine. I want to get her back with me, and, if you can open that safe as easy as you say, there's no reason not to do it."

"Let's go," said Spike. "I'm ready just any time."

Old Man Duggan and the admiring audience came from the saloon. "There she is, boys," said Old Man Duggan. "Biggest safe in the territory for the biggest little town. An' who hauls her? Duggan and Roberts, that's who. Best freighters a-goin'."

By noon the next day the safe was loaded and Buckshot Sever, the wagon master — five times indicted, but never convicted of murder — decreed a start. Old Man Duggan rode in the wagon with the safe. His shopping was all done, the Widow Fennessy's goods were loaded in the following wagons, along with miscellaneous supplies such as dynamite, fuse, and caps.

Duggan, accompanied by a quart of Chapman & Gore, reclined and refreshed himself. In his hatband was a sealed envelope containing instructions and the combination of the safe. Halfway down the quart,

Duggan took off his hat and found that sweat had loosened the mucilage of the envelope.

"*Hmm*," said Duggan. "Le's see."

Duggan could hardly read or write, but he could match figures. He knew the envelope contained the combination for he had been so informed. It was natural that he should remove the sheet of paper from the envelope and equally natural that he should try the combination. He missed a time or two, but, with a perseverance worthy of a better cause, tried and tried again.

Presently the safe door opened. Duggan, amazed and pleased with his prowess, closed it and repeated the process. By nightfall, when the wagons camped, he could open the safe every time; by the next night he could open it without referring to the combination in the envelope, and at noon on the third day, when the wagons swung into Gila City, Old Man Duggan could just about open the bank's new safe by sense of touch.

Dandy Bob Roberts was on hand to see the safe unloaded. To Dandy Bob, Duggan gave the resealed envelope, not mentioning his new accomplishment. Bob delivered the envelope to Sholto Fitzhenry and began the unloading, and Duggan, utterly worn out by his labors, took a drink at the Rajah Saloon.

From there he repaired to the adobe he shared with his partner, noting as he unlocked the place that someone had moved into the house next door. His curiosity was aroused but he held it down, peeled off his clothes, and took a nap. At six o'clock when Dandy

Bob, hot and tired, came to clean up for supper, Duggan roused.

"Get her unloaded?" he inquired.

"Got her in the building and set," Bob answered. "Why didn't you stay an' help?"

"I loaded her at Tucson," Duggan answered. "It was up to you to unload her. I didn't have no help. Who is livin' next door, Bob?"

"Fellow named Smith an' a man named Spike," Bob answered, groping for a towel to dry his face. "Spike's a hard-lookin' jasper. His face looks like he's been in an explosion. I've seen Smith somewheres, but I can't place him." Bob rehung the towel. "Duggan, I bought the Star Livery while you were gone. Gave the bank a mortgage on it an' on our outfit for the money. OK?"

Old Man Duggan's eyes widened. At one time Duggan had been a hostler at the Star Livery barn. "You bought it?" Duggan exclaimed, and then as the full impact came home to him: "You an' me own the Star Livery! Wait till I tell the widdy."

Old Man Duggan, without hat or coat, went flying out the door.

Grinning, Dandy Bob finished his dressing, then, taking the old man's neglected garments, followed him.

Duggan and the widow were in the Fennessy kitchen, the widow having relegated the parlor to Alice Moore and Joe Glennen. Violet Fennessy had not seen Bob since the purchase of the Star Livery, but the news was spread all over town and she had not been surprised at Duggan's announcement. But she was a little angry with Dandy Bob.

14

"Why didn't you come to me for the money, instead of borryin' from the bank?" the widow demanded.

Bob had not gone to the widow for good and definite reasons. Although Violet Fennessy was engaged to Duggan, she had not given up angling for a more suitable mate. Dandy Bob Roberts was on her list of prospects, and he had no desire to be indebted to the widow.

"Just tryin' to help the bank get started," Bob replied. "Anyhow, it's good business. All the directors need to have haulin' done an' they'll throw it our way now because we owe 'em money."

The widow sniffed, unsatisfied. She had an idea of Bob's real reasoning.

"An'," said Bob, "it wouldn't look right. Folks would say we was takin' advantage of you, because you an' Duggan are goin' to get married. They'd say he was marryin' you for your money."

Duggan *was* marrying Violet for her money. The attractions of the Limerick Girl far outweighed those of the mine's owner in Duggan's estimation. The widow opened her mouth to speak, closed it again with a snap. Sounds came from the parlor, then the front door banged.

"Now what do ye suppose is wrong?" the widow demanded. She hurried out of the kitchen.

Dandy Bob and Duggan waited a seemly time. They were about to go when the widow returned. "That Joe Glennen!" she said. "He asked Alice to marry him."

"What's wrong with that?" Duggan demanded.

"I dunno, but somethin'." The widow's face was wrathful. "Alice is cryin'. You two git. I don't want to be bothered with ye."

Bob and Duggan got, both filled with curiosity. In the Rajah Saloon they found Glennen drinking moodily and alone. "What's wrong, Joe?" Duggan asked, sidling up beside the young editor.

Glennen favored the old man with a long look. "None of your damned business!" he snapped, then downed his drink and left.

For the next few weeks things were pretty dark around the Fennessy cottage. Old Man Duggan, visiting his affianced, ran into trouble with every call. The widow's temper was black as Satan's. Alice moped about the house, helping her benefactress with the housework but saying very little.

There was still plenty of callers but Joe Glennen was not among them. The widow's evil temper could be traced partly to that fact, partly to her companion's moodiness, and partly to her feud with Luella Mae Fitzhenry. Violet Fennessy had taken Dandy Bob's advice, and, while she had all the materials necessary for a party, she issued no invitations.

Luella was holding all the cards and the widow was not fool enough to go against a stacked deck. The Gila City Literary Society was meeting once a week and once each week Joe Glennen faithfully reported the meetings in the *Herald*.

"That Joe Glennen!" the widow snapped to Bob. "I don't blame Alice for not havin' him. But" — her voice

16

softened — "she's in love with him. I know that. Bob, ye've got to do somethin'."

Dandy Bob shook his head. It seemed to him that, whenever anything went wrong, the trouble was packed to his door and left there. It was always up to Bob Roberts.

So, inevitably, the end of the month approached with pay day for the mines and the stamp mill, with the monthly clean-up from the Silver Dollar and other money-makers. Shipments came in via Wells Fargo, small, heavily sealed packages to be deposited in the bank's big new safe. Just two days before the month's end, Sholto Fitzhenry met Bob Roberts on the street.

"How are you, Roberts?" he greeted. "How is the freighting business?"

"Pretty fair," said Dandy Bob. "I've made a couple of contracts that ought to pay off in a month or two."

"Ah." Sholto cleared his throat. "Speaking of payments . . . I suppose you have your interest ready?"

"Why," said Bob, surprised, "I don't pay interest until I pay the principal, an' that ain't due for pretty near a year."

Sholto Fitzhenry shook his head. "Your note calls for monthly payments," he said. "Better look it up, Roberts."

Fitzhenry proceeded on his way. Bob hurried to the office of the Star Livery and dug his copy of note and mortgage out of hiding. He read it over, read it over again, and swore. Dandy Bob Roberts had set into a crooked and unfamiliar game. Bedazzled by Fitzhenry and the bank's lawyer, Bob Roberts had agreed to pay interest at the rate of eight percent per month, not per year — *per month!*

"What's the matter, Bob?" Old Man Duggan queried, entering from the barn.

Bob Roberts, with profanity intermingled, told Duggan what the matter was.

"We can borry from the widdy," Duggan commented, undisturbed.

"I know we can, but I don't want to," Dandy Bob rasped. "An' this makes me sore. I was a damned fool, an' let 'em rook me. Why, eight percent a month will take every dime we make. We'll never pay off. The bank will get the whole outfit. Damn Fitzhenry anyhow!"

Duggan was still placid. "You let me study on it some," he said. "I'll figger somethin'. I allus thought you was smart, Bob, but it looks like the old man would have to pull you outen this one."

Duggan strolled out. It was seldom that Old Man Duggan found Dandy Bob in a jackpot; generally things worked the other way. The old man was even a little pleased. He bought a quart of Chapman & Gore at the Mint and, carrying it carefully, repaired to the adobe he occupied with Dandy Bob. When the whiskey had been uncorked and sampled, Old Man Duggan chuckled.

"Looks like," said Duggan to the unresponsive walls, "Bob's caught with his pants down. Sure does."

A knock sounded on the door, it opened at Duggan's call, and one of the next door neighbors thrust in his head. "Got a little bottle?" he queried. "I'd like to borrow one."

"Why, cer'nly," said Duggan. "Half pint be big enough?" Rising, he brought an empty bottle from among those in a corner of the room. The neighbor spoke his thanks and went away. Duggan mused a while longer. Then, with dusk settling, he left the adobe, *en route* to carry out his suggestion and borrow from the widow. But upon application, he found Violet Fennessy adamant.

"If," said Violet Fennessy, "Dandy Bob needs money, let *him* come an' ask me for it. I'll not lend you any, Duggan. Send Bob to talk to me." There was a gleam in the widow's eye.

So repulsed, Duggan went to the livery barn. Bob Roberts was not there, nor was he eating supper at the Elite Restaurant. Duggan went to the Mint and took three drinks which, coupled with the Chapman & Gore imbibed in the adobe, built him a fine edge. Bob was not at the Mint. Duggan went on to the Rajah. There was Bob, bucking the tiger and losing. Duggan tried to talk to Bob, but was ordered off. He took two more drinks and, with whiskey fuming in his brain, walked out.

It was fully dark now. The old man moped down the street, pausing by the bank building. The new adobe structure showed no lights. Duggan scowled at the bank and then, like a comet flashing across the sky, an idea struck him. Cautiously and craftily Duggan crossed the street.

The bank door was locked and he prowled around the building, finding a window in its rear. New adobe settles unevenly and the window frame was warped.

19

There was a small space between the bottom of the sash and the sill.

Duggan grunted and hurried away. When he returned, he carried an empty grain sack taken from the feed room of the Star Livery and an old wagon spoke acquired at the same source. The spoke made a pry, the window went up with a shrill squeal, and Duggan crouched to listen.

There was no alarm. Satisfied of that, the old man crawled over the sill into the dark interior. He moved by sense of touch now, and presently his fingers encountered the smooth iron of the safe. Duggan chuckled as he touched the combination knob and rubbed its rilled surface.

He brought a match from his pocket, struck it, and, in the light of yellow flame, turned the knob, right, then left, right, and left again. There was a faint *click*. Duggan seized the handle, turned it, pulled, and the safe door swung noiselessly open.

CHAPTER
THREE

When Duggan had departed, the Widow Fennessy waited for a while, thinking that Dandy Bob Roberts would appear. Bob did not come and the widow got ready for bed. In nightcap and gown she went to the door of Alice Moore's room and looked in. The girl was still dressed and sitting by the small table, writing.

"Sure now, darlin'," the widow chided, "it's time for bed. You shouldn't be sittin' up so late."

Alice left her chair and came to the widow, putting her arms around the older woman. "You've been so good to me," she murmured against the widow's cheek. "So good. Promise me that, no matter what happens, you won't think badly of me?"

"An' how could anywan think bad things about a sweet child like you?" The widow patted Alice's back. "Go to bed now and sleep good. Good night."

"Good bye," Alice said, and kissed the widow.

"Good bye?" Violet Fennessy drew back in surprise. "Ye mean good night, don't ye?"

"Good night, of course," Alice returned. "Yes, of course, I meant good night."

"Good night, then," said the widow, and padded off to her room. The girl waited. Presently the sounds of heavy breathing came from Violet Fennessy's bedroom.

Cautiously Alice Moore moved. There was a small grip under the bed. She pulled it out. Her coat was in the closet. She put it on. Then, blowing out the lamp, she tiptoed from the room, through the kitchen, and out of the house. She paused there to look back and brush her hand across her eyes.

"Good bye," she whispered. "Oh, good bye."

With the grip dangling, she slipped along the street, through the shadows, toward the edge of town.

There was a light in the adobe house next to Bob Roberts's place, and horses stamped in the shed behind it. Reaching the adobe, the girl knocked. The door opened and she entered.

Kerr Joslin grinned sardonically at her, and Spike, beside the table, grunted.

"So you came?" Joslin drawled. "That was smart, but then you were always a smart woman. If you hadn't, I would have come for you. You haven't met my wife, have you, Spike?"

"I don't like this," Spike said bluntly. "I told you before I didn't like it. There's no use hamperin' ourselves with a woman."

"But Alice won't hamper us," Joslin said. He was watching the girl narrowly, his eyes thin-slitted and evil. "Alice will do exactly as I tell her. You see, Spike, my wife loves me very much, don't you, Alice?"

"I hate you," the girl said flatly. "You know that. I'd kill you if I dared." She lowered the grip toward the table top.

"Don't set that down," Spike snapped. Carefully he reached out and picked up a half-pint whiskey bottle, half full of an oily, yellowish liquid. "Jar this an' you could blow us all to hell. This is nitro."

Joslin laughed. "She would like that," he said, "wouldn't you, my dear? But then, if I were to die, you'd never know what happened to the boy, would you? You'd never find him. Put down your grip now. It's safe enough."

The girl set down her grip.

"We'll visit a while," Joslin said. "We've plenty of time. Sit down. I think . . ." He paused to listen. A door banged shut, faintly. "Our friends next door have come home." Joslin grinned. "Now, Alice, you will stay here when Spike and I are gone. When we come back, we'll ride away from Gila City. And if we reach San Francisco safely, perhaps I'll tell you what you want to know. Perhaps."

Time hung heavily. Joslin smoked, looked at his watch, and rolled another cigarette. Spike took a bar of yellow soap and kneaded it in his heavy hands. That soap would be used to seal the safe door and to build a cup in which the nitroglycerine would be poured. Alice Moore sat quietly watching first one man, then the other.

"Time to go," Joslin stated, his voice tense. "All right, Spike?"

Spike grunted and put the soap in his pocket, picked up the half-pint whiskey bottle carefully and put it in another pocket, added fuse and caps. "OK," he said.

Joslin lifted a heavy wagon sheet and spoke to the girl. "We'll be back. Wait for us." He and Spike went out the door.

The girl waited. Time wore on endlessly. She moved to the door, opened it, listened, and then returned to her chair, leaving the door open. A dull, muffled cough sounded, more a concussion of air than a real noise.

There was quiet and then, faint and far off, shots pounded in the night, and then came sounds of yelling. The girl sprang up, facing the door, her eyes dark pools. She heard the pound of running feet. Spike burst through the door, confronting her, hastily emptying his pockets of caps, fuse, and the almost empty bottle of nitroglycerine.

"They got Joslin," he rasped. "I'm gone!" Wheeling from the table, he ran out of the little adobe, and within seconds a horse pounded away. Still Alice Moore stood, transfixed.

Again steps sounded and now the girl moved, darting toward the door — too late. The steps were close. She moved back into the room and Old Man Duggan, eyes bleared, whiskey heavy on his breath, came shambling in.

"Say," said Duggan, "I heard some kind of racket. Sounded like a shot in one of the mines. Woke me up. Say!" The old man's eyes widened and his jaw dropped.

24

He struggled with his surprise. "Alice!" Old Man Duggan rasped. "What are you doin' here?"

The girl did not answer. Seizing Duggan's arm, she pleaded with him. "Take me home, Duggan. Take me back to Missus Fennessy's and don't let anyone see us. Please. Please, Duggan!"

"Sure," said Duggan. "Come on."

With the girl still clinging to his arm, he moved toward the door. A half-pint whiskey bottle stood on the table, a small amount of liquid in it. Duggan, passing the table, reached out, picked up the bottle, and dropped it into the pocket of his coat. A man never could tell when he was going to need a drink.

Old man and girl went out into the night. They moved through shadows, staying in the gloom, circling the center of town where there were lights and excitement. By devious ways they came to the back of Violet Fennessy's cottage.

"There you are," Duggan said. "Back door's open. She never locks it. G' night."

"You won't tell?" the girl pleaded. "Promise me you won't tell?"

"Ain't nothin' to tell," Duggan assured, anxious to join the excitement. "G' night."

He was gone, and Alice Moore, her little grip hugged close, tiptoed across the widow's back porch, opened the door, and slipped into the kitchen.

"Is that you, Alice?" the widow's sleepy voice hailed. "Something woke me up."

"Something woke me, too," the girl answered. "I got up to get a drink. I'm going to bed now."

Old Man Duggan, leaving the cottage, hurried to town. The saloons were alight, and a crowd milled by the bank. As Duggan joined the crowd, Sholto Fitzhenry, with Watson and Jim Frazee, came from the building. "Clean," said Frazee. "The safe's cleaned out. Everything taken." Fitzhenry's massive head hung on his chest.

"What happened?" Duggan demanded.

"Bank was robbed. Two fellers blew the safe, an' one got away with the money." The answer came, terse and sharp.

"What about the other one?" Duggan asked after a moment.

"He's over there." Duggan's companion nodded. "Dandy Bob Roberts was goin' home an' happened to be passin' the bank. This feller took a shot at Bob, an' Bob fixed his clock."

Duggan pushed on through the crowd. Dandy Bob Roberts, Frank McMain, Gila City's deputy sheriff, and half a dozen others stood in a circle around a body. Looking at the upturned face, Duggan recognized the man who had wanted an empty bottle.

"No use standin' here," McMain said. "Let's get organized. These fellows had horses staked out, you can bet on it. We'll organize a posse an' make a swing around the town. Soon as it gets light, we'll trail him. Let's go. Bob, I want you an' Frazee an' . . . " McMain continued, naming the members of the posse, giving them their instructions.

26

Old Man Duggan left, headed toward the Star Livery barn. The posse would want horses, and the sheriff's office was always good pay. Duggan would rouse the night hostler and get the barn open. He was filled with civic virtue, was Old Man Duggan.

CHAPTER
FOUR

On the day following the bank robbery, Gila City seethed and bubbled. McMain and his posse, returning empty-handed, found the citizenry in an uproar. The posse men repaired to the Rajah, the Mint, and other emporiums to slake their thirsts and learn what was going on in town.

Plenty was going on. Everybody was disgruntled and mad. Payrolls were missing, there was no money in Gila City, and miners, millers, merchants — everyone — blamed the bank. If there had been no bank, this could not have happened.

Gila City's wealth would not have been centralized but spread out in pockets, in company safes, in buried tin cans, and elsewhere. Sholto Fitzhenry and the bank directors were not popular, even with themselves. They held a meeting to see what could be done and there was another meeting scheduled for the evening. As stockholders they were liable for the loss, and, if they paid off, every one of them would be broke.

"No," Dandy Bob Roberts told Jim Frazee in the Rajah, "we didn't find him. The wind wiped out his tracks. Looks like you boys are stuck, Jim. Take about all you can raise to put the bank on its feet, won't it?"

"Looks that way," Frazee agreed dispiritedly. "That fellow you shot, Bob. He lived next door to you, didn't he?"

"They both did," Dandy Bob agreed.

"We searched their place," Frazee said. "Didn't find a thing but some fuse and caps."

Dandy Bob put down his empty glass. "I'm kind of glad you didn't ask me to buy stock, Jim," he drawled. "So long. I'm goin' home an' clean up."

Duggan was in the adobe when Dandy Bob returned. The old man was prone on his bed, gazing cheerfully at the ceiling. Bob sniffed, estimated that Duggan was fairly sober, and took off his coat.

"You won't have to pay the bank now that they lost the mortgage, will you?" Duggan queried.

That feature hadn't occurred to Bob. He paused in his undressing. "I guess we're stuck, anyhow," he said. "They'll have the mortgage recorded in Tucson."

Duggan rolled over on the bed and an unfamiliar crackling sounded.

"What's that?" Dandy Bob demanded. He looked up at Old Man Duggan.

"Somethin' under the mattress, I reckon." Duggan's reply did not sound quite natural. Dandy Bob walked over and looked at the old man.

"Sounded like paper," he said. Bending, he peered under the bed, then knelt and reached with a long arm. When he stood again, he held a package of crisp new bills. "Duggan!" Dandy Bob thundered, staring down at the money.

Before the wrath in that voice, Old Man Duggan quailed. "I was just tryin' to he'p out, Bob," he said. "I'd learnt to open the safe comin' down from Tucson, an', when the widdy wouldn't loan me the money, I was passin' the bank, so I went in."

"Get up!" Dandy Bob ordered. "Let's see."

Duggan got up. Dandy Bob rolled back the mattress. There, exposed to view was the loot of the First Bank of Gila City, money, papers, documents, everything.

"My Lord!" exclaimed Dandy Bob Roberts, and let the mattress fall back in place.

"I didn't mean no harm, Bob," Old Man Duggan began pleadingly. "I was just tryin' to he'p out."

Bob sat down on top of all that money and stared at his partner. This surpassed anything Duggan had ever done. "You ain't mad, are you?" Duggan queried tentatively.

Bob Roberts wasn't mad, he was scared. For just a moment, standing there, visions of wealth flashed through his mind, but fright dimmed them. Gila City was in a hanging mood, and, if the town ever discovered who had robbed the bank, Bob and Duggan both would decorate cottonwoods. It might be possible to get away with the money, but Bob was dubious.

"How much is there?" Bob demanded.

"I dunno," Duggan answered. "I was goin' to count it, but I ain't so good at figgers, Bob."

"If we get caught with this, they'll hang us," said Dandy Bob, "higher than hell. Do you know that, Duggan?"

30

Duggan shivered. "What'll we do, Bob?" There was a quaver in the old man's voice.

"I got to think," said Bob. He got up, selected a clean shirt, and unfolded it.

"Bob," said Duggan, "if I give it back to 'em . . ."

"They'll still hang you." Bob pulled the shirt over his head and tucked in the tails. "I told you I had to think. Now keep still!"

Old Man Duggan kept still. Dandy Bob finished dressing, cast a look about the room, and picked up his hat. "We'll go eat," he stated. "Come on."

They went to town, locking the door behind them. In the Elite Restaurant, Duggan displayed no appetite. Dandy Bob was well along in his meal when Watson, the assayer, walked in.

"We got a meeting of the bank directors over in Finebaum's store," Watson informed. "They sent me over after you, Bob. We got a proposition we want you to look at."

"Be right with you," Bob said. Watson went out, and Bob turned to Duggan. "You go home," he directed, low-voiced. "Don't you leave the place till I get back. Hear me?"

Duggan nodded and Bob walked out of the restaurant. As he reached the sidewalk, he bumped into Doc Speers.

"Excuse me," Bob apologized, recoiling, then, recognizing the doctor: "You're in an awful hurry, Doc."

"The widow called me," Doc Speers said. "That girl's sick again. Sorry I didn't see you, Bob." He hurried along while Bob crossed the street and entered Finebaum's store.

The bank directors, with Sholto Fitzhenry, were assembled in Sol Finebaum's office. Their talk ceased abruptly as Bob entered. He stood, tall and straight and immaculate as always, and looked around the room. "You wanted to see me?" he drawled.

"We did, Bob," Jim Frazee spoke for the directors. "We've got a job for you. Sit down."

Bob sat down, and Frazee, after a glance at his fellows, continued. "We want you to recover the bank's money, Bob. That's why we sent for you."

"Kind of a chore," Dandy Bob drawled. "That fellow got clear away, you know. We lost his tracks about fifteen miles north of town. The wind had blowed 'em out. We spent the day lookin' an' couldn't find a trace of 'em. You've sent out descriptions of him?"

"To Tucson, Lordsburg, Phoenix, every place we could think of," Frazee agreed. "We don't think they'll do much good. Here's the proposition, Bob . . . you know a lot of people that . . . well, you know a lot of folks."

Bob hid his grin. What Jim Frazee meant was that Dandy Bob Roberts knew a lot of the undercover population of southern Arizona — the bad boys who held up stages, ran contraband across the border, stole cattle, and otherwise stayed outside the law.

"Sure," Bob agreed, "I know a lot of people."

"And we thought," Frazee said, "that, if you went to work for us, you could learn something. We'd make it worth your while. We'd pay you five percent of whatever money you recovered an' no questions asked. There was fifty thousand dollars in that safe, Bob."

Bob pursed his lips in a soundless whistle, and did a little mental calculation. All that money lying under Duggan's mattress, and they would pay him five percent, $2,500, for getting it back. No questions asked. He looked at Sholto Fitzhenry.

"Ain't your customary rate eight percent?" Bob drawled. "Don't seem like you should ask me to work for less than you charge your customers."

Fitzhenry's face was red. "We do charge eight percent," Frazee agreed. His eyes circled the faces in the room again. "All right, make it eight percent."

Bob got up. "You've hired a man," he stated briefly. "Duggan will go with me, of course. I'll start to work on it. An' " — he paused and his eyes also circled the room — "if I find the money, I hope nobody here forgets what we agreed to." Dandy Bob Roberts went out.

On the sidewalk in front of Finebaum's store he paused briefly. He wanted to go home. He wanted to look at that wealth again because $4,000 of it was his. Then, recalling Doc Speers and the girl at the Widow Fennessy's, Dandy Bob started along the walk. As he passed the Rajah, Deputy Sheriff Frank McMain came from the door.

"Got a minute, Bob?" the deputy asked.

"I was goin' to the widow's," Bob answered. "Alice is sick an' they sent for Doc."

"I'll go with you," McMain stated, and fell into step.

The widow let them in. Joe Glennen was in the parlor, white-faced, sitting stiffly in a straight chair. The widow held a finger to her lips. "*Shh*," she warned. "Doc's with her now. He's goin' to give her somethin' to make her sleep sound."

Dandy Bob and McMain sat down while the widow tiptoed to a chair. "It's all me own fault," she berated herself. "Sure, we went downtown today, an' just as we was passin' Finebaum's warehouse, who should come out but Billy Lister, the undertaker, an' three Mexicans, carryin' a coffin. 'What have ye got there, Billy?' I says to him. 'Do ye really want to see?' he says, an' opens up the coffin top, an' there, layin' down inside the coffin, was a corpse.

"'Twas the man ye shot, Bob. Alice caught one glimpse of him an' turned as white as one of me sheets. 'Take me home, Vi'let,' she says. 'Please take me home.' So I brung her home. She went into her room an' lay down an' went to cryin'. I couldn't stop her, so I sent for the doctor."

Doc Speers appeared at the door. "I think she'll rest presently," he said. "I've given her a sedative. I'll just wait a while and see if it works." The doctor seated himself.

McMain, feeling in his pocket, cleared his throat. "That was what I wanted to talk to you about, Bob," he said. "I went through the guy before I turned him over to Lister. There was a letter in his pocket. I read it because I thought there might be somethin' about the bank, but there wasn't. It was all about a kid. Addressed to a convent in San Francisco. Here."

34

McMain brought out a letter, extending it to Dandy Bob. "See if you can make anything out of it."

Addressed to the Saint Catherine's Convent, Dandy Bob read from the envelope. Unknowingly he raised his voice a trifle. "There's . . ." Bob stopped.

There was a sound at the bedroom door, a gasping, choking sound. Alice Moore stood there, swaying, holding to the jamb for support. "Saint Catherine's," she gasped. "That . . . oh, Joe, Joe!"

Two long strides took Joe Glennen to her side and he caught the girl up in his arms. The Widow Fennessy was at the editor's heels and behind the widow came Doc Speers. Glennen carried the girl into the bedroom.

"Now what the hell?" Dandy Bob demanded of Frank McMain.

There was no immediate answer.

Presently the widow appeared. "Give me that letter," she ordered. Bob passed it over, and the widow returned to the bedroom.

Fifteen minutes later, Doc Speers came out, looked oddly at Dandy Bob and McMain, and picked up his hat. "I run into some of the damnedest things," Doc Speers announced conversationally. "And professional ethics keeps my mouth shut. Gentlemen, take my word for it, we aren't needed here. Joe and Missus Fennessy are doing all that needs to be done. If you'll go with me, I'll buy a drink."

Dandy Bob and the deputy followed the doctor. As they passed the bedroom door, they caught a glimpse of Joe Glennen kneeling beside the bed. They paused, and the widow closed the door in their faces.

Doc Speers bought the promised drink at the Rajah. When he left them, Bob and McMain discussed and surmised for a time, but Bob was uneasy. He was curious about the happenings at the widow's cottage, but he was even more concerned about the money under Duggan's mattress.

Bidding McMain good night, he left the saloon and made his way to the adobe. The lamp was lighted and Old Man Duggan, working on a fresh bottle, occupied the bed.

Bob hung up his hat and took off his coat. "Well," he said to Duggan, "we can get rid of the money now an' make some doin' it. The bank directors hired me to get it back for 'em."

"It's already back," Duggan stated, lowering the bottle.

"What?" Dandy Bob could hardly believe his ears hearing that information.

"I took it back." Duggan refreshed himself again. "I got to thinkin', Bob. When I make a mistake, I set it right. I knowed Fitzhenry was at that meetin' you went to, an' I just hypered home, put the money in a sack, an' carried it up to his place. The front door was unlocked an' there wasn't no lights, so I slid in an' dumped the sack behind the sofy."

Old Man Duggan retired behind the bottle. Dandy Bob, all the strength gone from his legs, sat down.

CHAPTER
FIVE

It took some time for the enormity of Duggan's action to sink in. Dandy Bob Roberts was more or less stunned. When he had recovered sufficiently to start cursing Duggan, he saw that the effort would be wasted. Duggan was asleep and snoring gently.

Dandy Bob undressed and blew out the lamp but he didn't sleep for a long time. 4,000 vanished dollars troubled his mind, and, when he did sleep, he dreamed about them. In the morning, when both awoke, Duggan was penitent, but so accustomed was he to being upbraided, so thick was his hide, that Bob's recriminations hurt not at all.

"Four thousand bucks," Bob said bitterly. "Enough to put us pretty near in the clear, an' you threw it away."

"Well," Duggan said complacently, "we c'n still borry from Vi'let. She wouldn't lend me the money, but she'll let you have it. You got to go an' see her, Bob."

Reluctant as he was, Bob knew that Duggan was right. The widow was the sole source of available wealth, and, now that the bank had recovered the mortgage, Bob must go to her. Accordingly he dressed in his best, shaved, and, after breakfasting at the Elite, he walked to the widow's cottage.

Mrs. Fennessy, face glowing, let him in. She gave Bob no chance to state his errand but began to talk immediately. "Ye'll never guess," said the widow. "It's that romantic ye'd never believe it. An' ye done it all, Bob. It would never have happened if it hadn't been for you."

"What wouldn't have happened?" Bob asked.

"Joe and Alice would never've got married." The widow fairly burbled with her pleasure.

"They ain't married," Bob said. He was just a little confused.

"Of course not. Not yet," the widow agreed, "but they will be. Come have a cup of coffee whilst I tell ye."

In the kitchen, drinking a superlative cup of coffee, Dandy Bob heard the story. Alice Moore, a stage-struck youngster and romantic by nature, had met Kerr Joslin in San Francisco and, bedazzled by him, had married the man. The girl's people were well-to-do and, although deploring the match, accepted it. In course of time a boy was born. Then Joslin, running true to form, had become involved in a scandal. Alice's parents had insisted on a separation and had taken their daughter and her child to live with them.

"He kidnapped the baby," the widow informed. "Stole it away, the divil, an' hid it."

Joslin had insisted that Alice join him, and, despite her parents' pleading, the girl had given in. There had followed an odyssey of travel with cheap shows, where Joslin had used his wife's beauty and accomplishments to make money. Delehenty had hired the two, and Delehenty, learning Alice Moore's story, had tried to help her.

"So Joslin kilt him," the widow concluded, "an' Alice was hurt, accidental. That's when I got her, an' I love her like she was me own daughter. Ye know the rest, Bob. The man came back, bad cess to him, an' scared Alice. She was goin' to run away from me an' join him again, hopin' she'd get her baby back.

"Then they robbed the bank an' you shot him an' kilt him dead entirely. It was the sight of him an' the thought of never gettin' her baby that made her sick yesterday. An' last night, when Frank pulled out that letter, it was like a voice from heaven. The baby's at Saint Catherine's Convent in San Francisco, an' Alice an' Joe are goin' to get married an' go an' get him."

"Well," said Dandy Bob, "that's fine."

"If only I could give 'em a party," the widow concluded, her voice wistful. "An announcement party. D'ye think I can, Bob?"

"I don't know," said Dandy Bob. "Maybe."

"If ye can fix it, there's nothin' I wouldn't do for ye," the widow said. "What was it ye wanted to see me about, Bob?"

Dandy Bob stated his mission. Mrs. Fennessy waved a large and careless hand. "Sure," she agreed, "all the money ye want. I'll get whatever ye need from Tucson. An', Bob, see about a party, will ye?"

Leaving the Widow Fennessy's, feeling a little easier in his mind, Dandy Bob started toward the Star Livery. He had almost reached the barn when he encountered

Jim Frazee and Sholto Fitzhenry. Bob expected to see these two in high spirits, sure that Fitzhenry must have found the loot where Duggan had deposited it. Surprisingly neither of the men mentioned such a recovery.

"When you goin' to start work on that job, Bob?" Frazee asked. "I thought you'd he headed for Tucson by now."

Bob looked at the postmaster, then at Fitzhenry. It was time to bluff, and Bob Roberts bluffed. "Maybe I won't go to Tucson," he said. "Maybe I won't go any place."

"Do you think it was a local job?" Frazee demanded eagerly.

Dandy Bob was looking searchingly at Sholto Fitzhenry and he caught the sudden flicker in Fitzhenry's eyes. In that instant Bob glimpsed his hole card and knew it was his ace. "I ain't sayin'," he drawled. "But I'm workin' on the business, Jim. Remember . . . you said no questions asked."

"That's right," Frazee agreed. "No questions, Bob."

"You goin' home pretty soon, Mister Fitzhenry?" Bob queried. "I'd like to see you if you are. Some things I want to know."

"I'm goin' home shortly," Fitzhenry answered. "Yes, I'll be there." He would not meet Bob's eyes.

"I'll see you then," said Bob. "So long, Jim." He walked on to the livery barn.

In the office of the Star Livery, which was also the stage stop, Dandy Bob sat down to think. He could hear Duggan out in the barn, giving orders to the hostlers. Duggan loved to boss the barn work, having once done it himself.

Dandy Bob smoked a cigarette and, through the trailing haze of burning tobacco, studied the ceiling. If what he thought was right, Bob had a lot of answers.

"'An' no questions asked,'" Bob quoted softly. Then, raising his voice: "Duggan!"

In answer to the roar, Duggan thrust his head through the door. "Yeah?" he queried.

"Come along," Bob ordered. "We're goin' up to Fitzhenry's."

"Fitzhenry's?" Duggan could scarcely believe what he had heard. "Why, Bob?"

"Because," Dandy Bob stated, "I've got him out on a limb an' I'm goin' to saw it off out from under him so he drops . . . hard."

En route to Sholto Fitzhenry's home on the Hill, Dandy Bob gave Duggan his orders. It was not necessary for Duggan to say a word; all he had to do was be present and obey his partner. Duggan promised faithfully to hold his silence, impressed by Dandy Bob's vehemence.

Bob rapped on the door of the Fitzhenry home and Luella Mae opened it.

"I'd like to speak to your husband," Bob announced.

"He won't —" Luella Mae began.

"If that is Mister Roberts, bring him in!" Fitzhenry called.

Surprise showing in her face, Luella Mae stepped aside. Bob and Duggan went in and met the master of the house.

"We won't need you, Luella," Fitzhenry said brusquely. "Come into the parlor, gentlemen."

In the parlor, with the door closed, Fitzhenry indicated chairs. "You wanted to see me?"

Bob had a twinge of admiration. Fitzhenry was a good poker player. "I did," Bob agreed. "You were at the meetin' last night when Frazee made the bank's proposition. I think you know why I'm here."

"I haven't the slightest idea," Fitzhenry said. "And I may as well tell you, Roberts, I was against employing you."

"Sure you were." Dandy Bob was bland. If Fitzhenry wanted to play it that way, Bob Roberts was agreeable. "I don't blame you for bein' against me. You knew I'd get the money back."

"But I *want* the money returned."

"Look," said Dandy Bob, "don't try that stuff with me. It won't work. You know an' I know that it was local talent that robbed the bank. Wait now . . ." He held up a hand to stay Fitzhenry's interruption. "Maybe the men who done the actual work wasn't local, but it was local brains directed 'em. I know where that money is, an' so do you!"

Old Man Duggan squirmed and Bob favored him with a scowl. There was a flicker of apprehension in Fitzhenry's eyes. "You're insane!" he snapped.

"Nope." Bob shook his head. "Mister Fitzhenry, the money's right in this house."

Sholto Fitzhenry jumped up from his chair. Bob's walnut-handled Colt slid out into his hand and covered the banker. "Sit down!" Bob rasped. "Duggan, you hike on downtown. Get Jim Frazee an Watson an' any more of the bank directors you can find. Bring Frank McMain. We'll search this place."

Duggan moved to obey.

"Wait!" Fitzhenry gasped.

"Wait a minute, Duggan," Bob seconded. The Colt covered Fitzhenry. "You don't want the house searched?" He grinned wickedly at the banker.

"There's some way we can work this out," Fitzhenry said weakly. He sank down on a chair. "I didn't rob the bank, Roberts. I didn't take the money. I found it hidden behind my sofa. I swear I don't know how it got there."

"Who is goin' to believe that?" Bob rasped.

Sholto Fitzhenry stared at him. The answer to Bob's question had been troubling him ever since he had discovered the loot.

"Nobody," Dandy Bob answered himself. "Go along, Duggan."

Once more, obediently, Duggan stood up.

"Wait!" Fitzhenry said again. "Don't do that. There's some way we can work this out, Roberts. There's got to be a way."

"Sit down, Duggan," Bob ordered. Duggan sat down. Dandy Bob stared at the banker. "I don't want to be hard on you," he said. "You're a married man an' likely you done it when you wasn't thinkin' straight. I don't really want you hung or throwed in jail." Thoughtfully Bob Roberts tapped his teeth with the muzzle of the Colt. "Yeah," he said, lowering the weapon, "I'll try to help you out."

Fitzhenry lifted his head. His face was eager.

"Tell you what," Dandy Bob said thoughtfully, "you turn that money and stuff over to me. Jim Frazee said I was to get it back an' there'd be no questions asked. I guess I'm the only man in Gila City who could walk in on them directors, dump down the money, an' walk out again."

"Of course!" Sholto Fitzhenry jumped up, relief flooding his face. "And they will pay you for doing it. Four thousand dollars. Of course, Mister Roberts. Why didn't I think of that?"

"Hold on a minute," Dandy Bob ordered. "The directors will pay me, sure, but this is worth a little somethin' to you, Fitzhenry. You don't get off scotfree."

The banker sat down slowly. "I haven't much money," he said. "I —"

"Not money," Bob interrupted. "There's other things, though. I don't like to pay eight percent a month on my loan. How about that?"

"That can be arranged," Fitzhenry agreed smoothly. "The monthly rate was a mistake. I'll change that."

"An' then," Dandy Bob drawled, "I wasn't asked to buy stock in the bank. It looks like that was a mistake, too. The directors voted you quite a little stock, didn't they? It didn't cost you a thing. How about splittin' with me, say for one dollar an' other good an' valuable considerations?"

Fitzhenry was silent for some time. Finally he nodded. "Is that all?" he asked.

"Not quite all." Dandy Bob was on the crest and he rode it. "Joe Glennen and Alice Moore are gettin' married. They're goin' on a weddin' trip, an' likely they'll adopt a baby while they're gone. When they come home, Missus Fennessy is goin' to give a party for 'em. You an' your wife will be invited an' so will everybody else. Seems to me you ought to go. The widow's good people."

Again a long silence. Again Fitzhenry nodded.

"An' that's all," said Bob Roberts.

"How do I know you'll keep your word?" the banker asked.

"You don't." Dandy Bob smiled cruelly. "But you can think it over."

Sholto Fitzhenry thought it over, recalling all the things he had heard about Dandy Bob Roberts. "All right," he said suddenly.

"Then," said Bob, "transfer the stock, fix up my note and mortgage, give me the sack, an' let me count the money. After that, Duggan an' me will pull out. We'll have to work this right. I'll have to leave town a while to make it look good, but you needn't worry."

"No," said Fitzhenry slowly, "I guess that's right. I needn't worry." He got up and walked out of the parlor. Within minutes he returned, carrying Duggan's bulging grain sack.

One hour later, Duggan and Bob Roberts walked down the Hill. Duggan carried a sack and looked furtively from right to left. They reached the Widow Fennessy's and were admitted.

"Joe an' Alice are goin' to leave for San Francisco tomorrow," the widow informed. "They'll be married there. They . . . What have ye there, Bob?"

"Something I want you to keep for me," said Dandy Bob. "Watch it, Violet, an' don't let anybody touch it. I'll be out of town a few days. An', Violet, figure to give Joe an' Alice a party when they get back. Send out your invitations an' be sure to invite the Fitzhenrys. Everybody will come."

"They will?" The widow clutched Bob's arm. "Ye're sure? Ye're positive?"

"I'm sure," replied Dandy Bob. "An' I'm not goin' to have to borrow any money from you, either. Thanks just the same. I'll pull out now. I got to catch the stage, an' Duggan's goin' with me. Come on, Duggan."

With a final regretful look at the grain sack, Old Man Duggan followed Dandy Bob.

CHAPTER
SIX

For one week Bob Roberts and his partner, Old Man Duggan, enjoyed the fleshpots of Tucson. The Old Pueblo welcomed the men from Gila City, entertained them, and then was glad to see them go. They returned to Gila City at night, and from the stage stop Bob went directly to Widow Fennessy's, there reclaiming his sack. Carrying the sack and followed by Duggan, who was armed with a sawed-off shotgun, Bob sought out Jim Frazee. In the postmaster's home he dumped the sack on the table.

"There you are," said Dandy Bob. "Remember, no questions asked, Jim."

Jim Frazee peeked into the sack, gave a yelp of sheer pleasure, and dashed out. Within half an hour the bank directors, including Sholto Fitzhenry, were gathered at Frazee's house. Bob stood by while money was counted, while papers and documents were hastily examined.

"It's all there," Frazee said at length. "Everything. Bob, you've saved our bacon."

Dandy Bob grinned. "You know," he stated, "I think I'd like to be in the bankin' business myself. I think I'll buy a little stock." His eyes were on Sholto Fitzhenry as he spoke. Fitzhenry grunted like a man hit low.

"An' now," Dandy Bob said, "me an' Duggan will pull out. We had kind of a rapid time, Jim. An' about that money we got comin' . . . just split the reward in two and deposit half to me an' half to Duggan. Remember, gents, if you get a new safe, me an' Duggan are in the freightin' business. We'll haul it for you." With Old Man Duggan trailing, Dandy Bob Roberts made his exit.

The recovery of the bank's money and documents was a nine days' wonder in Gila City. The citizens of that town gazed with awe on Dandy Bob Roberts. Bob had done it again, and, if the bank had sense enough to employ such a man as he, maybe the bank was all right, too.

This supposition became a certainty when Gila City learned that, by arrangement with Sholto Fitzhenry, Bob Roberts had become a stockholder in the bank. Accounts that had been withdrawn were reinstated. The bank was in the town's good graces again.

"They got a new safe ordered," Gila City said, "an' Dandy Bob's a director. Nobody's goin' to be fool enough to try to rob the bank again. Not with Bob Roberts to go against."

Duggan, of course, basked in reflected glory. He took plenty of free drinks and was asked plenty of questions, but Duggan maintained a discreet silence. Duggan was busy. The Widow Fennessy was giving a party, a reception for Joe Glennen and his wife who were expected shortly to return from their wedding trip to San Francisco. Violet kept Duggan trotting.

"She's got me runnin' till my tongue's hangin' out," Duggan told Dandy Bob. "Seems like them two ain't ever goin' to get here. I'll be glad when this party's over."

The widow also spoke to Bob Roberts. "I'm countin' on ye, Bob," the widow said. "Alice an' Joe will be back tomorrow, an' the reception's tomorrow night. Everybody's comin', an' I'm countin' on ye to keep Duggan sober."

"I'll try," Bob agreed.

He did try. Duggan, on hand with Bob and the widow when the eastbound stage arrived, was sober as a judge. With the rest, he welcomed a beaming Joe Glennen, a blooming Alice. With Bob and the widow, Duggan examined a sturdy two-year-old boy who stared back at him with round blue eyes.

Duggan behaved himself with care and, as a reward, was given the task of hauling the bride's trunk to the widow's home. And that was a mistake. Duggan was out of Bob's sight for half an hour.

Still no one knew that a mistake had been made. The old man and the trunk arrived by dray, and Duggan showed no evidence of anything wrong. True, there was a slight odor of cloves about him, but in the excitement of installing the Glennen family in the widow's spare bedroom, this fact was overlooked. Also overlooked was the brief trip Duggan made between the dray and the widow's back porch.

"You an' Duggan go get dressed now," the widow urged Dandy Bob. "I want ye to mix the punch, Bob, an' I want ye on hand when me guests begin to come. Go on now."

Bob took Duggan with him as he departed. "You've done pretty good, Duggan," Bob praised when they were in the solitude of the adobe. "Just keep it up."

Duggan grunted. "What you goin' to put in the punch?" he asked.

"Champagne," Bob answered, "an' oranges an' lemons and grape juice." He glanced at his partner. "Why?"

"Just askin'," Duggan said innocently.

"Well, then," Dandy Bob stated, "now that you know, shine your boots. You got to look nice tonight."

Back at the widow's, while Bob mixed the punch, Duggan stood by. Shrouded in one of the widow's aprons, he squeezed lemons and oranges and watched champagne and grape juice poured into the bowl. He stirred and tasted, he smacked his lips, but ventured the comment that the punch lacked authority.

"It's just right," the widow refuted, being called in to judge. "Now, Bob, come help me place the chairs. Duggan, bring the punch an' set it on the table in the parlor."

Bob followed the widow and placed the folding chairs, borrowed from Billy Lister, the undertaker, and presently Duggan carried in the punch bowl.

"More in the kitchen," Duggan announced, placing the bowl carefully on the table. "Want I should bring the cake?"

"I'll get it," the widow answered.

The guests began to arrive just as final preparations were completed. Mr. and Mrs. Jim Frazee, Mr. and Mrs. Watson, Dr. and Mrs. Speers, Mr. and Mrs. Sol Finebaum — couple after couple arrived to shake hands with the widow, to murmur polite congratulations to the bridegroom and felicitations to the bride.

Sholto Fitzhenry and Luella Mae came in, and all of Gila City's wealth and beauty was assembled, and still the party was not right. The men and their wives occupied folding chairs, they spoke small polite sentences, but constraint sat heavily upon the Widow Fennessy's cottage.

"They act like they was dead," the widow whispered to Bob Roberts. "They ain't havin' a good time, Bob. They act like so many corpses, they do so. What'll I do?"

Duggan, standing beside his partner, made answer. "Why don't you serve the refreshments, Vi'let?"

"I guess that's right," Dandy Bob agreed. "Let 'em eat an' go home, Violet." Bob Roberts scowled, for he felt responsible.

And so, with Alice helping, the widow served her guests, passing brimming cups of punch, serving angel food and devil's food cake. Plates and cups were accepted with polite aplomb. Cake was nibbled, punch sipped. Old Man Duggan entered from the kitchen with a pitcher and replenished cups.

And now, wonderfully, life began to enter the party, masked faces relaxed, eyes began to glow, voices were less subdued and more brisk. Dandy Bob Roberts, the widow, and Alice and her husband, the hosts and hostesses who had not been served, began to marvel.

"Looks like that was what they needed," said Dandy Bob to Duggan.

"Sure," said Duggan. "Punch."

"Punch!" said Dandy Bob, and hurried to the kitchen. One sniff, one taste was all he needed.

Duggan came in, his pitcher empty.

"Duggan," said Dandy Bob, "you spiked it! How much did you put in?"

"Four quarts," Duggan answered. "Didn't have no body to it before. Pretty good party, ain't it?"

It was a good party. Dandy Bob, observing from the kitchen door, saw Mrs. Finebaum in animated conversation with Alice. Fitzhenry, Watson, and Sol Finebaum stood with their arms around each other's necks, forming a line. "Come on, Bob!" Watson called. "We need a bass."

The widow pushed through her guests and joined Bob in the door. Over in one corner Luella Mae Fitzhenry, skirt lifted to expose a length of ankle, was demonstrating a polka step to Frank McMain.

"Look at her," the widow sniffed, "an' her so skinny that, if she didn't have an Adam's apple, she wouldn't have no figger at all. Look at 'em all, Bob. What's got into 'em? What happened to 'em?"

"Duggan," Bob answered gently. "He happened to 'em. They're havin' a fine time, Violet. They're enjoying themselves. You drink some punch, too."

On the back porch, seated on the step, Dandy Bob Roberts found his partner. Duggan sat, arms resting on

52

his raised knees, staring off into the night. "A waste of good liquor," said Old Man Duggan, sensing his partner's nearness. "I done my best, Bob, but I can't get no kick outen that punch. Wish I had some whiskey."

Methodically, almost mechanically, he began to search his pockets. His hand came up holding a half pint bottle containing a little liquid. It was the nitroglycerine Duggan had taken, and forgotten until that moment. Gently Dandy Bob Roberts took it out of Duggan's hand.

"Don't spoil it," he warned. "Joe an' Alice an' you an' me are the only ones that ain't drunk. It's a record, Duggan." Dandy Bob threw the bottle into the night.

There came a flash and a roar, a sharp shock of concussion. In the house the noises of the party suddenly ceased. Old Man Duggan came to his feet to stare into the night, to turn and look, eyes wide with terror, at Dandy Bob Roberts.

"Whiskey!" Old Man Duggan gasped. "I been drinkin' that. I . . . my Lawd! Oh, my Lawd! Don't touch me! I got a quart of that stuff in me!" Old Man Duggan's voice had ascended the scale as he spoke. Old Man Duggan's face was gray with fright. Old Man Duggan shivered, his legs gave way, and for the first and last time in his life Old Man Duggan fainted.

And now, in the house, a babble arose. Men came boiling through the kitchen to learn the cause of the explosion.

"What was that? What happened?"

"I don't know," Bob Roberts answered. "I just don't know, but I think that Duggan's goin' to swear off drinkin'. You-all go back into the house an' enjoy yourselves."

Jerico Takes
the Rough String

Jerico Jones, horse wrangler extraordinaire, made his first appearance in this story. It was published in *West* (8/17/32), very early in Bennett Foster's career. In fact, since the appearance of his verse poem, "Circuit Rider" in *West* (3/19/30), his first published work, *West*, a biweekly magazine published by Doubleday, Doran and Company, Inc., was Foster's principal market, and would remain so until the middle of 1934.

Jerico Jones hung his chin on the top bar of the corral, looked inside, and then brought a freckled hand up to rumple the unruly shock of brown hair that no barber's comb had ever been able to subdue.

"I'll be damned!" announced Mr. Jones. "I sure will be damned!"

There was a noise on the stoop of the Manassa House, behind the self-condemned Jerico, and he turned quickly to ascertain its cause. A sleepy eyed, somewhat obese, and rather greasy individual stood on the stoop. Jerico beckoned to the man.

"Come here," he commanded, and then, when the greasy gentleman had gained his side: "Say, did I or didn't I put twelve horses into this here pen last night?"

The greasy one eyed Jerico dubiously, looked into the corral, rubbed his eyes, and answered. "Why, yeah," he said. "You put twelve horses in there. Why? Ain't they here?"

Jerico shrugged broad shoulders eloquently. "Do you see 'em?" he countered. "They sure ain't here. I reckon them broncos must've sprouted wings or somethin'. The next time I pen a bunch of horses, I'll put 'em to bed an' sleep with 'em, by golly! I'll . . ."

Jerico did not finish his sentence. The man from the hotel was hoisting his bulky body over the corral rails and Jerico paused in his speech to watch him. The hotel man dropped heavily inside the corral, started to stride across it, and, halfway, stopped suddenly, stooped, and picked up a clod. He examined the bottom of the clod, looked at the place from whence it came, and then stooped again and put it back.

"Find 'em?" questioned Jerico, interested.

The greasy man looked at his questioner with dull eyes. "Why no . . . " he began. "Say, they ain't here, are they?"

"I been tellin' you," replied Jerico patiently. "Is horses in the habit of disappearin' around here? I'd say that this country sure makes free with a newcomer."

The man in the corral looked at Jerico, his face a blank, then looked away again toward the open door of the saddle shed behind the corral. Something he saw caused him to move toward it.

Jerico, following the man with his eyes, swore softly again to himself. The greasy man stopped at the farther side of the corral.

"They's some saddles gone, too," he announced complacently. "They was six saddles in the shed last night when you run your horses in, an' now they's only one. I reckon . . ."

Jerico craned his neck and peered across the corral into the saddle shed. "An' the one that's left ain't mine," he announced. "By damn . . ."

From the highway, stretching in front of the Manassa House, an automobile horn sounded hoarsely. Looking

58

toward the road, Jerico could see a dust cloud whirling under the early morning sun. The cloud resolved into an automobile that drew rapidly nearer and presently stopped with complaining brakes. From the front seat of the car a heavy-set man ponderously detached himself and nodded curtly to the driver who sat motionlessly behind the wheel. From the rear seat four men, each bearing a rifle, swarmed out. The hotel man in the corral lumbered across the enclosure toward Jerico. One of the men from the rear seat of the car ran down the road, rifle in hand, and disappeared behind the hotel.

Jerico faced the approaching newcomers and waited. A star, revealed by his swinging coat, gleamed on the vest of the ponderous man. Flanked by his companions the star bearer approached Jerico and stopped.

The unkempt man in the corral, seemingly aroused from his lethargy, spoke. "Howdy, Sheriff," he said. "Out kinda early, ain't you?"

The pompous man grunted.

The hotel man tried again. "Lookin' for somebody?" he asked.

"I'm lookin' for five men that held up the Farmers' and Stockmen's Bank in Littlecreek last night." The sheriff's voice was a heavy rumble. "You seen anythin' of a car come from that way last night or early this mornin'?"

The hotel man paused and considered the question. Presently he answered it. "Why," he said brightly, "I dunno."

"You dunno nothin'." The sheriff snorted his contempt. "Didn't you see a car? Didn't you hear nothin'?"

The hotel man scratched his head and shifted his weight from one foot to the other. Presently the sheriff got his answer. "I dunno," the flunky again announced.

"Hell," said the sheriff.

The posse man who had gone behind the hotel came breathlessly around the corner of the building and hurried toward the group. "There was a car through here, Purdy," he announced as he reached the standing men. "Come through just before you telephoned Hyson last night. I reckon it was them."

Again the sheriff said: "Hell."

"Must've been them," insisted the posse man. "Hyson said he stayed up the rest of the night, watchin', an' there ain't been no other cars."

"Where's Hyson?" demanded the sheriff.

"Comin'."

The official turned a cold and lackluster gray eye in Jerico's direction. Apparently he noticed Mr. Jones for the first time. "Who are you?" he demanded abruptly.

"Jones," said Jerico instantly.

"Jones, huh? Why didn't you say Smith? It's commoner. What you doin' here?"

"Just listenin', up to now." Jerico's tone was tinged with sweetness. "If you got time, I'd like to tell you that twelve horses I had back in that corral last evenin' are done gone."

"Gone?" said the sheriff.

60

"Gone," repeated Jerico. "Vamoosed . . . went. I don't talk Dutch or I'd tell you in that."

The sheriff overlooked the insult. "Twelve of 'em?" he insisted.

"Twelve of 'em," replied Jerico. "Nice horses, too. They had tails and four legs, every one of 'em. They's five saddles gone, too."

The sheriff pondered. The posse remained silent. Jerico waited, and the hotel man bent over and picked up a straw that he chewed assiduously.

Presently the sheriff began to rumble again. "They took 'em," he announced. "Them five that robbed the bank. They come through town here, stopped, an' come back, an' then rustled your horses. Didn't they, boys?"

Two of the four posse men nodded, one said, "Yes," and the remaining one, the youngest of the group, remained silent, a grin overspreading his face.

"You got 'em well trained," observed Jerico.

The sheriff paid no attention to Jerico's remark. He stood deliberating for a long instant, and then lifted a heavy hand and pointed a ponderous finger at the youngest posse man.

"You, Tom," he said, "you stay here an' find out about this feller's horses. Look around. Mebbe them fellers will come back. There ain't no doubt about it, they're the bunch that robbed the bank, an' they took to horseflesh here. The rest of us will go out to the Half Triangle an' get mounts. We'll circle an' cut their trail between here an' there. Come on, boys."

Jerico started to speak, thought better of it, and grinned while the ponderous sheriff turned and, still flanked by his cohorts, made his way to the waiting car. The posse climbed into the machine, there was a growl as the driver meshed his gears and let in the clutch, and the car moved away down the road. Jerico turned to the posse man who had remained.

"Do you think they'll come back, mister?" he asked, his lips quirking in a smile.

Tom, the youngest posse man, jerked his hat from his black thatched head, flung it down viciously, and swore. "Of course, they won't come back," he said when he had finished his tirade. "Of course, they won't. Purdy, damn his time, allus leaves me when there's anythin' interestin' comin' up! I allus get the jobs of findin' pet dogs that's lost or horses that's strayed. By the horns of hell!"

"Now, don't you go losin' your temper," consoled Jerico placidly. "It won't do you no good, an' you may need it. Let's you an' me look into this horse matter a little. Mebbe them fellers will come back, after all, an' if they do, an' if they're the birds that took my horses, I'll bet you two bits that somebody gets shot."

The young deputy sheriff stared alertly at the speaker. There was something in Jerico's tone that told more than the spoken words. The deputy asked a question. "What do you mean, mebbe they'll come back?" he demanded. "What do you know that you ain't said?"

Jerico smiled gently. "Why," he said, "them twelve horses I had in here was part of Lew Madrid's buckin' string. There was three horses that could be rode an' the rest of 'em was plumb bronc's. Nope. I'd say, offhand, that them fellers ain't gone far if they're dependin' on my horses to carry 'em."

The deputy stood open mouthed, staring at Jerico. In the corral, the fat hotel man put a foot tentatively on the bottom bar. "Well," he said, "I got to get breakfast," and then began to climb over.

Jerico put his hand on the deputy's arm. "You an' me, too," he said, echoing the roustabout's sentiments. "Let's go eat an' I'll tell you about the horses an' you tell me about the bank robbery. How's that?"

The deputy nodded. "I'll go with you," he announced. "I'm hungry as a she-wolf, an' I'd sure admire to know how you come to be with Madrid's buckin' string. Why didn't you tell the sheriff about it?"

"Did the sheriff ask me?" countered Jerico. "Nope. He said for you to find out about the horses an' you're findin' out. Come on." He moved off in the direction of the Manassa House.

The two went into the dining room of the hotel. The deputy hung up his hat. Jerico, having left his room in haste when he had discovered the empty corral from his window, had no hat, and went directly to a table. The deputy joined him and they sat down. Across the table they sized each other up and each liked what he saw.

Jerico spoke first. "My name is Jones," he said. "Jerico Jones. I'm from Texas an' I'm goin' to Littlecreek. I met Madrid in Uvalde last year, an', when I drifted up this way, I looked him up. He was sendin' his string to the rodeo at Littlecreek an' I drifted 'em over this far for him to save shippin' charges. That explains me, I reckon."

The deputy across the table nodded. His black eyes were bright, staring into Jerico's blue ones. "That explains you, I reckon," he concurred. "I'm satisfied, an', if Purdy ain't, he can wire Madrid. My name's Barr, Tom Barr, an' I'm just a damn' enough fool to be a deputy for Purdy till somethin' better turns up."

Jerico solemnly extended a hand and Barr took it. They shook and both smiled.

A waitress, coming from the kitchen, approached the table and the two broke off their conversation to give their orders. When that was done, Jerico addressed Barr again.

"Tell me about this bank robbery," he urged. "When did it happen?"

"Last night," replied Barr. "Must've been about six o'clock."

"An' you're just gettin' out here?"

"We didn't find out about it till around midnight." Barr was apologetic. "Purdy phoned all around, an', as soon as it was light, we started."

"How did it happen, anyhow?"

Barr leaned forward on the table. "Why," he said, "seems like las' night, when the bank was closin', five fellers drifted in. Old Man Pruit, that owns the bank, keeps open late at the end of the month as a general thing, so it was around six-thirty or mebbe seven when this happened."

"That's right, today is the first, ain't it?" interrupted Jerico. "Excuse me, go ahead."

"Well, Pruit was in his office, an' the feller that works for him, Gibbs is his name, was behind the counter.

Pruit heard somethin' outside the door of his office an' he went to it. He just had time to see that there was five men when a gun was stuck into his middle an' a blanket throwed over his head. Next thing he knowed, he was tied an' slung on the floor. We got all this later from Pruit, you understand?"

Jerico nodded. "What about the man that was workin'?" he questioned. "Gibbs, you said, didn't you?"

"I was comin' to that. It wasn't till about twelve o'clock that Pruit managed to squirm around an' get his feet against the window. He sure kicked the glass out an' raised a rumpus. Somebody heard him an' went for the sheriff, an', when Purdy got there an' broke in, he found Pruit still tied in the blanket an' Gibbs was behind the counter, deader'n a herrin', with a knife stuck right square in his gizzard." Tom Barr paused dramatically.

"Dead, huh?" Jerico spoke musingly. "Sounds kinda like a . . . never mind. Go on with your yarn."

"Well, the vault was rifled. They had about twenty thousand in it, Pruit said, an' everythin' was gone except some silver an' some coppers. They'd made a clean haul an' got away."

"How'd you come to learn that they'd took an automobile?"

"Pruit heard one leave from in front of the bank after the door closed. He figgered that the robbers had gone in it."

"He was right, likely." Jerico stared blankly at the tablecloth. The waitress brought their orders and distributed them. Both men fell to eating. Presently

Jerico poised a fork full of sausage before his mouth and asked another question.

"Didn't Pruit get any description of them fellers at all?"

"Not much of a one," Barr answered. "Pruit's near-sighted and he didn't have much time to get a look. He says that they was five of 'em, that they all wore dark suits an' caps, an' that's about the limit of it. Purdy thinks that it was some city gang."

Jerico masticated the sausage. "I reckon he's changed his mind about now," he announced when he had swallowed. "No city gang would've took horses."

Barr nodded. "You're right," he said. "I want a description of them horses, too. Purdy said to get one."

"I'll give it to you," assured Jerico. "Say, let's you an' me do a little thinkin'. It ain't painful an' sometimes it's right productive."

Mr. Barr nodded and wiped his mouth, signifying that he had finished his meal. "I'll go you," he replied. "Let's get a drink before we do it, though. Thinkin' is sort of dry work."

Jerico nodded. "All right," he replied. "Say, I'll pay for breakfast an' you buy the drinks. How'd that strike you?"

It seemed to strike Mr. Barr suitably, and the two rose from the depleted breakfast table. Leaving the dining room, they went into the hotel lobby where Jerico paused briefly to pay the proprietor, who lounged behind the desk, and then, accompanying Mr. Barr, pushed through the door that led into a wing opposite the dining room.

It was a narrow barroom they entered. Behind the bar, which ran down half the length of the room, was an amiable man who was nonchalantly polishing a glass. He nodded a greeting as the two entered.

"Hyah, Billy," greeted Tom Barr. "Got any whiskey that's fit to drink?"

"I *allus* got good whiskey," announced the bartender. "Want some?"

"A drink apiece, Billy," assured Mr. Barr. "This here is a friend of mine. Mister Jones, Mister Holmes. He's had a little hard luck."

Billy Holmes set out two glasses and a bottle. "That's what I heard," he said. "Kelden was tellin' me that him an' you found your horses gone this mornin'. He says that Purdy thinks the bank robbers stole 'em. Purdy's wrong, I reckon. Them robbers was city dudes. They wouldn't steal no horses."

Jerico, his drink poured, nudged Tom with his elbow.

Barr, pouring his drink, appeared to choke suddenly. "What do you know about the hold-up, Billy?" he asked, raising his drink and nodding in Jerico's direction.

"I heard about it from Hyson last night," returned Holmes. "He come in an' tole me. He was out lookin' for the car them fellers got away in."

"Much goin' on around here, Billy?" asked Barr.

The placid Mr. Holmes shook his head. "Big poker game upstairs yesterday an' most of last night," he said. "Six-handed. Tipon, from the Half Triangle, an' Moss from the store, an' a couple of Tipon's cowhands, an' Burrel from over by Littlecreek, an' another feller in it.

67

They kept Kelden hoppin' most of last evenin', cartin' 'em up drinks."

"Kelden the night man here?" questioned Jerico.

"General flunkey," replied Holmes. "I guess there was some big pots in that game. They was sure quiet."

Jerico nodded. "I didn't hear 'em," he observed.

"You wouldn't." Mr. Holmes moved the bottle invitingly toward his two customers. "They had it up in Tipon's room, over the bar. He keeps that room just for poker parties an' such. It's off from the rest of the hotel."

"Uhn-huh." Jerico appeared incurious. "Say, Tom, I got to be goin'. Got to go to the depot an' send Madrid a wire, an' then I'll browse around a little. I'll be seein' you."

"Goin' to do anythin' about your horses?" Barr swung on one elbow and faced Jerico who had moved toward the door.

"I reckon the sheriff will find 'em," replied Jerico placidly. "Anyhow, I'm goin' to send that wire. I'll see you before dinner." And with that he was gone.

When he left Tom Barr and Billy Holmes, Jerico went on out into the little lobby of the Manassa House. Here he paused briefly to exchange comments and surmises with the proprietor of the hotel. The hotel man was sorry about Jerico's loss and said so. Jerico also was sorry. The tall Mr. Jones managed to break away shortly and went upstairs to the room he had left so hurriedly at an earlier hour. Here he rummaged in a pair of saddlebags that were his sole luggage. From one of the bags he brought out a shoulder harness and a scabbard containing a very short-barreled Colt. Without more ado Jerico put on the harness and followed it with his vest. He pulled the scabbard through the armhole of the vest, fastened the bottom tab to the top of his trousers, and then slipped into his coat. After trying the gun in its spring-clip holster a time or two, Jerico was satisfied, and, picking up his hat, he left the room. He felt now that he was properly dressed for company.

Again passing through the lobby and leaving word for Barr to wait for him, that he would be back soon, Jerico sallied out upon the single street of Cisco.

The street was short enough. There were, beside the hotel, three stores, another saloon, and at the end of the street a depot. Toward this yellow painted building Jerico made his way. He went in, got a blank from the agent, and, after chewing a pencil for a short time, wrote a telegram to Lew Madrid. Having paid for his message and informing the agent that a reply would find him at the Manassa House, Jerico went out of the station and back up the street. He had something on his mind and stopped at the first store he saw.

Entering, Jerico inquired of a clerk if the establishment had any ready-to-wear clothing. There being none in stock, Jerico went on out and sought the next store. Here again his question brought a negative reply and again Jerico passed on in his search.

His next stop was at the third store, a larger and more imposing edifice that bore a sign across its front bearing the slogan, **MOSS'S GENERAL**

MERCHANDISE. Again Jerico engaged in conversation the clerk who waited upon him. The clerk was elderly and not overly bright. Finding that Jerico wished to purchase ready-to-wear clothing, the clerk led his customer back into the dim recesses of the building and stopped beside a showcase.

"We might have some," he said, opening the showcase. "I think we got in a shipment a while back, but I didn't unpack 'em." He reached inside the case and brought out a hanger. On it were three suits of clothes. These the clerk exhibited with some pride.

"Ain't many stores in little towns like this that carry anything but overalls and shirts," he announced. "Mostly the fellers around here go in to Littlecreek to buy their clothes."

Jerico fingered the suits, saw that they were either gray or brown, and decided not to buy. He thanked the clerk and left the place, going on down the street. At the corner of the building that contained Moss's store, Jerico stopped as though struck by an idea. He paused a moment, and then turned and walked down the building to the back. Here he stopped again and stood looking over the litter that was in the yard, back of the store. There was a packing box there, a new box with **Smart Clothes Co**. stenciled on its side. Jerico nodded with satisfaction and went on toward the Manassa House.

In the lobby of the hotel Jerico found his friend Tom Barr waiting for him. Barr was somewhat impatient. "Did you wire Madrid?" he questioned, when Jerico came up.

"I did," returned Jerico.

"What'd he say?" demanded Mr. Barr.

"How do I know?" retorted Jerico. "I telegraphed him, I didn't phone him. Likely he'll cuss a little when he gets my wire."

"How about a description of them horses?" questioned Barr practically.

Jerico shrugged. "It ain't important," he answered, "but I'll give you one."

Barr brought out a pencil and paper. "Have at it," he invited. "I must say you're a curious jigger. You seem to think that them horses will come back by themselves."

"Not by themselves," corrected Jerico, "but they'll be back. Well, here goes." He fell to describing horses and brands while Barr made notes. When Jerico had finished, he rose from the chair in which he had been seated and grinned down at Tom Barr.

"Now," he said, "I seen a pool table in that saloon down the street. What do you say we go play a little rotation?"

Barr scowled at Jerico, glanced around the lobby, and then nodded. "Might as well," he replied. "I ain't got nothin' to do till Purdy comes back."

"I got an idea he'll be back pretty soon, too," announced Jerico. "When he comes back, he'll likely want to go into Littlecreek an' organize a big hunt. You might as well go on in with him, but, if you really want to do some huntin', I'd suggest that you resign from his posse an' come back out to Cisco. You got a car, ain't you?"

Barr, puzzled, nodded. "Yeah," he said.

"Get it an' come on out," advised Jerico. "This is about as interestin' a town as you're apt to find, an', anyhow, I need somebody that knows the country around here."

Barr stared at his companion. "You're the coolest duck I've seen for a long time," he announced at last. "Here you lost a string of horses an' your saddle an' all you do is wire the feller that owned the bronc's. Well, it's your funeral."

Jerico shook his head. "I ain't been to my funeral yet," he observed placidly, "an' I don't aim to go to it for quite a while. By the way, when you're goin' in with the sheriff you needn't say nothin' about them horses bein' Madrid's buckin' string, unless he asks you. Somehow I don't like that sheriff much."

Barr grunted. "I won't," he assured. "He'll probably know it anyhow. Come on, let's go play that pool game."

They played the game of pool and four others. Jerico bought a drink and Barr returned the compliment. They had exhausted the time-killing devices of Cisco and were squatting against the front of a building, smoking and simply loafing, when the car with Purdy and his posse men returned and stopped before them in the street. The sheriff leaned over the door and gestured to Barr without alighting.

"Couldn't find no trail!" he yelled as Barr arose. "We're goin' in to Littlecreek an' organize a regular manhunt. Come on, Barr."

Jerico looked up and winked at his friend, and Barr, a scowl on his tanned face, shook his head. "I'll be back," he said, low voiced, and strode out into the street and got into the waiting car. From the other side a man, carrying a rifle, climbed down, and, with a clash of gears and a roar of the exhaust, the sheriff's car was gone.

The man with the rifle strode over and stopped before Jerico.

"You the feller that lost the horses?" he demanded.

Jerico nodded. "My name's Jones," he said. "I take it that you're Hyson, the deputy here."

The man with the rifle nodded in his turn. "That's me," he said briefly. "We didn't find no sign of your saddle stock at all. We went out to the Half Triangle an' got mounts, an' then come back toward town. We circled, figurin' to cut the trail, but we never cut it. I reckon the fellers that took your horses hit out on the highway. It's hard surfaced an' there's no sign on it that we could read."

Jerico nodded. "It beats me," he observed, "why them fellers would take to horseflesh instead of stayin' with a automobile. If they wanted to take to the hills, you ought to've found some sign of 'em leavin' the road."

Hyson grunted and spat. "We would've if we'd had anything but a damn' belly-wobblin' politician for a sheriff," he replied. "That damn' fool Purdy don't know as much as a hog knows about Sunday. Well, I hope you get your stock back."

"Thanks," said Jerico, rising. "Mebbe I will. 'Bout time to tie on the nose bag, ain't it? I reckon I'll go

73

down to the hotel an' see what the cook's ruined for dinner. So long."

Jerico ate his noon meal at the Manassa House and, chewing a match, left the dining room and again repaired to the lobby. He exchanged a few words with the fat proprietor, and then asked a guileless question.

"That feller Kelden that works here," he said, "he around?"

"Out in back, I guess," observed the proprietor. "Want to see him?"

"I might," replied Jerico, and moved over toward the door that led to the hotel barroom. "I'm goin' to have a drink . . . have one?"

The hotel man shook his head. "Never use it," he said. "Thanks just the same."

Jerico nodded and drifted out of the lobby. He went to the back of the hotel, and there encountered Kelden sitting on the back steps of the kitchen engaged in peeling potatoes. Jerico sat down on the steps beside the man, reached into his pocket for his knife, opened it, and then fell to peeling potatoes.

"Quite a time we had this mornin'," he said cheerfully.

Kelden nodded. "That damn' sheriff thinks he's smart," he said, placing a peeled potato in the dishpan beside him.

"Uhn-huh," said Jerico. "You must've been pretty sleepy last night."

"I was. Them fellers an' their damn' poker game kept me up most of yesterday an' last night."

"Soooo?" Soothingly.

"Yeah. About every fifteen minutes they'd want a drink an' I'd have to take it up to 'em."

"Did you see much of the game?"

"Not a damn' bit. They'd stamp on the floor an' Holmes would fix up a tray with glasses an' send me up with it. Burrel would take it at the door an' shove out a tray with the empties, an' I'd go back down. He never let me in once, never give me a damn' cent, neither."

"Kinda close is he?"

"Hell, he's closer than the next second. Everybody knows that Burrel's a damn' tightwad."

"Kinda funny that he'd be takin' in the trays all the time."

"Not if you know Burrel. He'd want to be sure that he got his drink first."

"I wonder why they didn't buy a bottle an' keep it up there." Jerico put a peeled potato in the pan and reached for another. "That would've saved you a lot of steps."

"They wasn't worryin' about that," replied Kelden bitterly. "Hell, I'm just their dog. I'd have to go out an' up them dark steps every trip, too."

Jerico looked toward the wing of the building that contained the saloon. The hotel was three-storied with two sprawling wings, and, above the saloon, there was a half story, roofed and windowed, with an outside stair leading up to its door. The Texas man shrugged.

"You been up since they left?" he questioned.

"No, but I got to go pretty soon. I got to clean their damn' mess up before tonight. Tipon told me they was goin' to play some more."

"Let's go up an' do it now," suggested Mr. Jones. "I'll help you. Likely they left some money up there for you for a tip."

Kelden rose to his feet and straightened the flour sack that he wore for an apron. His dull face brightened. "Mebbe they did at that," he said. "Come on."

The two left the potatoes, and with Kelden in the lead went up the steps that led to the room above the barroom. Kelden opened the door with a skeleton key and they went into Tipon's room. There was a bed in one corner of the room, but it had not been occupied. In the center of the room was a round poker table with a slot for the banker. There were a few cigar and cigarette butts on the table's edge, chairs were pushed back from it, and there was a litter of cards on its green surface. Across from the bed and table, and closer to the door, was a cupboard. While Kelden, with some profanity because there had been no money left for him, began to clean up the floor about the table, using a broom that he took from a corner, Jerico strolled over to the cupboard, opened it, and looked inside.

"Seems like them fellers would've used the liquor they had up here, instead of makin' you trot them stairs," he commented, peering into the cupboard.

"What liquor?" snarled Kelden. "They didn't have no liquor up here before they began to play. All they got was what I had to carry."

76

"Is that right?" Jerico appeared interested. "How do you know?"

"Because Tipon never keeps no liquor in this room ... an', anyhow" — defiantly — "I looked in here yesterday mornin' before they began their game an' all I seen was a couple or three empty bottles."

"Must've brought it up with 'em, then," said Jerico.

"They didn't do that, neither. They all met in the bar before they come up an' I know they didn't have no liquor."

"Well, there's some here now," said Jerico. "Here, lemme have that broom an' you straighten up the chairs an' the table."

He took the broom from the willing Kelden and, while that worthy set the table and chairs to rights and generally straightened up the place, Jerico finished sweeping. When they had finished, he accompanied the hotel employee down the stairs again and left him to his potato peeling. Jerico walked around to the front of the Manassa House, entered the lobby, and there, sitting in a chair, leaned back against the wall, and with his hat tipped down over his eyes, devoted himself to some serious thinking. It was in that position that Tom Barr found him when he entered the lobby later in the afternoon.

Jerico was glad to see Tom. He got out of his chair and invited the young deputy to have a drink. Tom, who had left his car outside, accompanied Jerico into Billy Holmes's bar and they indulged in a modest libation. With that accomplished they returned to the lobby.

Barr had a good deal to tell Jerico and Jerico was more than willing to listen.

"They ain't found out nothing more in Littlecreek," announced Barr. "The State Bankers' Association has got out a reward of a thousand dollars apiece for the fellers that done the job, an' Purdy has got a posse 'most organized. They'll be out through here, some of 'em, right away. Purdy thinks now that the bank robbers might've gone some other way. There was a car with men in it that answered their description, that went out of Littlecreek, headed south, right after the robbery. He thinks that mebbe your horses have just been stole by some local talent or mebbe a drifter. He heard that there'd been some stock missin', an', when he was out to Tipon's Half Triangle, Tipon told him that this was part of Madrid's buckin' string."

"Nice an' obligin' of Tipon, wasn't it?" questioned Jerico, his blue eyes narrowed in a squint. "How'd he know they was Madrid's horses? I didn't tell him."

Barr shrugged. "How do I know?" he said. "I didn't tell him, neither, but he knew all right. What you find out?"

"I found out that there ain't no ready-made suits in this town," replied Jerico, "but there's been some. You know —" He broke off abruptly. "Say, do you like to play poker?"

Barr was plainly puzzled by the sudden change of subject.

"Why, yeah," he said. "Say, what's playin' poker got to do with all this? What you drivin' at?"

"I like to play a little, too. Do you reckon we could get up a little game?"

Barr scratched his head, ruffling his black hair, and squinted at Jerico. "We might," he replied finally. "You're just too damn' agile for me. Your mind skips around like a flea on a griddle. What do you want to play poker for?"

"For instruction." Jerico was grinning broadly. "Let's you an' me go into the saloon an' do some talkin'. I'd like to get into that game that Tipon is puttin' on tonight in his room."

Barr shook his head. "No chances for that," he said. "Didn't you hear Holmes say that it was already six-handed? That game's about full up."

"But it mightn't be tonight," urged Jerico. "Come on. I'm a optimist."

Followed by the puzzled Barr, Jerico went into the saloon that adjoined the Manassa House. There, after buying a drink, he indulged in considerable conversation, flashed a sizeable roll of bills, and otherwise laid himself open to inspection. Jerico was adroit. Tom Barr followed his leads, and, with such gentle manipulation, it was Billy Holmes himself who suggested that Jerico's pining for a game of chance might get its fulfilment when Tipon and his party arrived.

"If Tipon's game ain't full up," said Holmes, "you might get into it. I'll ask him when he comes in. You goin' to be around?"

"Later on in the evenin'," replied Jerico. "I'd sure be obliged if you'd suggest it to him. Let me know, will you?"

Holmes said that he would, and Jerico and the puzzled Tom Barr left the saloon again and returned to the lobby. The hotel dining room was open and the two went in and ate supper together. When they returned to the lobby after the meal, it was almost dark outside.

"Let's go in an' see how our chances are for that poker party," suggested Jerico, crossing the lobby. "I hope that they're comin' all right."

"You're sure rarin' to lose some money," grumbled Barr, following Jerico. "Damn it! I'm about ready to quit you an' go home. I don't think . . ."

"Wait till mornin' before you quit," urged Jerico, opening the door to the barroom. "Gosh, feller, don't run out on me now. I need you."

At the bar they found Holmes talking to a bulky, somewhat gray man who turned and scanned them with cold gray eyes as they entered. Barr nodded shortly. Apparently he knew the gentleman talking to Holmes. The bartender beckoned Jerico over and introduced him.

"This here is Mister Tipon, Mister Jones," said Holmes. "I was just tellin' him about your wantin' to play a little poker tonight. He thinks mebbe he can accommodate you."

Neither Jerico nor Tipon extended a hand. Both nodded, each to the other, and each stared with steady eyes. Tipon was the first to speak.

"I reckon we might get you in," he announced, his voice a hard rasp. "The game's six-handed, if everybody shows up, but we could make it seven."

"I'd take it mighty kindly," Jerico drawled. "It's kind of lonesome just waitin' with nothin' to do."

"You're the feller that lost the horses, ain't you?" Tipon asked abruptly. Jerico nodded. "Heard anythin' of 'em?"

"Not yet, but I'm expectin' to 'most any time. I'll be droppin' around later. I got a little business to tend to, an' then I'll look you up. I'm shore obliged." Jerico half turned.

"What time will you be comin'?" Tipon's words checked Jerico's movement.

"I reckon around nine or nine-thirty, if that's all right with you," Jerico answered the question. "I'll try to make it by then."

"We'll count on you at nine-thirty." Tipon was definite in his statement. "I'll look for you then."

Jerico nodded. "Nine-thirty it is," he said. "Come on, Barr. I'm shore obliged, Mister Tipon." With Barr trailing him, Jerico went back to the lobby. Well away from the saloon door, he stopped and whirled on the sulky Barr. "You dressed for business?" he snapped.

Barr stared at his questioner. "Why," he said, his puzzlement showing in his voice. "I got a gun in the car. Do you want me to get it?"

Jerico shook his head. "You heard him say nine-thirty, didn't you?" he snapped. "Let's go!"

With Barr hurrying after him, he almost ran from the lobby and climbed into the seat of Tom's car.

Barr slid in behind the wheel and clicked the ignition switch. "Where to?" he questioned.

"Out toward the Half Triangle," said Jerico. "I'll tell you while we're goin'."

With the car started and sliding smoothly up the road toward the north, Barr ventured a glance at the man who sat beside him. Jerico was staring straight out into the headlights' beam and, despite his promise of a moment before, was singularly uncommunicative. Barr, impatient with his status, spoke somewhat sharply.

"Well," he said, "you said you'd tell me. Do it!"

Jerico took a long breath and expelled it. "I'm afraid to think I'm right in what I think," he said somewhat ambiguously. "Still, it's got to be that way or else my brains are lyin' to me along with a lot of facts. Tom, what would you say if we run into my horses out at the Half Triangle?"

"I'd say that they'd picked 'em up for you," responded Barr promptly.

"Yeah" — dryly — "so would I. About one o'clock this mornin', or thereabouts."

"What you mean? Do you think that Tipon an' the Half Triangle men stole 'em last night? Why, you're crazy!"

"Somebody's got to be crazy. If Tipon didn't take them horses, or else order 'em taken, then I'm shore enough nuts."

"You shore are." Barr slowed the car. "If you're goin' out to the Half Triangle, figgerin' to find your horses out there, I'd say you were plenty loco."

"They're there if they are in the country." Jerico was very positive. "You trail with me, Tom, an' I'll prove I'm right."

"Then you think that Tipon an' them fellers was the ones that robbed the bank in Littlecreek? Why, they couldn't've done it. They was all upstairs over Billy Holmes's place, playin' poker, when the bank was robbed. They couldn't't've."

"I told you it sounded crazy," reminded Jerico. "Listen, Tom. This mornin' I made some inquiries concernin' ready-to-wear clothes in Cisco. I found out there wasn't but a few in town, but there had been some at Moss's store an' they *hadn't* been sold! Not only that, but Tipon was mighty anxious to get me into that poker game tonight. Then, this afternoon, before you come back, I got to visit Tipon's room a little an' I found some liquor there. That set me thinkin' more than ever because Kelden had been busy all last night, cartin' up drinks. Tom, I'll bet you that Tipon an' his Half Triangle men not only took my horses, but I'll go further than that . . . *I'll bet they was in that bank robbery at Littlecreek.*"

Tom Barr took his foot off the gas, and the car drifted along, losing speed. He stared at Jerico, his eyes incredulous in the light from the dash. Finally he spoke. "You're crazy," he said hoarsely.

"I told you," reiterated Jerico. "Just the same, when I was in the Rangers, I've gone on crazier things than this. I . . ."

Barr's eyes widened. "Are you *that* Jones?" he snapped. "The feller that run that bunch out of Uvalde an' —"

"I'm that Jones," interrupted Jerico. "Speed it up a little, will you, Tom?"

Barr made no reply save to increase the speed of the car, and they tore along the level highway in silence save for the noise of the motor. Presently Barr slowed and negotiated a turn from the main road. They struck off to the right on two narrow, deeply printed ruts.

Jerico stirred in his seat. "This the road to the Half Triangle?" he questioned.

"Yeah." Barr was laconic.

"Stop before we come to the ranch," requested Jerico. "Mebbe it would be a good thing if you stopped before they could hear the noise of the car there."

"I still think you're bughouse," reminded Barr, "but I'll go with you a piece. Wouldn't do to have a nut trailin' off alone. I'll stop in plenty of time."

"That's all I'm askin' you to do," retorted Jerico. "It won't be long now before we see whether I'm crazy."

Barr grunted.

The narrow road twisted and turned. Presently Barr took his foot from the throttle and began to apply the brakes. "We're about a quarter of a mile from the ranch," he said. "I —"

In front of Tom Barr the windshield shivered into a thousand pieces. Concurrent with the crash of glass came the smashing report of a rifle. Jerico, his short-barreled Colt in his hand, dived over the door and lit, sprawled in the road. Behind him the runabout came to a halt. In the dim light of the dash lamp Jerico could see Tom Barr opening the left-hand door. Another rifle shot came with its accompanying tinkle of glass and the right headlight went into darkness.

"You all right, Tom?" Jerico called softly.

84

A muffled curse came in answer and Jerico grinned in the darkness. Barr was all right or, at the worst, had a very slight wound. The tall Texan wormed his way from the car toward a clump of soapweed close to him. "Stay down," he warned, low voiced.

His answer was a rifle shot that whined by, singing shrilly. Jerico hugged the earth. From the other side of the car a Colt began a hoarse bellowing. Apparently Barr had taken his gun with him when he had left the car. The staccato roar of the Colt was punctuated by the sharper, more emphatic *crack* of the rifle. Jerico saw a red flash and in the next second was on his feet, running toward it. He zigzagged in his run, felt the hot breath of a bullet in his face, replied to the shot, and the next instant was upon a man who half rose and tried to meet him. The short Colt in Jerico's hand described a swift arc that ended on a head. Jerico felt the man beneath him go limp and, breathless, Jerico crawled to his feet.

"Quit, Tom!" he called. "It's all over!"

Barr, stuffing shells into a gun, crossed the beam of the single headlight and came toward Jerico. "What in hell was this all about?" he demanded as he came up.

"We didn't start stoppin' soon enough," explained Jerico. "This feller didn't want no visitors."

Barr lit a match and bent over the man on the ground.

"Why, it's Stuffy Ellis!" he exclaimed, amazed. "What in hell could have put him on the prod?"

"Know him, do you?" questioned Jerico.

"Yeah. He works for Tipon."

"He's the feller that was goin' to bring back my horses, chances are," observed Jerico, busying himself with a neckerchief that he took from his captive. "We'll tie him up an' go a little further into this."

"I'm commencin' to believe you, Jerico." Tom Barr's voice was grim.

"Uhn-huh." Jerico tugged a knot tight on Ellis's wrists. "Lets take him over to the car an' go on to the ranch. If I'm right, it's goin' to get more interestin', an' it shore looks like I'm right."

Barr was lifting the inert man's feet as Jerico took up his head. "Interestin'?" he asked. "Mebbe you could call it that, but I want to know . . ."

"An' you'll find out," assured Jerico. "What you worryin' about? You're havin' a good time, ain't you?"

"Oh sure" — sarcastically — "I'm havin' a regular whale of a time. Here's the car. Do you want to put him to bed in it?"

"Nope." Jerico heaved his end of the body onto the seat. "I just want him to rest easy. Now, let's lash his feet to the steerin' post an' go on about our business."

While Jerico acted on his own suggestion, Barr opened the hood of his roadster and lit a match. The match went out, but Barr's profanity rumbled on.

"Ruined!" he announced. "That slug that hit the lamp went on an' plugged the vacuum tank. We're stuck."

Jerico came around the car. He had finished his tying job and now he, too, lit a match and bent over the engine. Tom had been right — the vacuum tank of the car was pierced by a jagged hole.

Jerico blew out his match, and he straightened. "An' I got a date to play poker at nine-thirty," he said softly.

"An' I got a ruined car." Barr was so mad that he was almost crying. "By damn, Jones! This is the blamedest, craziest —"

Jerico interrupted the tirade. "One good thing," he said softly, "they'll be a place in that poker game for you now."

"I don't give a damn about that poker game. My car's shot an' . . ."

"We'll all get half shot when it's over," assured the hopeful Mr. Jones. "Come on. Let's go to the house an' see if we cain't find somethin'."

Tom Barr was too mad for further speech. Without a word he set off along the road, and Jerico, grinning placidly in the darkness, followed his seething companion.

It took the two men perhaps ten minutes to reach the Half Triangle ranch house. There was a light in the kitchen window, and Jerico, after a cautious investigation, returned to Barr and informed him that there was no one at home in the place. Barr didn't care and said so. He had lost his temper very thoroughly and he sullenly followed Jerico around the house and to the barn, beside which was a corral. There were horses in the corral that shied and moved away at the approach of the two.

"That's them," asserted Jerico. "That's that damn' bunch of wild eyes I was trailin'. I'd know 'em any place. I'll bet they wasn't here when the sheriff come out. Tipon had 'em cached an' brought 'em in tonight."

"You cain't see," reminded Barr. "You don't know for sure. I *still* think you're crazy. What the hell would Tipon be doin' with Madrid's buckin' horses?"

"He didn't want Madrid's buckin' horses," explained Jerico patiently. "He'd never've took 'em if he'd knowed they was a rough string. That's why he was goin' to return 'em tonight. When I was peacefully gettin' rooked at poker about ten o'clock, these horses was due to be delivered at the Manassa House corral. Come on. Let's go see if we cain't find a saddle."

"But I don't figger . . ."

"If I had time, I'd draw you a picture," snapped Jerico. "I'm right so far, ain't I? Well . . . now, where in hell is that saddle shed?"

Silenced, Mr. Barr conducted the way toward the desired room in the barn. Once inside the tack room Jerico lit a match and looked around. His glance fell upon a familiar object and he stepped toward it, picked it up, and held it out toward Mr. Barr.

"Here's my saddle," he announced triumphantly. "Now, what'd I tell you? This . . . *Ouch!* Damn it!" The match he held had burned his finger and the rest of Jerico's speech was unintelligible. Finally he took his finger out of his mouth long enough to command aggrievedly, "Get you a saddle," and, lugging his own furnishings, tramped out of the saddle room.

When Barr, carrying a saddle that he fondly hoped would fit him as to stirrup length, joined Jerico beside the corral fence, the tall man was unfastening his rope from his saddle and whistling tunelessly.

"I'm goin' to get you that gray horse," announced Jerico, placing a foot on the bottom rail of the corral. "See him?"

Dimly in the darkness, Barr could discern a gray object in the corral. "Yeah, I see him," he said.

"Well" — Jerico crawled over the corral fence and dropped inside — "he don't pitch much. I'll snare him out for you."

"What one you goin' to ride?" Tom could see Jerico's arm move as he shook out a loop.

"I dunno that I'm goin' to ride." Jerico's voice was dry. "I'm goin' to make a hell of an effort though. Most any of them hellers is bad enough, but we ain't got time to be pickin' an' choosin' tonight. I'm goin' to spread a wide loop an' . . . *Ugh!*" This last as his rope fell and he dropped the end across his thighs and set back on it.

"Here's your gray horse, Tom."

Barr swung his saddle up on the fence and climbed over. He was beginning to believe that his companion was right in his wild guesses. Jerico was going up the rope, hand over hand, and the gray horse stood quietly.

When Barr had slipped a bit into the horse's mouth and fastened the throat latch on the bridle, Jerico took off his rope.

"Lead him out a ways," he requested. "I'm apt to fasten on to a wil'cat this time."

Barr did as requested, leading his horse over toward the fence and his saddle. When he had adjusted the blanket and was swinging up his saddle, he heard Jerico grunt again and knew that a second horse had been roped.

Apparently Jerico was having trouble with this one. Barr heard a *thud* and a scramble and some lurid profanity. He tugged tight his latigo and, fastening the reins to a fence rail, hurried to help his companion.

But Jerico did not need help. "He's standin' like an old cow, now. Just fought a little at first," Jerico informed Barr when the latter came up. "I'll get my saddle on him all right, but I don't know what from then on. The way he's actin' I think he's Ol' Blue, an', if he is, I'm in for it." As he spoke, he started up the rope, gingerly. Barr stood still and awaited developments.

"It's Blue, all right," announced Jerico cheerfully. "I won't need no help to saddle him. I wish you'd open the gate."

"These horses will drift out," objected Tom.

"They won't go far from water," replied Jerico, "an', anyhow, I'm goin' to need a couple of acres to ride this devil in. Whoa! You damn' jughead! Don't you swell under this saddle."

Barr untied his own horse and, leading him, went to the gate. He let down the bars and awaited developments. There was still some speech inside the corral. Apparently Jerico was trying to talk the blue horse out of the notion of bucking. Barr chuckled and swung into his saddle. He was pleased to find that his choice had been good. The stirrups were long enough and the saddle was easy. There was a commotion inside of the corral, a wild yelp, and then a horse and rider shot out of the gate toward the house.

90

Where the light from the lamp in the window gave a dim glow, the blue horse stopped his sudden bolt, ducked his head, and went to work. And there, before an audience of one, Jerico Jones put on an exhibition. He rode that blue horse free and easy. He raked him and beat him with his hat while the blue tried to drive his hoofs into the hard earth and arch his back to the skies at the same instant. The blue sunfished and fence-rowed, reared, and stood almost straight on his front hoofs, and then, as suddenly as it had begun, it was over. The blue horse bawled once and his head came up. He lunged out of the light and his hoofs beat the mad tattoo of a gallop. From the dark Jerico's voice floated back to Tom Barr.

"Come on! Let's go to town!"

Barr, awe in his face, kicked the gray horse into a run and set out after Jerico.

When Tom Barr caught up with his companion, the blue horse was bucking again. Barr could tell by the erratic pound of hoofs and the thwacks as Jerico's hat struck the blue that there was a ride in progress, but he could not get close enough to see much of it. Jerico yelled to Barr when the blue let down a little in his pitching, instructing him to go to the car, see if their captive were still tied fast, and turn off the single remaining headlight. Barr spurred ahead to perform Jerico's wishes, and had just made sure that Ellis was still securely fastened, when the blue horse pounded by. Barr flicked the car light into darkness, swung up on the gray, and followed.

The blue roan bucked spasmodically all the way into Cisco. At times he would run madly, then down would go his head and up would go his back. It was a much pounded and shaken Jerico Jones who managed to climb down from the blue close by the Manassa House and lead the horse toward the corral. Tom Barr, without instructions, followed Jerico's lead. They stripped the saddles from their mounts inside the corral, and Jerico hastily made what toilet he could in the light that came from the Manassa House windows. When he had rearranged his attire and straightened himself up as best he could, he spoke earnestly to Tom Barr.

"Now, listen, Tom," he said. "I'm goin' up to that poker game. You come along. You foller what I say an' don't make no comments. If it comes to trouble, remember that there's times when one man alone has a big advantage an' don't you go hornin' in. I've damn' near been killed twicet by well meanin' friends tryin' to save my life. You trailin' with me?"

Barr nodded. "An hour ago I thought you was plenty crazy," he said ruefully. "Now, I reckon I am. Findin' them horses at the Half Triangle has plumb upset me. I don't know nothin' an' I'm not a damn' bit sure of that. I'll foller your lead, Jerico."

Satisfied, Mr. Jones turned and went toward the outside stair that led up to Tipon's room. There were lights in the room and Jerico, as he progressed toward it, furtively felt under his coat and made sure that the Colt was in its holster. A thought struck him and he stopped, jacked an empty shell from the gun, and replaced it, then slipped another shell into the chamber that he usually kept empty. With that done, he resumed his progress, reached the stairs, and ascended them. Barr followed close at his heels.

At the door of the room, Jerico knocked and a voice from within demanded his identity. Jerico answered and was bidden enter. He pushed open the door and went into the lighted room. Just inside, he stepped to the right and Tom Barr came in. Jerico blinked until his eyes adjusted themselves, and then he nodded to Tipon who had half risen from a seat at the table.

"I brung Barr up with me," announced Jerico. "He hadn't nothin' to do, an' I thought he could loaf here a while. That all right with you?"

"Why . . ." Tipon hesitated. "I reckon so. You don't want to play, do you, Barr?"

"No." Barr shook his head. "I'm just killin' time."

"That's all right, then." Tipon sank back, apparently relieved. "Stuffy Ellis is comin' up later, an' I told him I'd save him a place. That'll make the game seven handed. We could take in another, but . . ."

"I don't want to play," Barr said again. "I'll just sit around a while an' look on."

Tipon turned from Barr to Jerico. "You don't know these fellers, do you, Jones?" he questioned. "This here" — pointing to a heavy set man at his right — "is Ross Gates, my foreman. That's Moss that keeps the store here. This here's Burrel," he continued, indicating a long, lank man with a drooping mouth and a great predatory nose. "Burrel runs a garage at Littlecreek. That there is Cartwright from San Antone. Fellers, this is Mister Jones. Now we're all acquainted . . . we can play some cards."

As Tipon spoke, he had pointed out each of the men named. Moss was short, his hair graying, and deep lines were etched in a rather white face. Cartwright was a wiry man of medium height, and one eye squinted badly. He looked steadily at Jerico as if seeking some sign of recognition, but Jerico's face remained impassive. Jerico nodded to each man in turn, then, when the introductions were finished, stepped to the table and pulled back a chair. Tom Barr, his face as blank as Jerico's, stepped halfway around the table and took an empty seat, tipping back in it. Jerico, in that moment, admired the black-haired, black-eyed Wyoming boy. Barr was good. He was in a place and a situation that he didn't know anything about, but he was backing the man who was with him. Jerico turned to Tipon.

"What we playin'?" he asked.

"Draw," replied Tipon. "It's the only game there is that's worthwhile. We play straight draw with no joker runnin' wild, nor nothin' else. Every time the deal goes clear around, we play one hand of stud. That suit you?"

"Suits me," replied Jerico. "Table stakes?"

"Yeah," Tipon told him, "an' you can play back as much as you like. The ante's a dollar an' it's a fifty-dollar limit. Let's cut for deal."

Jerico nodded and settled into his chair. From his pocket he brought out a roll of bills, peeled off $100, and shoved the money toward Tipon, who sat at the banker's slot. "I'll take that in chips," said Jerico, "an' I'm playin' a thousand back of it."

The other men in the game bought chips, stacked them neatly before themselves, and the cards were cut for deal. Moss won the deal, riffled the cards, and slid them out.

As a poker game it was interesting. Jerico played a leather vest game. He trailed in the betting, losing his ante time and again in order to see how the men about the table played their cards. It was half an hour and the deal had been clear around before Jerico loosened up. Then, when the stud hand was dealt, he bet, caught a pair back to back, got the third one on the fourth card, and won the pot. As he gathered in the chips, he grinned.

"My first pot," he announced. "I'll buy a drink on that. You got any liquor here?"

Before Tipon could answer, he was on his feet and striding to the cupboard in the corner. The filled bottle he brought out was plainly astonishing to the men about the table. Jerico was grinning cheerfully as he brought it back.

"Didn't expect I'd find no liquor, did you?" he observed. "Now, where in hell's the glasses? Glasses? Glasses?" He stared about the room. Tipon had slid back his chair and was staring at Jerico and the full bottle.

"There's another where this come from," assured Jerico cheerfully. "Don't appear to be no glasses here. Oh, well, we can drink from the bottle, cain't we, Squint?"

At the question, Cartwright half rose, and then slumped back again into his chair, his face a mask of hate and every muscle tense.

Jerico uncorked the bottle and, holding it in his left hand, passed his right across the mouth to wipe it. "You know," he remarked conversationally, "it's a heap better for us to take a drink like this than it is to keep Kelden trottin' up an' down them stairs like we done the other night. Besides, we don't need no alibi, tonight, do we, Burrel?" He half raised the bottle.

Burrel, his face white, managed a question. "What . . . what'd you mean?" he half gasped.

"Oh, nothin' much." Jerico lowered the bottle and stood it on the table. "You're shore tight, Burrel. You ought to've got rid of this whiskey and not tried to save it. But, hell, that's nothin'. You fellers all made plenty of mistakes."

Cartwright was crouched in his chair. Moss was tilted back, the tips of his fingers touching the table. Gates sat and stared, his slow wits not equal to the task confronting them.

Tipon rasped a question. "What are you talkin' about, Jones?"

"I'll tell you," replied Jerico easily. "Before I do that though, I want to compliment you. Havin' a poker game is shore a slick way of dividin' up the loot. I'll say that." He paused. Not a man about the table stirred. Jerico noted with satisfaction that Tom Barr had put his chair upon all four legs and was sitting tensely in it.

"Several mistakes," resumed Jerico, his voice musing. "Leavin' that packin' box that the clothes come in, out

96

back of your place, Moss. That was a mistake . . . an' Burrel's savin' this whiskey. My . . . my! Then pullin' Squint Cartwright in on the deal. The knife play had all the earmarks of that job you done in Laredo, Squint. Your name wasn't Cartwright then, though. Mistakes? Hell, the whole damn' thing was full of 'em, but I reckon the worst one, outside of robbin' the bank, was stealin' my horses. Tryin' to steal a rough string. I cain't figure —"

But Squint Cartwright, with a squeal of rage, had leaped from his chair to the table top, a knife glinting in his hand. Tipon was on his feet, his hand flashing back toward his hip. Moss had dropped to the floor and rolled under the table. Burrel was up, tugging at a gun. Only Ross Gates, a vacant expression on his face, still held his seat.

Jerico's hand dived beneath his coat and the short-barreled Colt came out in a dull blue arc. It crashed once and Cartwright, on the table, folded in the middle and went down, finished, a slug where his belt buckle should have been. Tom Barr came out of his chair as if on springs. A gun flashed in his hand and bellowed, and the light, hanging over the table, swayed wildly and crashed down. As it fell, Jerico could see Barr going under the table after Moss. With the fall of the light came total darkness. A gun flashed redly to Jerico's left, and he threw a swift shot in reply, dropping to his knees immediately after he had fired. Apparently he had missed, for the gun flashed again. Following its crash came a scream, unearthly and awe-inspiring, and then a *thud*. From the direction of the scream a voice came harshly:

"Damn it, you killed Gates!"

Jerico fired twice in the direction of the voice, dropped flat, and rolled swiftly. He was just in time, for three guns answered his fire. The table, heretofore still standing, fell with a crash and there came the *thud* of a blow.

Jerico, flat and still on the floor, moved his hand out cautiously. His fingers encountered a booted foot. Jerico grabbed the boot and jerked with all his strength. The man above him toppled, tried to recover his balance, and fell. Jerico, rolling cat-like, was on top of him, swinging his Colt. The first blow missed the man's head, but the second went home. Jerico was left with two opponents and a possible third. He discounted the latter possibility, however. He had seen Tom Barr go under the table and he believed that Tom had taken care of Moss. From somewhere above him and to his right came a hoarse panting. Jerico, coming to his knees again, listened intently, swinging his Colt in the direction of the sound. He had fired three times. There were three more shots in his gun. When they were gone, he would be at the mercy of the men about him until he could reload.

Steps pounded up the stairs outside. Jerico waited, holding his breath. The hoarse breathing near him changed its position. The door of the room swung open and a lamp was thrust inside. For a moment the room was lighted and in that moment Jerico saw Tipon, still on his feet, swinging his big body toward him. Both men were off balance, both out of position, still two shots roared together. Jerico felt a burning pain along his side, and lurched. The lamp was swiftly withdrawn — went out. Again there was utter blackness. In the room a man groaned. There was a staggering step, and then a heavy *thump* as a body struck the floor. Again there was silence.

The silence lasted forever, it seemed to Jerico. It beat and pulsated about him. He wanted to scream, to shout, to pull the trigger on the remaining shots in the Colt. Still he waited, his iron will controlling every jumping nerve in his body. A voice spoke softly and yet it roared in his ears:

"Jerico."

Jerico did not answer.

Again came the voice. "Jerico. This is Barr."

"You all right?" questioned Jerico. "There's another one, Tom. You . . ."

A match flamed from behind the table and Tom Barr rose to his feet. "They're all down," he said softly. "You damn' heller!"

Again came the *thud* of feet on the stairs. Light flooded in through the open door. Billy Holmes, holding a lamp in one hand and a cocked double-barreled shotgun in the other, stood in the opening.

"What the hell?" he demanded angrily. "What . . . ?"

"Come in, Holmes," said Jerico wearily. "Come in. This, I reckon, is the end of the bunch that robbed the Littlecreek bank."

★　★　★

About two o'clock that afternoon, seated in the lobby of the Manassa House, Jerico Jones, his feet stretched out before him, spoke softly to Tom Barr who sat at his side. In the corral back of the Manassa House were twelve horses, part of Lew Madrid's string of buckers. On the road to Littlecreek were two cars. One of those cars contained a much-puzzled sheriff named Purdy, two deputies, and two prisoners, Moss and Stuffy Ellis. The other car held a disgusted deputy sheriff and four dead men: Tipon, Cartwright, Ross Gates, and the lanky Burrel.

For the third time, Jerico was explaining things to Tom Barr.

"Now you see," said Jerico patiently, "they took my horses to throw the sheriff off the track. They had to return the car they'd used, because it was Burrel's, an' he couldn't have it turn up missin'. So they borrowed my horses to make it look like they'd took to the hills. Tipon's men had come in on horseback, an' they just drove my bronc's out, dodgin' the deputy that was watchin' the road for a car. The saddles went in Tipon's car, and the deputy let it get by without searching it, because it was a local car. They'd had Moss order them blue suits. He could do it, bein' in the business, an' their wearin' clothes like that was a good disguise. Nobody'd ever seen any of 'em in them kind of clothes. Moss leavin' the packin' box outside his place, where I could see it, was a mistake, like I said. Cartwright done the knifin'. I figgered that when I seen him, an' Moss said so. Cartwright pulled a knife stunt in Laredo when I was in the Rangers. He called hisse'f Carrel, then. We

100

caught him an' he was sent up for life, but he made a getaway an' drifted up here. He was shore a bloodthirsty little cuss. They left Burrel here to call for drinks an' act like there was a poker game goin' on. That was their alibi. Kelden trotted up an' down them stairs most of the night, cartin' whiskey, an' Burrel was too damn' stingy to throw it out. That saved whiskey helped hang it on 'em."

"Funny about Burrel," commented Tom Barr. "He just died of fright, I reckon. The coroner didn't find a scratch on him. Said he had a bad heart an' it quit on him."

"I reckon," said Jerico absently.

"But how'd they get out an' leave here?" questioned Barr, after a moment's pause.

"It wasn't hard," replied Jerico. "That outside stair made it pretty easy. They just kept goin' up an' down till Holmes an' Kelden got used to it an' then, one at a time, they'd forget to come back. They had Burrel's car cached outside town, an', when they all got congregated, they went off in it."

"Umm," Barr sighed thoughtfully. "I'm awfully dumb, I reckon."

"You ain't too dumb to make a break that give me a chance," rejoined Jerico. "Shootin' down that light wasn't a dumb stunt by no means."

"Umm," again Barr sighed, then he straightened in his chair. "But how'd you know they was goin' to bring them horses back last night?" he demanded.

"I didn't know," returned Jerico. "I just figgered they would. When Tipon seen the brands by daylight, he was bound to know that they was Madrid's horses. Tipon had followed the rodeos some, Moss said so, an', havin' done that, he'd know the horses. I figgered he had 'em hid when he told the sheriff they belonged to Madrid. He didn't want no truck with a bunch of outlaw bronc's. They didn't fit into his scheme, so he was goin' to turn 'em back into the corral. That would've muddied things up a lot more. Don't you see?"

Tom Barr shook his head. "No," he said, "I don't see. That is, I don't see how you doped it out, but then, like I said, I'm dumb. What you goin' to do now, Jerico?"

Jerico scratched his head, then reached meditatively for the makings. "Go to Littlecreek for the rodeo, I reckon," he replied. "Then . . . say, Tom, you said a while ago that you was figgerin' on a little ranch some time pretty soon. I been figgerin' the same thing. Why don't you an' me take what we got an' go look for one? Think you could stand it?"

Tom Barr grinned at his companion. "I dunno," he said slowly. "If the last two days is a sample of your goods, I dunno whether I could stand the pace or not. But I'll tell you, Jerico, we'll try it a whirl."

102

$teers

This was Bennett Foster's second Jerico Jones story. It appeared in *Short Stories* (12/25/35), a monthly magazine owned and published at the time by Doubleday, Doran & Company, Inc.

CHAPTER
ONE

Jerico Jones liked the looks of the kid in the corral. He liked the business-like way the young fellow set about saddling the blindfolded pony that was tied to the snubbing post, and he liked the way the kid went on with his work and paid no attention to spectators. The kid was a hand.

Sitting the gray horse, Stranger, that he had bought in Vado, one booted foot cocked over the horn of his saddle, Jerico prepared to enjoy himself. There was going to be a show and Jerico had a reserved seat.

With the saddle on and cinched down tightly, the youngster stepped back a pace and surveyed his handiwork. Apparently finding it good, he loosened the pony from the snubbing post, caught a stirrup, and went up into the saddle. There he collected the long end of the loose rope he had knotted to the hackamore, tucked one end in his belt, took a good hold with his left hand, and, leaning forward, slipped the blindfold from the trembling horse.

The pony stood stockstill for a moment, collecting himself, and then went straight up in the air. The boy rode easily. He didn't spur like a contest rider, nor did he pull off his battered Stetson and fan the horse. He sat the saddle, anticipating his mount's movements by the fractional second that marks the rider and, anticipating them, shifted his weight adroitly. The chunky bay horse was a bucker. Jerico leaned forward in his own saddle to watch the show.

The kid was riding clean, and so engrossed was Jerico that he failed to note the advent of another rider beside the corral. Jerico was riding that bucking horse with the kid and sweating just about as much as the kid was. The bay spun, sunfished along the side of the corral, hit the ground with all four hoofs, and sucked back under the saddle and the kid stayed there. Jerico, brought to his senses by the odor of burning hair, plucked the cigarette from his lips and threw it away. For perhaps the 4,000th time he had singed the close-cropped brown mustache that shaded his lips. He swore petulantly at the mustache and, turning his head, saw the other rider.

Jerico nodded a greeting and with lifted reins moved Stranger over toward the newcomer. He was filled with admiration for the job going on in the corral and he wanted to share his enthusiasm with someone else.

"Makin' quite a ride of it, ain't he?" said Jerico when Stranger stopped.

The man he addressed merely grunted, and Jerico spared a glance from the exhibition in the corral. He didn't particularly like what he saw. The man was swarthy. His full lips were petulant, pouting a little. His black eyes were hard as he looked at Jerico, and his clothing was entirely too good. Jerico dressed pretty well himself but his taste ran more to boots and hats. Give Jerico Jones a pair of $40 shop-made boots and a $50 Stetson and he didn't care particularly what was between them. Jerico took his eyes from the black-haired man and watched the show.

The chunky bay horse was pretty well bucked out. The kid tried a tentative spur and renewed activities for a moment, but it was evident that the bay was through. A few more jumps and the horse quit, standing with heaving sides and head down. The kid waited as a gentleman should, to see if there was anything more his opponent had to do. The bay was quiet and the kid climbed down and fell with adroit, adept movements to removing the saddle.

The black-haired man beside Jerico spoke for the first time. "When I want my horses rode, I'll tell you, Macklin!"

Macklin, the kid in the corral, pulled his saddle from the bay. He dropped it in the dust, pulled off the hackamore, and turned.

"He ain't your horse," said the kid levelly.

"He's my horse an' this is my place," snapped the black-eyed man. "You got your notice to vacate yesterday."

"An' tore it up," answered the boy. He lifted the heavy saddle and, carrying it, came to the corral fence. Depositing the saddle atop the fence, he climbed up and over to stand to Jerico's right. Jerico reined Stranger back out of line. Evidently he had butted into something here in Rock Rib Valley.

"You'll get off this place." The black-eyed man seemed very certain of his ground. "It was mortgaged to me an' I'm goin' to take it over. You're dispossessed."

"He don't seem to know it," said Jerico dryly.

"Keep out of this!" snarled the black-eyed man, glancing at Jerico.

Jerico's blue eyes were mildly amused.

"This is my place!" Macklin, the youngster on the ground, spoke harshly. "I own it. The mortgage ain't for enough to cover it all. Sturgis, you maybe can pull that on some, but you can't on me. Now get out!"

The black-haired man backed his horse a step or two. For a moment Jerico thought that he was going to take the order. There was a look on the man's face that Jerico didn't like. There was something coming. Sturgis had a hand hidden by the skirts of his coat. There was a gun in that hand, Jerico was sure. Macklin, the kid, didn't have a gun. A man doesn't ride buckers with a hogleg on his hip. Jerico's own right hand stole up and caressed his mustache. Six inches down from that brown adornment, under his coat was a spring-clip holster and a .45 with a four and a half inch barrel. Several men had mistaken mustache stroking for a gesture of indecision.

"No, sir," said Jerico softly, and yet there was command in his voice. "The kid ain't got no gun on him."

Neither Macklin on the ground nor Sturgis in his saddle looked at Jerico. Apparently they were waiting for something. Sturgis spoke, his voice as soft as Jerico's.

"Get off my land," said Sturgis, and added a name that will bring a fight wherever English is spoken. Macklin's face went red. He lunged forward, reached with angry hands for the man on the horse. As he moved, Sturgis brought a gun from under his coat, and from the corner of the log barn, close by the corral, a rifle blasted. Macklin's lunge became a fall. He pitched down, full length, rolled convulsively, and for a moment Jerico had a picture of an awful face, the eyes wide and staring and the forehead gone where a soft-nose slug had torn its way through bone and brain.

In the next instant Stranger leaped under the thrust of spurs. It was not a moment too soon, that leap. The rifle slammed again from the corner of the shed and lead smacked viciously through the air.

Jerico's own gun was out. Atop the plunging Stranger, Jerico threw two slugs toward the barn. From his left a Colt roared and Stranger ceased his plunging and leveled off in a run. Sturgis was shooting, Jerico knew. He pulled back on his reins to check the running Stranger, and the left rein snapped. There was blood on Stranger's neck. The leather dangled uselessly in Jerico's left hand. He twisted in the saddle and threw two shots back at Sturgis beside the corral. He had the satisfaction of seeing Sturgis throw himself out of the saddle, then the rifleman beside the barn resumed practice and Jerico flattened himself out and devoted his attention to getting the most out of his horse. Eight years in the Rangers had taught Jerico the fallacy of going up against a man with a rifle, particularly when that individual is hidden and is a good shot. Stranger went over a rise of ground with his belly almost touching the ridge, covered an intervening draw with a leap, and took to the other hillside. Jerico pulled hard on the rein left him, swung his weight to the right, and the running horse curved down from the hillside and went down the draw. There was no use in trying to stop Stranger. Jerico straightened in the saddle, swung his body with the wild run of the horse, and fell to jacking out used shells from the .45. His face was white beneath its tan, and his brown mustache stood out dark against the whiteness. He had just seen cold-blooded, premeditated murder committed, and he hadn't been able to do a thing about it.

The gray horse, Stranger, had ideas of his own about being stopped. A bullet crease along his neck had cemented those ideas in his mind, and Jerico was some distance away from the little cluster of ranch buildings where he had witnessed tragedy before he brought the gray down to sanity again. When he did gain control, he stopped the horse and dismounted. Then, taking a length of his rope for a rein, he repaired the damage wrought his bridle as best he could, soothed the trembling horse, and, mounting again, rode on at a hand's pace. Jerico knew that there was no use in returning to the scene of the shooting. He would either run into hot lead or, and this was more probable, find the killers gone. He carried a distinct picture in his mind of the dark-faced Sturgis. The actual killer he had not seen.

CHAPTER
TWO

There was a town, Niroba, somewhere to the south of him. The gray had run south, and Jerico judged that he was within ten or fifteen miles of the place. The proper thing for him to do, he felt, was to ride into Niroba and report the killing he had witnessed to the authorities. Still, Jerico was a canny sort of individual. In his thirty odd years he had seen a moil of strife and trouble and he was not in the habit of going off halfcocked. Before he did any reporting, he told himself grimly, he would do a little scouting around. The name Sturgis seemed to find some responsive spot in his memory. Somewhere he had heard that name, but he could not exactly make a connection. So, grim faced, Jerico rode on, and the gray Stranger, placid once more, set a steady running walk that ate the distance.

Striking a road that ran south Jerico swung into the ruts. He followed the road, passing a cluster of buildings over to his left where lights were already beginning to glow. Quite a pretentious ranch the size and number of buildings indicated. Probably a place where a wandering rider might find bed and board. Still Jerico rode on and within five miles his efforts were rewarded. The sun had dropped behind the Rock Ribs

111

and dusk was heavy in Rock Rib Valley when, crowning a low rise, Jerico saw, scattered before him, the lights of Niroba. Stranger checked the running walk and Jerico let go a long breath. This was town.

He watered Stranger at the trough in front of the blacksmith's shop near the edge of town and, riding easy, let the gray horse travel down the street. There was a graze on Stranger's neck and a rope bridle rein to back Jerico's story, and that was all. Reflecting on these facts, he did not immediately seek a livery stable and rest for the horse, but rather well toward the middle of Niroba's single dusty street he stopped and, tying the horse to a deserted hitch rail before an unlit store building, proceeded afoot. Caution and circumspection had served Jerico well before this. A man who rides the lone trails, be he outlaw or officer, learns to progress carefully until boldness is demanded. In front of a well-lighted building the sign of which informed the uninitiated that it was **The Stag Saloon,** Jerico stopped. He beat dust from his clothing with his gray Stetson, settled the shoulder rigging of his gun, and, with his coat shrugged down in place, walked through the swinging doors. Instantly light and sound beat upon him.

The Stag was populous. From the rear of the room came the musical *clink* of glasses, the fainter, softer flutter of cards being shuffled and poker chips touching each other. Smoke from cigarettes, pipes, and cigars curled up toward the two big lamps that hung from the ceiling and shone against the bracket lamps on the walls. The *thump* of booted feet came, and over all these sounds was the steady diapason of voices, drawling, soft-spoken voices. This was a cow town. Jerico felt weight drop from his shoulders. In a hundred towns in ten states he had been greeted by just such sounds. This was home.

As he walked toward the bar and a waiting bartender, Jerico became aware of a group of men clustered loosely under the nearest of the lights. Range men these were with the twang of Texas in their voices when they spoke. They were not doing much talking, Jerico noted. In the center of the group was a tall giant of a man, white-haired, hook-nosed, keen blue eyes showing beneath bushy white eyebrows, sweeping mustachios above his thin lips. Jerico knew the man. He was Old Man Larey of the Long L north of Marfa. Idly Jerico wondered what Larey was doing so far from home. No one knew how many acres the Long L controlled or how many cows wore the brand. Surely there was enough and more to keep the old man busy back in Texas. Shortly Jerico told himself, he would walk over and speak to Larey. They had sided each other some years before in a minor bickering near the border and Jerico knew that Larey would be glad to see him.

Jerico gave the bartender his order for whiskey and, when the glass and bottle were shoved out, poured a modest drink. He wanted information rather than whiskey. The bartender might give it.

"Pretty good business?" suggested Jerico.

The barman nodded. "Always good," he answered. "Niroba's a good town."

"You got quite a territory," said Jerico, putting down his glass. "Many ranches?"

The bartender shrugged. "Not so many as there was," he said. "We got one big one though, an' that's plenty. The fall work's about done an' there's lots of Bar S men in."

"Bar S?" questioned Jerico.

"Sturgis's outfit," said the barman. "Have one on the house?"

Jerico poured his drink and slid $1 out on the bar. There was a little fire creeping up in his mind. Sturgis! That was where he had heard the name. In Vado, where he had left the railroad in his quest, they had told him that there was not much use going south, that Sturgis owned the country. Men had been passing and repassing behind Jerico's broad back as he talked. Now the bartender nodded and Jerico half turned. He saw a broad-faced, sandy-complexioned man return the bartender's greeting. There was a star on the vest of the broad-faced man.

"Deputy sheriff," said the bartender as Jerico turned back. "Lance Touhy."

"Good man?" suggested Jerico mildly. He would have business with the sheriff's office presently.

"Plenty good," said the bartender. "Used to be a Bar S wagon boss. He spends most of his time around here. There was a killin' north of town today, an' I reckon Lance is lookin' into it."

"A killin'?" Jerico appeared to be slightly interested.

114

"Fella named Macklin," said the bartender. "Sturgis an' Webb Greves brought him in. Sturgis seen the fella that shot him."

"Well," said Jerico thoughtfully.

" 'Nuther?" questioned the bartender, eyeing the bottle.

"One more," agreed Jerico. "Where's a good place to eat?"

The bartender's eyebrows lifted. "Tired of eatin' at the yards with your bunch?" he asked.

Jerico saw that he had made a mistake. He hastened to rectify it. "I'm plenty tired of burned grub," he growled.

From his left, toward the clustered group of Texans, came a voice that caused Jerico to put down his partially filled glass. He had heard that voice, heard it during the afternoon. It was a hoarse, rasping voice, and, without turning, Jerico identified the owner. The speaker was Sturgis.

"That's the proposition. Take it or leave it!" snapped Sturgis.

Quiet seemed to settle in the Stag's long room following that announcement. Jerico turned slowly keeping his glass in his right hand. The movement brought his hand across his coat, nearer the .45 that lurked in the shoulder harness.

"Sturgis, you're a dirty crook!"

That was Old Man Larey's deep voice. Jerico, eyeing the old man saw that his mustache was bristling, a sure sign of impending trouble.

"You bargained for them steers last spring an' you know it."

"Have you got a scratch of paper to prove that, Larey?" Sturgis was apparently as angry as Larey. "You come bargin' into the yards with a thousand head of Chihuahuas an' expect me to take 'em off your hands. I won't do it. Not at the price you ask."

This was interesting. Jerico leaned forward a little to get a glimpse of Sturgis's face. He saw it, the same swarthy, full-lipped, black-eyed features that he had seen at the corral. Behind Sturgis was another man, almost an albino. As Jerico peered, he caught a glimpse of a pair of washed-out blue eyes as the man behind Sturgis looked up.

"I'll give you fifteen thousand dollars," rasped Sturgis. "Not a cent more. You can take it or leave it, Larey."

"Hell, they stand me twenty thousand the way it is," growled Old Man Larey.

"I can't help that." Sturgis lifted his hand and Jerico could see a slip of pink paper in it. "Here's the check."

There was a soft murmur among the cowpunchers near Larey. These were Long L hands, Jerico surmised. They were taking their temper from the boss.

"To hell with you!" Larey snapped the words. "Damn you, Sturgis, you crooked me an' you know it. You an' that white-eyed skunk behind you think you own the earth an' got a fence around it. You . . ."

The man behind Sturgis stepped away from the bar. Between Jerico and the tall Larey, men pushed themselves away. These were local men. Apparently they had an idea that something was coming. Jerico had seen that movement before, that ripple of men along a bar front. Usually it presaged a shooting. He stood calmly, his left foot on the bar rail, his right hand holding his glass.

"You talkin' about me, Larey?" snarled the light-eyed man.

Jerico, watching narrowly, wondered why it was that men like the speaker never became accustomed to the climate. They were always burned and never tanned. The speaker was sunburned and his nose was peeling and red.

From Larey's left a fresh voice came, a smooth, flowing voice with a touch of the South in it. "He was talkin' to you, Greves," said the voice. "Any remarks?"

Jerico looked at the speaker. He was young. Very young. His face looked as though it had never felt a razor. Smooth the boy was, smooth sloping shoulders, smoothly muscled body, smooth hair where it showed under his pushed back hat. The hands were long and brown and smooth. A heavy gun, butt swung a little forward, hung in a carved leather holster that seemed to hug the boy's thigh. Sure he was young and smooth and, Jerico judged, just about as forked a proposition as ever straddled a horse. The light-eyed man, Greves, would do well to take a backward step.

"Shut up, Pat!" snapped Old Man Larey angrily. "I'm old enough to look out for myse'f. Sure I was talkin' to you, Greves. To you an' Sturgis. I'll talk some more. I'll make you a proposition, Sturgis. I'll

117

write you a check for a million dollars even. I'll give it to you for the Bar S, lock, stock, an' barr'l. I aim to start me a steer ranch up here. What'd you say?"

Sturgis's face darkened with a sudden surge of blood. "I say you're crazy," he snarled. "You couldn't write a check for a million dollars. You —"

"Try me an' find out," flared Larey. "If you won't take me up, then pick up your two bits an' go home. Fifteen thousand dollars!"

Sturgis's fingers ripped the slip of paper he held. The pieces of the check dropped in a little pink shower. "You'll start a steer ranch," he snarled. "*You'll* . . . " His eyes met Jerico's, and he stopped short. The breath he had taken came out in a long gasp.

"Lance!" he yelled. "Come here, Lance! There's the man that killed Macklin!"

There was confusion as the deputy sheriff pushed forward. Men moved swiftly out of the way, pushing back toward the wall. Jerico waited, tense. This was pretty, very pretty, he thought. For an instant he took his eyes from Sturgis's face and glanced at Old Man Larey. Old Man Larey's eyes met his. Old Man Larey's eyebrows went up a little in surprise. Old Man Larey's voice boomed.

"Where?" he demanded.

"Him!" Sturgis's pointing finger was rigid.

Old Man Larey's look followed the pointing finger. Apparently he saw Jerico for the first time. Old Man Larey's voice boomed again.

"Him?" repeated Old Man Larey. "Hell! That's Jerico Jones. He's been with me all evenin'. How'd you leave things down at the yards, Jerico?"

Lance Touhy, the deputy, had stopped short at Larey's words. Sturgis's face was a mixture of surprise and wrath.

Jerico spoke calmly. "All right, Mister Larey," he answered.

"But I tell you . . ." cried Sturgis.

"You cain't tell me nothin'!" roared Old Man Larey. "Think I don't know my own men? Come on, boys, le's get outta here. Come on, Jerico."

Hard-faced Texans closed in about Jerico Jones. Old Man Larey seized Jerico's arm. He was swept along by the current of brawn about him. The door of the Stag loomed blackly. He was swept out through that door into the darkness of the street. Old Man Larey bent down. In a whisper that almost deafened Jerico Jones he asked a question.

"What hellishness you been into now, Jerico?" he demanded. "Hell, that was bad back there."

Jerico freed his arm from Larey's grasp. His hand sought and found Old Man Larey's. "Le's get where we can talk, Frank," he said, low voiced. "You're damn' right that was bad back there."

"The hotel," decided Old Man Larey. "Pat, you come along. The rest of you can hell around till twelve o'clock. You go back to camp then, an', if a damn' one of you is drunk, by God, I'll have his hide!"

Around Jerico Texans chuckled. Pat, the smooth-faced youth, with melancholia on his long, tanned countenance, groaned, and Old Man Larey seized Jerico's arm again.

"It's a damn' long time since I seen you, Jerico," said Old Man Larey. "You come on. I got a bottle in my room."

The men about the three dispersed, and Jerico, walking with the giant Frank Larey on one side and the smooth-faced Pat on the other, went down the street. They had gone but a short distance when Jerico recalled his horse.

"I got a horse back there with a bullet burn on his neck," he said, stopping short. "I reckon I better look after him."

Larey and Pat had stopped when Jerico did. Larey shook his head. "You let that horse alone," he commanded. "What for lookin' kind of a horse is he?"

"Gray," replied Jerico. "He's tied to a hitch rail back there in front of a store. One bridle rein's rope. I'd like to get him stabled."

"Bullet burn, you said?" questioned Larey. "You let that horse alone. You'll make a damn' liar out of me yet, Jerico. Pat, you go look after that horse. Take him down to the yards an' feed him. Then come back."

Without a word, the youth, Pat, turned back, and Larey, tucking his arm through Jerico's, drew him along.

Larey was stopping at the Hoffman House, Niroba's one hotel. He got his room key from the clerk behind the desk in the lobby, and, followed by the clerk's curious glance, he and Jerico climbed a flight of stairs, went down a corridor, and let themselves into a room. Larey lit the lamp, threw his hat on the bed, and, sitting down beside the hat, began the laborious process of removing his boots. Jerico chose a chair and, bringing out papers and tobacco, rolled a thin quill of smoke.

"Where you been these last few years, Jerico?" asked Larey, tugging at a boot.

"Here an' there," replied Jerico. "After I left the Rangers, I ranched it for a spell. Then I took to buyin' cattle. That's my business now."

Larey's boot came off, and he almost fell over backward. "I tol' you to look me up when you got tired of the Rangers," he chided. "What you doin' up here?"

"Lookin' for some grass to lease," Jerico answered. "I got a chance to get a little bunch of steers, an' I thought I'd hold 'em on some grass this winter an' go to market next fall. The price of cattle is lookin' up."

"The cow business is a good business," said Larey sententiously. "I've allus found it such. I got some steers, Jerico."

"So I heard." Jerico's voice was dry.

"Damn that Bond Sturgis!" flared Larey. "The cheap little crook."

Jerico was silent. Larey, both boots off now, stretched himself out on the bed with a contented sigh. "What kind of a jackpot are you in?" he demanded suddenly. "What did Sturgis mean callin' you a killer?"

Jerico knocked the ash from his cigarette toward a corner. "I'll tell you," he said. With brief laconic sentences he described the happenings of the afternoon. Larey listened attentively, nodding now and again.

"It looks to me," said Jerico in conclusion, "as though it was the same old story. The big outfit hoggin' the grass. When a little man starts up, he's a rustler an' treated as such. That's the way it looks."

"I run a big outfit," drawled Larey. "Iffen you ask me, most of these little grangers *are* rustlers."

"I don't deny it," Jerico spoke slowly. Suddenly anger flared in his voice. "Damn it, though, Frank. I liked the looks of that kid. He was a rider an' a hand an' he never had a chance."

There was a knock on the door. Larey boomed — "Come in!" — and the smooth-faced youth entered the room.

"I took that horse down to the yards," he said, reporting. "Fed him an' put the saddle over by our stuff. Cookie ain't there, Mister Larey."

"Out gettin' drunk, likely," grunted Larey. "Jerico, this here is Pat Fallon, my wife's sister's kid."

"The last name is Jones," said Jerico, rising and holding out his hand.

There was a flicker of interest in Pat Fallon's hazel eyes. "You used to be a sergeant in the Rangers, didn't you?" he asked, shaking Jerico's extended hand.

Jerico said, "Yeah," and Pat walked over and squatted down against the wall. There he rolled a smoke and lit it, his eyes squinted against the curling fumes of tobacco.

122

"Jerico was just tellin' me about a little trouble he seen," commented Larey. "A man was killed north of town today an' they're tryin' to hang it on Jerico. You don't reckon none of the boys will talk too much, do you, Pat?"

"They heard you in the Stag," said Pat briefly. "I reckon they'll keep their mouths shut."

There was silence for a moment. Jerico studied Pat Fallon, squatting against the wall. Pat was examining his cigarette. He spoke suddenly.

"What do we do tomorrow? Get cars an' start them steers back for Texas?"

An oath boomed from Frank Larey's lips. "Not by a damn' sight!" he exclaimed.

Pat Fallon was silent and Jerico looked over at Larey. "What's the trouble, Frank?" he asked.

"That damn' Sturgis," swore Larey. "Last spring he was down to the ranch, lookin' things over, an' he give me an order for a thousand head of steers, laid down here. We agreed on twenty-five dollars, with him havin' the privilege of cuttin' back five percent an' buyin' 'em for fifteen dollars. I thought his word was good an' I wrote him we was shippin' an' started the steers. I didn't hear from him so, after I'd waited a while, I packed up an' come. You heard what happened down in the Stag?"

"I heard you offer him a million dollars for his layout, yeah," said Jerico dryly.

"I'd've give it to him, too," boomed Larey. "The dirty double-crossin' skunk."

"Well?" said Jerico. "It looks like a tough spot, Frank. You got the shippin' money in them steers an' you're stuck."

"Not by a damn' sight I ain't stuck," flared Larey. "I'll get a place an' run them steers myse'f before I'll let him put it over on me."

Jerico's eyes narrowed. "You got it in for Sturgis, then," he said slowly. "So have I. Damn it, every time I close my eyes I see that kid."

"What kid?" Pat Fallon spoke from beside the wall.

Jerico looked at him. "The kid I saw killed," he said gravely. "He was about your age."

Again he repeated the story he had told Larey. Pat Fallon listened silently, his face expressionless. Jerico finished his tale. Larey stirred on the bed. The old man was restless.

"I'd like to teach Sturgis a damn' good lesson," he muttered.

"You can," Jerico said simply.

Larey sat up on the bed. "How?" he demanded.

Jerico moved a hand gently. "Why," he said, "I'm lookin' for steers. I ain't in shape to pay no twenty-five thousand dollars for a bunch, but if I was to find a little place an' lease it, an' you was to give me some steers to run on shares till next fall, I don't reckon anybody'd be the loser. I reckon a man could pick up a place around here, a little place."

Larey leaned back on the bed again. His eyelids formed thin slits through which blue gleamed faintly. Pat Fallon's face was still expressionless.

"An' you think you could find a place around here?" questioned Larey at length.

124

"Pretty sure of it," said Jerico. "If the Bar S is treatin' all the little fellows like I seen today, there's bound to be somebody that wants to pull out from under."

There was silence for a moment. Each of the three was thinking. Pat Fallon spoke suddenly. "I like this country," he said. "You can pay me off, Mister Larey. Mister Jones, could you use a man?"

"You damn' fool!" growled Frank Larey. "Shut up an' let your betters think."

Silence again. Presently Larey shook his head. "It won't do," he said, half aloud.

Jerico got to his feet. "That's that, then," he commented, his voice level. "Frank, I'm obliged to you for what you done tonight. I reckon . . ."

"Set down, you damn' fool," said Larey. "A thousand head ain't enough. This here country is open range, most of it, ain't it?"

Jerico sat down. There was something coming. "From what I hear, it is," he answered.

Again Larey withdrew into his mind. Over against the wall Pat Fallon rolled a cigarette and studied Jerico with blank, expressionless eyes.

Larey sat up swiftly. "The Long L is goin' to start a steer ranch," he announced abruptly. "I'm pickin' out Niroba because it's close to market an' all. Jerico, you're foreman with a workin' interest in the cattle. Pat, you're straw boss. Maw has been after me to start you in the cow business, anyhow. Besides that, I'm tired of your wet nursin' me. We'll lease a little place an' put around a thousand head of steers on it. Then, owin' to favorable reports from my foreman, I'll ship about two thousand more. Three thousand Chihuahuas ought to make a purty pitcher in anybody's front yard. So, Pat?"

Pat Fallon let go a long, thin jet of smoke. "A mighty pretty picture," he corroborated. "I'll take back that quit I made a while ago, Uncle Frank."

"Jerico?" questioned Larey.

"We can try her," replied Jerico doubtfully. "Of course, there's some things to think about. Range hogs ain't popular, you know, an' there's bound to be trouble."

"Trouble!" Old Frank Larey worried the word like a dog does a bone. "Since when did you start considerin' trouble, Jerico? There's other things to think about besides that. There's my steers, f'instance, an' that kid, an' . . ."

"Why sure," said Pat Fallon. "Cert'nly."

"All right," agreed Jerico. "I'll be a reckless fool kid again with you, Frank. I got nine thousand dollars to throw in for an ante."

Larey shook his head. "You don't ante money in this game," he said. "I'm puttin' up the money an' the cattle. I take half the net profit. You take a fourth, an' Pat gets a eighth."

"That leaves an eighth," objected Jerico.

"That's a bonus." Larey grinned. "You an' Pat can get it if you do the job."

Jerico's face was hard. "My gun ain't for sale," he announced harshly. "I —"

"An' I ain't hirin' it," flared Larey. "You're too damn' touchy, Jerico. We'll just leave that eighth hangin' up for a bonus."

126

Jerico leaned back in his chair. "All right," he said slowly. "That's that. The eighth's a bonus. Now we got things to talk about. There's a crew to get, an' saddle stock, an' an outfit, an' a place to lease. There's . . ."

Larey waved a hand. "Start earnin' your bonus," he commanded. "Them things are your look-out. I ain't furnishin' ridin' stock or an outfit or a crew. I'm just furnishin' the steers and the money."

Pat Fallon got to his feet. "You're right about that except for one thing," he said flatly. "That's the crew. We got a crew, Mister Jones. Uncle Frank is furnishin' it. When I talk to the boys, I *know* they'll like this country."

Larey laughed. "There's a bottle in my grip," he said. "Le's take a drink to the Long L steer ranch."

Pat Fallon brought out the bottle and it went the rounds. When Larey had handed it back to Pat, Jerico spoke again. "There's still some things to settle," he said.

Larey nodded. He had risen from the bed to drink, and now, sitting down, he reached for his boots again. "We got to get 'em settled, too," he announced. "There's a train out of here at one o'clock . . . an' I'm goin' on it."

Jerico was thoughtful. He wished that the old man would stick around at least long enough to see that the Chihuahuas were out on grass, but, if Larey wanted to go, why he, Jerico, was willing. He was perfectly competent to see that those steers were taken care of.

"You better write out a power of attorney for Fallon, here," he said. "An' we're goin' to need some money."

Larey finished with his boots. "Why not make the things out to you?" he asked.

"Might be some trouble over that shootin'," answered Jerico. "Besides, Pat here will want to talk to your boys an' . . ."

"All right," Larey grunted. He searched his pockets, produced a short stub of pencil and a brand book, and on an empty page, with his lips working as he wrote, scrawled for a short time. When he had finished, he tore out the page and extended it to Pat Fallon.

"Here's your power of attorney," he announced. "Now, how much cash you goin' to need?"

"I dunno," Jerico spoke doubtfully.

"We —"

From his hip pocket Frank Larey produced a plethoric purse. He opened it, looked at the contents, grunted, and, putting the purse on the bed, delved beneath his shirt. "I been travelin' heeled for considerable time," he commented as he performed a series of contortions. "Now if that damn' safety pin . . . There." From beneath his shirt he pulled a long leather strap. There were pockets on the strap. It was a money belt.

"Thousand be enough?" questioned Frank Larey, looking at Jerico.

"For now," agreed Jerico. "I got a little myself."

The old man opened a flap on the belt. A thick wad of green currency came from the flap. The old man wet a thumb and began to peel money from the roll. Fifteen times the thumb slipped off a bill. There was still money in the roll when Larey finished.

128

"There's fifteen hundred," he said. "Now . . . I'm goin' to throw my duds in my war sack an' get to hell out of here."

As the old man packed his few clothes, Jerico and Fallon sat on the bed and talked. Plans were considered, events foreseen as best they might be, and, when finally the three left the room, Pat carrying Larey's worn old telescope grip, things were pretty well arranged. At the desk Larey paid his bill and all three went down to the depot.

They had half an hour to wait, which they spent in the waiting room, smoking, talking low voiced, and, when finally the eastbound train wailed its station call, they went out to the platform.

The train pulled in. Jerico and Fallon accompanied Larey to the chair car. The old man shook hands with them both. "I'll keep the steers comin'," he promised. "You let me know how things are. You can wire me. Mainly I want that you boys should take care of yourselves. Pat, I'll tell Maw that you're all right. Be good." He swung up on the step and grinned back at the two on the platform. Down the line a lantern waved, a brakeman called — "ALL aboard!" — and with the clanking and a snort from the train Larey started back to Marfa.

When the train was gone the two men left behind looked at each other and grinned slowly. "Well," said Jerico.

"Well," said Pat Fallon, "what do we do now, Mister Jones?"

129

"Jerico," said Jones firmly. "'Mister' is for the boss. I reckon we better round up the boys, Pat, an' get 'em down to where you're camped. It looks like a heavy day tomorrow."

"The old man told 'em midnight." Pat grinned. "That means by mornin'. I guess we might as well look around a little an' pick up what we can."

Turning, side-by-side, they started back from the depot toward Niroba's still lighted and busy street.

Rounding up the Long L crew was easier said than done. Some of the men were playing poker. Two were in a game of Kelly pool and wanted to finish it. They failed entirely to find the cook, and so presently Jerico and Pat gave it up. Old Man Larey had paid his hands that afternoon and the Long L men were spending their money. It was well toward two o'clock when Jerico and Pat Fallon walked down to the stock yards and stopped, close by the fence, where the Long L had established a temporary camp.

"The old man believes in holdin' his men close together," said Pat wryly when they reached the campsite. "He travels with bedrolls an' a chuck wagon even when he's on a train."

"You got saddles with you?" suggested the practical Jerico.

"Sure," answered Fallon. "We figgered to mebbe drive these steers to wherever Sturgis wanted 'em delivered. We got bedrolls, saddles, an' a cookin' outfit. We even got a cook. I tell you we traveled in style, eatin' in the caboose, an' all. Hell, down around Marfa the old man owns the country an' the railroad, too. They even give us a way car to come through with the cattle."

Jerico was silent a minute. Fallon seated himself on a bedroll, and then got up. "It's awful quiet," he remarked.

"Just what I been thinkin'," rejoined Jerico.

"I wonder . . . " began Pat. He walked over toward the white-paneled fence of the yards that gleamed dully in the semidarkness of the night. Jerico waited a moment, and then followed. They reached the fence and peered through the panels. Pat shook his head as though he didn't believe his eyes.

"There was steers in this pen when I left," he said.

"Mebbe," said Jerico.

Pat swore softly. "Mebbe, hell!" he snapped. "I'll bet . . ."

He left the fence and moving swiftly, Jerico beside him, went around the long wing of the pen. On the far side he stopped. The gate was open. Pat went through the gate and across the empty pen. On the far side of the pen they came to another open gate.

"The damn' . . . " began Pat.

Jerico laughed softly. There was a hard, grim note in the laughter. "Saved us some trouble, didn't they?" said Jerico Jones. "Them steers won't have to be fed, come mornin'. They been turned out to grass."

"I'll save Sturgis some trouble." Pat Fallon's voice was hard. "I'll . . ."

"We don't know that Sturgis had a thing to do with this," snapped Jerico. "We cain't prove a thing on him. No."

"Then what do we do?" challenged Fallon. "Lie down an' take this like a bogged calf?"

"We go to bed," said Jerico slowly. "We turn in like we hit camp too drunk to know a thing. In the mornin' we get up and be surprised as hell. Then we buy some horses, get a wagon an' grub, an' start out to round up these steers."

"You're the boss." There was a tinge of contempt in Fallon's voice.

"So I am," said Jerico sweetly. "That's why we'll do what I say. There's always a break in a thing like this, an', if you're just innocently trailin' along with both eyes open, you're sometimes in shape to take the break when it comes. Let's turn in, Pat. In the mornin' we'll get strung out. Mebbe this ain't so bad, after all."

Fallon grunted, seemed ready to say something, and, thinking better of it, closed his lips in a straight firm line and began to unlash a bedroll. "I reckon you better crawl in with me," he remarked, when the bed was unrolled.

"Why, sure," returned Jerico cheerfully. He sat down on the unrolled bed and began to pull off a boot. "Don't you think too hard of me, Pat," he said when the boot came off. "I'm gettin' an idea that this is just the start of it. I got an idea that, in the mornin', we'll run into some grief that *is* grief. Just keep a-lookin' forward . . . that's my motto. They's always an end to a road."

Fallon grunted. He, too, was tugging at a boot. "I aim to be there," he said briefly. "Right there when the end of the road comes around."

"Why," drawled Jerico Jones, "so do I, Pat. So do I."

Undressed, they rolled and smoked good night cigarettes in silence, and then, sliding down between the soogans of Pat Fallon's bed, each arranged himself for comfort and said a brief good night. There was quiet over the little camp. In perhaps half an hour Pat Fallon stirred and propped himself up on an elbow.

"Jerico," he said softly, "are you asleep, Jerico?"

Jerico rolled over on his back. Pat waited a moment. A faint snore arose from Jerico. The snores gained in volume. Pat Fallon slumped back on his blankets. Mister Jerico Jones, apparently without a worry in the world, was sleeping the sleep of the just.

CHAPTER
THREE

It was fully five o'clock before the Long L camp stirred. Men crawled out from blankets with sullen curses, rubbed the sleep from their eyes, and spat from mouths that were dry as cotton and tasted like an old boot. Having rubbed away the sleep, some of them discovered the empty yards. Immediately there were curses and turmoil. Pat Fallon, up, dressed and bright-eyed, listened to the Long L hands. He let them curse themselves out before he said more than a word or two. When finally the first surprise had worn off and the Long L men were clothed, he called them together.

"The old man's gone," he said briefly. "So are the steers. We got a job to do. This here is Jerico Jones. He's in charge."

Jerico, who had stood by, was now the center of interest. The Long L men stared at him. There was a muttered curse or two. Jerico took a step forward.

"Mister Larey an' me went into pardnership last night," he said. "We're goin' to lease a place an' run steers up here. Fallon said that we might pick up a crew from you fellows."

A little banty of a man close by Jerico spat disdainfully. "Where in hell are the steers?" he queried.

Jerico grinned and waved an arm. "Out there," he said, gesturing toward the brown range that stretched away toward the rolling Rock Rib hills.

Pat Fallon spoke. "I told Jones that we could get a crew here," he announced. "If any of you don't want to stay, there'll be a train out of here this afternoon an' we got passes."

No one moved. Jerico stared around the little circle of hard, weathered faces that clustered about him. For the most part these men were young. The cook, tanned and worn, was the oldest of the lot; next to the cook was a man of perhaps fifty. Except for those two, there was not a Long L man over thirty.

"I'd like to know these fellows' names, Pat," said Jerico.

Pat Fallon pointed to the cook. "That's Doughgod Smith," he said. "He's Nebraska Williams," — pointing to the older man next the cook. "That little bitty fello' is Marty Rafferty. Nig Bell is next him an' that big towhead is Swede Hanson. The kid next to him is Blake Wade. That's the size of the pile."

Jerico nodded to each in turn. "Le's set down," he said.

Smith, the cook, had built a little fire. The men squatted around it, Jerico with the rest.

Doughgod spoke up. "I know you, Jones," he said. "I was ridin' for Frank Larey when that li'l trouble come up over to Marfa."

"I thought I'd seen you," replied Jerico. "I got somethin' I want to lay out to you fellows. You heard Old Man Larey claim me last night?"

There were nods around the circle. "Well," said Jerico, "you knew the old man was lyin'. Here's what happened."

Briefly then he told the listening men of what had happened at the lonely ranch. They listened intently. Now and again one looked at another. When Jerico finished, there was dead silence.

"Now," said Jerico, "these Chihuahua steers you been nursin' are gone. We figgered to run a little spread up here, Larey an' Pat an' me. We thought mebbe we could lease a little place an' put sev'ral steers in this country. Larey figgered she'd graze about three thousand head."

Around the circle faces lightened. Slow grins cracked weathered gravity.

"Of course," continued Jerico, "we'd want men we knew. Fellows we could sort of depend on. You know . . ."

Old Nebraska, weathered and wise, spat into the fire. "I'd never figgered to winter this far north again," he mourned. "You fellers are goin' to need sheepskins an' hair pants."

Marty Rafferty, nervous fingers curling brown paper about tobacco, grunted contemptuously. "Hair pants!" he scoffed. "What you goin' to wear, Nebrasky? A silk nighty?"

"You get us some horses an' we'll start roundin' up our little bunch of steers *pronto*," suggested Nig Bell, his dark face split in a grin. "It'ud be a shame to have 'em eat all this good Bar S grass."

Jerico grinned back at the circle of faces. "Le's eat breakfast," he suggested, "then mebbe we can go to work."

Pat Fallon, beside Jerico, spoke four soft words: "We got a crew."

Doughgod stirred up breakfast. The crew ate, threw their soiled dishes in the pan, and the cook and Blake Wade, the kid of the outfit, fell to washing the dishes. Jerico and Pat Fallon strolled apart from the others.

"Notice that my horse is gone," said Jerico. "Where'd you put him, Pat?"

"In an empty pen," answered Fallon. "Your saddle's with the rest, though."

"Yeah," said Jerico. "Bridle, too. Bridle's got a rope rein."

"Might get that fixed," said Fallon. "Nig," he called, "come here a minute, will you?"

Nig Bell came over.

"Jones has a rope rein on his bridle," Fallon informed Bell. "I wonder if we cain't get it fixed. There might be some questions asked if the law come around."

"I got a pair of bridle reins in my war sack," said Bell. "I'll put 'em on. What do you want said if the law does come?"

"Just that Jones was with the old man yesterday. The old man didn't get in till noon an' come right over here, you remember?"

Bell nodded and turned away.

"What do we do now, Jerico?" asked Pat.

Jerico looked at his watch. "Let's see where we can find some horses," he said. Fallon nodded. The two went back to the fire, informed the men there that they were going uptown and gave orders that the Long L hands were to stay close to camp. Then, side-by-side, they strolled toward the town.

The Stag was their first calling point. The bartender there on early shift suggested one or two men who might supply them with mounts. "Sturgis might sell you some," he said innocently. "The Bar S has got plenty of ridin' stock."

Pat and Jerico grinned at each other, found out where one of the horse owners lived, and went on out.

Carpenter, the man to whom they had been directed, was at home. He had just finished breakfast and was at the barn back of his house, hitching a team. When Jerico and Pat introduced themselves and made known the purpose of their visit, Carpenter stopped his operations and listened. When they had finished, he announced that he might be able to supply their wants. There was some talk of prices, and then Jerico drew Pat aside.

"You go on out with him an' look over what he's got," directed Jerico. "We got to trade pretty close. We ain't got a lot of money when it comes to buyin' horses."

"What you goin' to do?" asked Pat.

"Stick around town. I got an idea that there's goin' to be somethin' movin' around here an' I want to be in on it."

Pat shook his head. "You come along," he said. "We'll take Nebraska with us. He can bring back what we buy." He stepped away from Jerico and addressed Carpenter again. "How far out is your place?"

Carpenter finished hooking a tug and looked up. "Ten miles," he said. "Take a little over an hour to get there."

Jerico and Pat again entered into consultation. "These are broomtails he's got," said Jerico. "Suppose we just take all the boys out? I don't want 'em layin' around town. They might talk too much an' they might get into trouble."

Pat grunted and spoke again to Carpenter. "How many of us can you take?" he asked.

"Two or three," answered Carpenter.

Jerico shrugged. "Let's go," he said.

They got into the buckboard with the horse owner, and Carpenter drove on down the street. He stopped at a store to load some supplies, and then took his two passengers to the camp at the yards. There Jerico and Pat loaded in their saddles, picked up Nebraska Williams, and, leaving orders for the other members of the crew to stay close to camp, climbed back in the buckboard and were whirled away.

It took them a full hour and a half to reach Carpenter's ranch. There was not much talk on the journey. When they arrived at their destination, Carpenter sent a man out to run in a bunch of horses and another hour elapsed before the bunch was brought in and penned.

For the most part the animals were young, unbroken, and wild as hawks. There were a few broken animals in the bunch, however. Jerico and Pat made selections, haggled back and forth with Carpenter, and finally, at the end of some three hours, made the deal. Jerico paid over $750, and Carpenter made out a bill of sale for twenty-six head. With the business transacted the men went to the house and ate dinner, and, when the meal was done, Pat, Nebraska, and Jerico went back to the corral, roped out broken horses, and saddled them. Mounting, they then pushed the horses out of the corral and started back toward Niroba.

Riding together in the rear of the little bunch, Jerico and Pat, once they were well away from the ranch, fell into conversation.

"Pretty good bunch," Pat said, referring to the horses.

Jerico grunted. "Goin' to be a man-size rodeo when we start out," he commented. "About half of them horses are just stake-broke an' that's all."

Pat grinned. "They'll get rode," he prophesied. "The next week or so will see them horses broke."

Jerico bent his horse away to turn a bay gelding that tried to break back. When he rejoined Pat, he, too, was grinning. "Broke horses cost more than we can afford, Pat," he said. "How are the boys on exercise?"

"They like it," Pat returned. "Look out for that bay."

Jerico swung away again and sent the bay back into the bunch.

It didn't take as long to return to Niroba as it had to go out. They swung their horses wide of the town, came into the yards from the east, and pushed their bunch into a pen. When the gate was closed, the three riders dismounted. All the Long L men were at the fence looking over their prospective mounts.

"Anythin' goin' on while we was gone?" Pat asked Marty Rafferty.

Marty spat into the dust. "That damn' deputy was down, hintin' around," he answered. "Say, Pat, how about givin' me that roan an' that dun horse in my string? I like the looks of 'em."

"We'll draw straws for first pick," answered Pat. "You hear what he said, Jerico?"

Jerico nodded. "That's what I was afraid of," he said. "What did the sheriff say, Marty?"

"Asked about you," answered Rafferty. "We sent him off talkin' to himself."

Jerico stood for a moment, looking into the corral, then he turned, walked away from the fence, and called the men to him. "Listen," he said when they were assembled. "It looks like mebbe I was in for some grief. There's all the signs. Now get this an' get it straight . . . when I'm gone, Pat's the boss. He carries the ramrod. Lackin' Pat, Nebraska takes charge. Get that?"

There were nods around the circle.

"What you think is goin' to happen?" queried the irrepressible Marty. "You think that Sturgis an' that deputy are goin' to start somethin'? If they do, we'll —"

"You'll stay out of it!" snapped Jerico. "First, last, an' all the time, you're workin' for the Long L an' there's a thousand head of steers out there for you to look after. Get that?"

Again heads nodded, slower this time.

"We're goin' to start a roundup," pronounced Jerico. "We're goin' to get away from here before dark. Blake, you're horse wrangler. You'll nighthawk for us. Doughgod, you take some money an' go uptown. Buy what grub you need an' get a couple of pack saddles. This is goin' to be a pack outfit from here on. When you boys pick your horses be sure you get a broke horse that'll carry a bed. Nebraska knows 'em. That old gray an' the claybank are pack horses . . . Doughgod gets 'em for the chuck. Now you can pick your strings, an', remember, no matter what happens, you got to look after them steers."

The faces of the Long L men were serious. There were slow nods of understanding. Jerico turned abruptly and walked away from the men and after a moment Pat followed him.

"What do you think is comin', Jerico?" questioned Pat when he had caught up. "Do you think . . . ?"

"I think they're goin' to make it as tough on us as they can," Jerico returned.

Pat made no comment. Back by the camp Marty Rafferty was pulling a straw from Doughgod's clenched hand. His wild whoop of glee carried to Jerico and Pat.

"I reckon Marty gets the roan." Jerico grinned.

There was a great deal of confusion after the lots had been made. Jerico, as boss, naturally had first pick and Pat Fallon followed Jerico. They pointed out the horses they wanted, each taking one broken horse and two broomtails. Blake Wade, as horse wrangler, got two well-broken mounts, and Doughgod, a broke horse and two pack animals. The others singled out their mounts — Swede Hanson, the unlucky last, getting the leavings. When the horses had been picked, Doughgod and Nebraska went uptown for supplies, and Marty, Swede, and Nig, on one pretext or another, also departed. Jerico, Pat, and Blake Wade remained at the camp. The men who had gone to town were to return as quickly as possible, for Jerico wanted to get away.

Doughgod and the others had been gone for perhaps fifteen minutes when a man strolled around the corner of the yards and came toward the piled bedding of the Long L men. It was Touhy, the deputy sheriff. As he strolled into the camp, Jerico rose from a bedroll to meet him.

Touhy stopped, nodded to Pat Fallon and Blake Wade, and then looked at Jerico. "Your name's Jones, I hear," he said slowly.

"Jerico Jones," affirmed Jerico.

"You was with Larey all day yesterday, I reckon?" Touhy drawled the words.

"That's what Larey says," replied Jerico, eyeing the officer.

"What do you say?" Touhy was blunt.

"You wouldn't have me make my boss out a liar, would you?" Jerico grinned faintly.

"Somebody's a liar." Touhy's narrow eyes were fixed on Jerico. "Bond Sturgis swears that you're the fellow that was at Macklin's yesterday."

"Does he?"

"Yeah. More'n that he says you're the fellow that shot Bob Macklin."

"You come down to arrest me for that?" Jerico was as blunt as the officer.

Touhy shrugged. "No," he answered. "Kinda tough about your steers."

"Kinda."

"Got any idea how they got out?"

Jerico grinned. "*You* got any ideas?" he asked pointedly.

Touhy shook his head. "I hear that the watchman was drunk," he answered. "The agent says he's goin' to fire him."

"Good idea." Jerico was playing his cards close to his vest.

Touhy strolled over and looked down at the bedding and the riding gear. "Where's Larey?" he asked.

"Headed home." Jerico walked over and stood beside Touhy.

The deputy moved away from the beds. "Too bad." Touhy stopped beside the cooking outfit. "Mebbe Larey an' Sturgis could've dealt for them steers."

"You got a warrant for me?" Jerico's sudden question was blunt.

Touhy shook his head.

"If I had, I'd serve it," he said, his eyes staring levelly into Jerico's own.

Jerico said slowly: "I believe you would."

"Don't never make no mistakes about that." Touhy's voice was not hard, it was simply firm. "I'm workin' as deputy sheriff. I try to do the job."

144

"An' no other?" Jerico asked softly.

"An' no other," agreed Touhy.

"Well, then?" intoned Jerico.

"Larey said you was with him. Sturgis said you wasn't. There's no warrant been swore out." Touhy paused.

"You *could* make an arrest," suggested Jerico.

"I could, but I won't. I've heard of Frank Larey. So has others."

"I see," assented Jerico.

Suddenly Touhy grinned, the wrinkles at the corners of his eyes crinkling. "I'll go sell my papers," he announced. "So long, Jones."

"So long," Jerico said absently.

Touhy, still grinning, walked away. As soon as the deputy was out of earshot, Pat Fallon spoke. "Workin' for Sturgis," he muttered.

Jerico shook his head. "Nope," he drawled. "Didn't you *sabe* what he was tryin' to tell me, Pat?"

Fallon shook his head. "I *sabe* that he used to be Sturgis's wagon boss," he announced.

"He was tryin' to tell me that he'd tend to his business, that there wasn't no warrant out for me, an' that Larey's bluff last night had got over with Sturgis. I believe he's a good square-shooter, Pat."

Pat Fallon grunted his disbelief.

"That's right," insisted Jerico. "I kind of like that old boy."

"Mebbe." Pat was doubtful.

"I been thinkin'," Jerico spoke slowly, marshalling his ideas, "we want a place to hold these steers, sort of a headquarters that will give us some rights in this country."

"Yeah?" Pat was noncommittal.

"Yeah. Why wouldn't Macklin's make us a good place? I've a mind . . ."

"A mind to do what?"

"A mind to ride out there an' see."

Pat Fallon revolved the idea. "It might not be bad at that," he agreed finally. "If you want to prod Sturgis . . ."

"Sturgis has been doin' all the proddin' up to now," reminded Jerico. "It's time we done a little. That would sure make him ringy. We'll pull out when the boys come back. Go up the railroad till we hit wood an' water, an' then make camp. Tomorrow I'll ride over to Macklin's an' talk business with whoever's over there. Mebbe I can pull it off."

"*We'll* ride over," amended Pat. "Nebraska can start the boys on circle tomorrow. We'll need somebody that knows the country, too. You thought of that?"

"I reckon we can get somebody," agreed Jerico. "Here comes Marty back from town . . . an' Nig's with him. Let's get started, Pat."

CHAPTER
FOUR

The Long L pulled out of Niroba without difficulty. To be sure one of Doughgod's pack horses put up an argument against the load, and both Nig Bell and Marty Rafferty chose unbroken horses — "Just for the hell of it" — and there was a little rodeo before the bronc's were subdued, but, as far as interference by Touhy or any of the townsmen was concerned, there just wasn't any. Jerico started the men and the outfit up the tracks, and some six miles above the town, with dusk falling rapidly, they reached a little stream and a bunch of cottonwoods. There they camped.

At Jerico's orders night horses were kept up. Wood was brought in, a fire flickered, and Doughgod started supper. Jerico and Pat, sitting on their bedrolls, talked over the work with Nebraska who sat close by.

"My idea," said Jerico, "is that those steers was give a good push. I don't think they're scattered much, I just think that they was turned loose and pushed out to grass. I don't think Sturgis will spread 'em."

"I think that he would," contradicted Pat. "I think that likely they was split up in little bunches and shoved in all directions. That's what I'd do."

"Yeah," drawled Jerico, "but you don't own the country, Pat. Sturgis does. He's goin' to play a hand with us an' he's dealt the cards. I don't think he's so worried about the steers . . . I think he's goin' to lay into us."

There was silence for a moment, and then Nebraska spoke up. "We can make a little circle in the mornin'," he said. "I think that what was done was this . . . I think that the steers was pushed a ways, and then let drop out. These fellers are cowmen. They'd make it look natural."

"Mebbe," said Jerico. "Anyhow a little circle will show. You'll have to take the boys out, Nebraska. Pat an' me are goin' to make a ride in the mornin'."

Nebraska looked his question.

"Over to Macklin's," explained Jerico. "We're goin' to try to lease the place."

Nebraska said — "Oh!" — thought a moment as though about to ask a question, then thought better of it.

From the fire Doughgod called: "Come an' git it!" The Long L men rose and shifted toward the blaze.

Jerico kept a look-out at the camp that night. Blake Wade stayed with the horses and the others took turns just as though they were standing guard on a herd. There was no disturbance. The camp was peaceful, and, when morning broke and the men crawled from their soogans, there was some amusement and some kidding concerning the precautions that had been taken. Still, all the crew knew that those precautions had been necessary and there was no complaint.

148

With breakfast finished and the horses run into a rope corral in the cottonwoods, each man singled out a mount. Marty Rafferty was told to day-herd the horses. Blake Wade rustled wood for Doughgod and then turned in, and Nebraska, under Jerico's direction, started out with Nig and the Swede.

"Stick close together," warned Jerico. "Tomorrow, when Pat an' me are with you, we'll cover the country. Right now, we're just lookin' it over. If you find any cattle, bring 'em in, but don't burden yourselves."

The three nodded their understanding and rode off. When they were gone, Jerico and Pat also mounted and, with Jerico leading the way, rode north.

Jerico had the faculty of seeing a country once and keeping it in his head. He had left the Macklin Ranch in a hurry and with lead flying after him, but he pointed straight for it. Pat rode along beside Jerico, not asking questions as to the direction they took, but rather filled with curiosity as to what they would do after they got there.

Jerico shook his head to Pat's queries. "I don't know what we'll do," he said. "I don't know who's at the place or nothin' about it. We may just be wastin' time. From what I heard Sturgis say, he dispossessed the Macklins. Mebbe that means he done it legal or mebbe it means he was just throwin' a bluff. We'll go see."

That was all the satisfaction that Pat could get and he had to be content with it.

With Jerico pointing the trail, they made steady progress and presently Jerico reined in his mount. "This," he informed Pat, "is the gulch I crossed when I left the corral. You stay here with the horses . . . I'm goin' to 'coon up to the top of the ridge an' take a look."

He swung down from his horse, tendered a rein to Pat, and then started up the ridge. Near the top he crouched, crawled a little distance, and then, pulling off his hat, lay flat and crawled farther. At the top, he stopped and lay for some time looking over the ridge. Then he reversed his trail and presently was back at Pat's side.

"There's somebody there, Pat," he said. "There's two horses at the corral fence an' the door is open. We can follow down this draw an' come in back of the barn. I reckon that's what we'll do."

"Why?" asked Pat. "Why don't we ride right on in, Jerico? I don't get this sneakin' around an' . . ."

Jerico smiled grimly. "Why, Pat," he said. "I reckon I should've told you. The rig on one of those horses belongs to Sturgis. I got a good look at his saddle when I was here before. I reckon we'll do a little eavesdropping."

Pat, reassured, held out Jerico's rein. Jerico took it, mounted, and, turning his horse, rode down the draw, with Pat following close at his heels.

The draw curved north. Some distance below their first stop, Jerico halted again. Both men dismounted. Both secured their horses to convenient clumps of scrubby growth. Jerico again took the lead, went up the slope of the draw, crouched at the top, and then advanced at a hasty run. Pat followed Jerico's actions exactly and arrived, panting a little, behind the log barn at Jerico's side.

They waited there a moment or two, then reconnoitered, and, again with Jerico leading, went around the corral, negotiated a fence, and arrived close against the side of the house. Here they paused, and then went forward until they were at the end of the building with only the porch in front of them. The two stood listening. Voices came to them, voices that were indistinct. Jerico shook his head. All their precautions had been useless.

Pat tugged at Jerico's shirt. "Window," he whispered, pointing to the one above their heads.

Jerico nodded. Pat, standing fully erect, put his hand against the window and pushed gently. It slid up a crack, noiselessly. Now they could hear.

A girl's voice came distinctly. "I have three months," it said. "I'll stay here until the redemption period is over."

Jerico's elbow jerked into Pat's ribs with such force as almost to arouse a startled grunt from the surprised youth.

"You can't stay here alone." That was Bond Sturgis's voice. "You haven't any money, by your own statement. You know that this place is mortgaged and that it's useless to stay. You —"

"You say you are a friend of mine, Mister Sturgis," the girl interrupted. "You come here offering to give me money for my equity in this place when you have only to wait for three months and take it. That's what you said, you know. I'm going to stay. This is my home. I —"

"You're a little fool!" Sturgis's voice was harsh. "I'm doing you a favor and —"

"And I won't accept it. If you want to do me a favor, find the man who killed Bob. You say you saw him."

Jerico's elbow jerked toward Pat Fallon again and struck empty air. Jerico turned swiftly. Pat had stepped away from behind him and was walking unconcernedly toward the front of the house. Jerico took a step to follow, and then thought better of it. Again he crouched by the window. Pat's boots clumped on the porch. There was the sound of a sudden movement inside the house. Pat's knuckles beat on the door, and then came Pat's deep drawl.

"Oh, excuse me. Am I buttin' in?"

A pause followed the question. Jerico could hear movements in the room, but he did not lift his head above the window to peer in. At the moment he was Pat's ace in the hole, and he relished the rôle.

Then came Sturgis's voice. "What do *you* want? What are you doing here?"

"You own this place?" Pat was evidently talking to Sturgis for the girl's voice answered.

"*I* own it. Was there anything I could do for you?"

"Yes, ma'am." Pat took his time. The words came slowly. "I want to lease a place around here. I . . . that is, we . . . got a thousand head of steers out on grass. My boss, Frank Larey of the Long L, is startin' a steer ranch in this country. We want a place for headquarters

152

an' to give us some water rights an' grazin' rights on the gov'ment land around here."

There was a pause. Jerico would have given a good deal for a view of Sturgis's face. He raised himself cautiously, peering over the window ledge. Bond Sturgis was sitting, the side of his face toward Jerico, staring at Pat who stood in the doorway. Across from the window sat a girl, smooth-haired, red-lipped, her face distraught now, and eyes red from crying. Jerico liked her looks. There was character in the small, firm chin and in the eyes that were turned toward Pat. There was another man in the room. His back was toward Jerico but even by the back Jerico recognized Webb Greves.

Pat's slow drawl went on evenly. "Is this place for lease, ma'am?"

Bond Sturgis started up from his chair. His face was dark with the angry flood of blood. His voice snarled. "No, it isn't!" he rasped. "Get out, you two-bit . . ."

"Easy!" Pat Fallon lost his drawl and his voice was hard. "I'm talkin' to a lady!"

The girl, too, came out of her chair. Her voice was eager. "I'll lease the ranch!" she said. "I —"

Jerico Jones pushed up the window. He had seen Webb Greves move. Greves's elbow was sliding back. Jerico knew the meaning of that movement. In turn he entered the conversation.

"Hold still, Greves!" warned Jerico. "Hold jus' as still as you can."

Greves froze. The elbow that had been inching back was immobile. The eyes of the others, Sturgis, the girl, and Pat Fallon, flashed to the window. Jerico stood there, looking through. For a moment all three were speechless, then the girl gasped, and Sturgis, finding his voice, rasped hoarse words.

"That's him. That's the man that killed your brother!"

Jerico flung Sturgis's words back in his teeth. "You lie, Sturgis!"

"I saw you!" Sturgis sprang up from his chair.

Jerico had neglected Greves too long. He had been looking at Sturgis too intently. Greves, noting that Pat Fallon was staring at Sturgis, took his chance. He came up out of his chair, and, as he moved, his hand went down and back. Jerico snatched for the gun under his left arm and dodged back from the window, for Greves was turning. Pat Fallon went into action like a smooth machine. One long step he took, and his left fist, backed by his weight, lashed out at Greves. The blow did not land fairly, but sent Greves reeling back, his gun half drawn. Jerico, gun out now, caught the window, threw up a leg, and was halfway into the room in time to stop Bond Sturgis's sudden movement. Jerico Jones was in command now, and he made the most of his moment. Greves had regained his balance but his hand fell away from his gun as he saw the weapon in Jerico's hand. Sturgis, too, stopped his draw.

There was a killing light in Jerico's blue eyes. "You lie, Sturgis," he repeated deliberately. "You lie an' you know it. It was you out by the fence when Macklin was killed, an' it was your own pet killer, Webb Greves, that was by the barn an' that shot the boy! Greves .—"

Webb Greves broke under the strain. Guilt and the menace of Jerico's gun were too much. Webb Greves spoke five words and with those five confirmed Jerico's statement. "You never seen me. I —"

Jerico swung up his other leg, preparatory to sliding into the room. The movement made Pat Fallon shift his eyes, and, as he did so, Greves seized his opportunity. Lunging at Pat, he threw the youth off balance and sprang for the door. Pat, reeling back, masked Greves from Jerico. Jerico was now inside. He leaped toward the door, thrusting Pat aside. Sturgis, caught in the whirlwind of sudden motion, took a step and stumbled. Pat caught his balance, slapped the gun from his holster, and leveled it at Sturgis. Jerico, at the door, raised his gun, and then lowered it slowly. Greves had reached his horse. Jerico might have shot him, but checked. Greves was weakening; he might break completely. There was a woman in the room. Jerico stepped back and slowly sheathed his gun.

"Put it up, Pat," he said wearily. "I reckon you heard him, ma'am?"

The girl's face was white. She stared first at Jerico, then at Sturgis. Pat Fallon, disregarding Jerico's orders, kept his gun on Sturgis.

"Git out!" snapped Pat Fallon. "Git out, Sturgis!"

Sturgis looked first at the girl, and then at the grim-faced Jerico. His gaze shifted to Pat's hot eyes. He opened his mouth to speak but the words refused to come. Staggering a little, so angry that he could not control his muscles, he went toward the door. At the door he paused. "I'll . . . " he began.

"Git out," ordered Pat again. Sturgis's boots clumped on the porch. Pat stood at the door, gun still out and ready.

Jerico faced the girl. "He's accused me of killin' your brother," said Jerico slowly. "You heard what Greves said, I reckon."

"Who are you?" demanded the girl hoarsely. "What are you doing here?"

"My name's Jones," answered Jerico.

Pat Fallon shifted uneasily beside the door. Jerico gnawed at one corner of the close-clipped brown mustache. The girl gripped the arms of her chair. Plainly she was fighting to control herself, trying to hold her emotions in check. Both men witnessed the struggle and its final successful outcome.

It was Jerico that broke the awkward silence. "We heard some of what was said, ma'am," he announced gently. "If there's any way we can help . . ."

Polly Macklin, holding herself on a tight rein, interrupted. "They said you killed Bob," she began. "They said . . ."

"Ma'am," said Jerico earnestly, "I never killed your brother an' I never harmed him. I was there. I seen . . ."

The girl leaned forward. "Tell me!" she commanded.

Jerico collected himself. He took a long step, shifted the chair that Greves had occupied, and seated himself. "I'll tell you, ma'am," he agreed. "This here is just what happened."

He kept the emotion from his voice as he recounted the story. He omitted nothing, glossed nothing over, his words were a monotonous drone. The girl listened.

156

Once she covered her eyes with her hands and Jerico stopped and waited for her to regain control before he continued.

"That's the truth," he said, finishing his recital. "It's hard, ma'am, I know. I didn't see the killer, but I did see Sturgis. I think it was Webb Greves by the barn. You heard me throw that at him an' you heard what he said. I reckon he done it. Provin' it is a different thing."

The girl lifted her head wearily. "We buried Bob yesterday," she said slowly, and paused, choking back a sob. Pat Fallon took two short steps from the door, his hand half outstretched, stopped, and stepped back. Jerico waited.

"What am I to do?" queried Polly Macklin, utter futility in her voice. "I believe what you say. There is talk concerning Sturgis and the Bar S. I heard what Greves said. What must I do?"

"I don't know, ma'am," answered Jerico. "I been accused of this. I never done it. I'm going to stay here until I prove who did."

"But . . . " began the girl.

"We'll lease your place," offered Pat Fallon awkwardly. "Mebbe if you had some money, you could go away an' . . ."

Sudden anger flared in Polly Macklin's eyes. "I'm going to stay," she declared. "I'm going to stay here and find out who killed Bob. I can fight, too."

"Set down, Pat," drawled Jerico. "You don't know us, ma'am, an' I reckon it's askin' a heap for you to trust us, but there's this thing we can get together on. We'll lease your place for six months. We'll pay you cash, so

157

you know you won't be cheated. We'll talk to anybody you want us to talk to. An' " — he paused a moment — "if there's trouble," he concluded slowly, "I reckon we can take care of it."

A long silence followed Jerico's words. Jerico sat stockstill. He wanted to help this girl, wanted to do all that he could for her. He looked at Pat Fallon. Pat was watching Polly Macklin as though trying to read her mind.

Polly Macklin lifted her head. "I'll lease you the ranch," she said suddenly.

Jerico got up from his chair. "Good," he drawled.

The girl, too, arose. "You come back this evening," she ordered decisively. "I'm going to town to talk to Abe Whitaker. He was father's lawyer. I'll bring him out. You can talk to him tonight."

Jerico moved toward the door. "We'll get you a horse," he offered, "or if you want a team hitched . . ."

"I'll ride in," Polly Macklin decided. "There's a horse in the barn."

Pat Fallon went through the door to the porch. Jerico stopped at the doorway. "I'll get our horses, Pat," he said. "You saddle up for Miss Macklin. I reckon we'll side her toward town a ways."

As the three rode south toward Niroba, Jerico tried to keep a conversation going. He asked questions concerning the extent of the land that the Macklins owned. He made queries as to the winters, whether they were hard or open. While she answered him, Polly Macklin made no effort to hide the fact that she didn't want to talk, and finally Jerico gave up and they rode in silence. Perhaps two miles out of Niroba, the two men left the girl and turned back toward their own camp. They watched her out of sight, then crossed the railroad tracks and rode back toward the north.

At the camp they found Doughgod and Blake Wade. Jerico and Pat dismounted, unsaddled, and staked their horses. Wade was asleep and Doughgod had nothing to report. Jerico and Pat ate a lunch, smoked, resaddled, and were ready to ride out to make a short circle when they saw a string of cattle coming in toward the cottonwood motte. They rode out to meet the drive.

Nebraska, Swede, and Nig were all with the animals. Jerico, riding toward the three, made an estimate of the number in the drive. There were about 100 head. He drew up alongside Nebraska.

The grizzled veteran made his report. "Just found these in a bunch," he drawled. "I was right, Jones. Them fellers just gave 'em a push, an' then let 'em dribble off."

"Where'd you find these?" asked Jerico. "North?"

"North an' east," answered Nebraska. "We could've picked up a lot more if we'd took everything we seen. They're all mixed. What we need is about twenty men an' a wagon. If we're goin' to round this country up, we got to have a bigger crew. We . . ."

"They're all on grass, ain't they?" asked Jerico.

"Of course." Nebraska looked his surprise.

"Well" — Jerico thought a moment — "as long as they're all gettin' a full belly every day, there don't seem to be much sense in movin' 'em."

159

"I thought you wanted 'em bunched." Nebraska looked at Jerico from beneath raised eyebrows. "You said . . ."

"It looks like mebbe we've leased a place," said Jerico. "I want a little bunch of steers that we can handle easy. I aim to close herd that bunch in one place. With the rest of 'em, I just reckon we'll work along a line an' throw 'em north. Just regular cow work."

"Huh?" said Nebraska, not comprehending.

"We'll pick up another hundred head," explained Jerico. "Then we'll move 'em south an' play like we was herdin' sheep."

Nebraska got the idea. "Just rubbin' a sore spot," he grunted.

"Sure," agreed Jerico, "an' gettin' it sorer."

"You must like a fight," said Nebraska flatly.

"Well . . . " drawled Jerico, and left Nebraska to draw his own conclusions. Nig Bell, who had ridden close to the two, grinned and swung away to where the Swede was pointing the bunch.

At camp Jerico stayed with the bunch, loose herding them. The others rode in. Marty Rafferty brought the horses in over a hill. When Nig rode out to relieve Jerico, he wore a broad grin. Evidently Pat had been answering questions.

"There's just one question I got to ask," announced Nig as he reined in beside Jerico. "When you had a gun on Greves, why didn't you let her go off?"

Jerico looked at the rider. "Would you've done that?" he said dryly.

Nig's grin broadened. "Nope," he said cheerfully.

In the afternoon, leaving Nig with the gathered bunch, Jerico, Pat, Nebraska, and the Swede rode out to pick up more Long L steers. They found it an easy thing to do. About five miles southeast of the camp the country seemed literally covered with Long L brands. The steers had not scattered much and evidently had not been pushed any too hard. The Long L men picked up approximately 100 head and started them back. Jerico and Pat left Nebraska and the Swede to make the drive once it was well started. They had other business and rode on ahead. Back at the camp, they ate again and then began their return to the Macklin Ranch.

As they reached the ranch, they saw Polly Macklin's horse in the corral with two other horses. Riding on in, they saw the girl come from the house. There were two men with her. Dismounting, Jerico and Pat tied their horses to the corral fence and approached the house.

One of the men on the porch with the girl was short, spare, and middle-aged. The other was young, square-built, and chunky, a typical cowhand. Jerico and Pat stopped at the porch steps. Polly Macklin made the introductions.

"This is Mister Whitaker," she said, gesturing toward the older man. "Mister Jones and . . ." She looked at Pat.

"Pat Fallon," said Pat, blushing.

"Mister Fallon," the girl concluded. "This" — looking at the younger man beside her — "is Lon Dennis. He . . ."

Jerico walked up the steps. "Hello, Dennis," he said, holding out his hand. "Ain't you from Hereford?"

Lon Dennis grinned broadly. "Sure," he answered. "I know you. You're Jerico Jones." Dennis turned toward the girl and Whitaker. "This is him, all right," he announced.

Whitaker put out his hand to Jerico. "Dennis said that he thought he knew you," he announced. "Seems like he was right. From what he says you were in the Rangers at one time."

"Yes," agreed Jerico. "Suppose we talk some business. Fallon an' me are representin' Frank Larey of the Long L. I reckon Miss Macklin told you about our proposition?"

Whitaker nodded. "Let's go inside," he suggested.

The little party trooped through the door and into the house. There, when they were seated, Whitaker proceeded directly to business. Terms of the proposed lease were discussed. The limits and acreage of the Macklin Ranch, the Seven M, were defined. Pat produced his power of attorney from Larey and Whitaker inspected it.

Finally the lawyer summed it all up. "You can take this lease," he said slowly. "If you can put up some cash, I think that I can protect you legally. We can satisfy the mortgage against the place, for the redemption period is not yet up. Sturgis may fight in court, but it will take some time to settle that." He smiled thinly as he made that statement, and Jerico grinned in sympathy. He knew that Whitaker was smart enough to cause plenty of legal delay.

162

"We can put up some cash," Jerico stated. "Not much right now, but some. Then, when we get hold of Frank Larey, I reckon a loan could be managed to take care of the whole thing. Frank seemed to be right anxious to run steers up here."

It was Whitaker's turn to smile in sympathy. "I understand that Sturgis managed to step pretty well on Larey's toes," he said.

"All over 'em," agreed Jerico.

"That will be satisfactory then," the lawyer resumed. "I'm satisfied with what you say, and, as I've said, I think I can look after the legal angle. As for the rest I can't say. I might as well tell you that the talk in town is that you killed Bob Macklin. Polly here" — he looked at the girl — "seems to discount that talk. Lon says he knows you and . . ."

"Sure I know him," Lon Dennis blurted. "There's no more use sayin' he was mixed up in a murder than in sayin' I was."

Whitaker lifted his hand and Dennis stopped. "We're all satisfied here," the lawyer announced. "The thing is that there will probably be a warrant issued for your arrest. If there should be trouble when it is served, I can't say what will happen. You understand that?"

Jerico nodded. "We'll take care of that when the time comes," he said. "Let's go ahead with this lease."

Whitaker nodded. "I've prepared some papers," he announced. "We can go over them."

The lawyer produced a long envelope from his pocket and tendered it to Jerico. Jerico opened the envelope, took out the papers, and, with Pat looking over his shoulder, scanned them carefully. When he finished, he handed the lease and agreement back to Whitaker.

"We got around seven hundred dollars cash," he said bluntly. "You got two thousand acres here that you own. We ain't interested so much in what's owned as in what's controlled. How about that?"

Whitaker's smile was bland. "A lease gives a man a legal foothold in the country," he said. "This range is open and it is largely Public Domain. How is Public Domain usually controlled?"

"By custom," affirmed Jerico.

Whitaker nodded slowly. "And in this case?" he asked.

"You guess!" returned Jerico.

Again Mister Whitaker nodded. "How many steers did Mister Larey contemplate putting up here?" he questioned guilelessly.

Jerico's sudden grin spread beneath the brown mustache. "Why," he drawled, "this here is a special case. The old man talked about three thousand head."

Surprise showed in Whitaker's eyes for a moment, and then was banished. "I see," he intoned. "And you think that a two-thousand acre lease would entitle you to graze that many?"

"How many does Sturgis graze?" parried Jerico.

"I've understood that he has perhaps ten thousand cattle." Whitaker's voice was precise.

"An' how much land does he own?" persisted Jerico.

"Offhand, I should say about five thousand acres."

Jerico lifted his hand and brought it down gently on the arm of his chair. "Custom's custom," he announced cheerfully. "From now on there'll be two hogs at this trough."

The lawyer frowned for a moment, and then laughed. "Hogs," he said gently.

Jerico turned abruptly and faced Lon Dennis. "You know this country?" he asked.

Dennis nodded.

"Could you use a job?"

Dennis thought for a moment. "I ain't no warrior," he said doubtfully.

"An' I ain't hirin' guns," grated Jerico.

Dennis looked steadily at Jerico, hesitated a moment, and then spoke. "I'll hire out," he agreed.

Jerico turned back to the lawyer. "Let's sign that thing," he said. "You'll be wantin' to go back to town, you an' Miss Macklin."

Polly Macklin rose from her chair. "I'm not going back to town," she stated firmly. "I'm going to stay here."

"But . . . " Jerico and Whitaker expostulated at once.

"There's no need of arguing about it," stated Polly Macklin. "I'm going to stay here."

Despite the statement, there was an argument. Both Whitaker and Jerico did the best that they could. Even Lon Dennis entered into the debate, and in the end the one determined woman had her way.

"You can move into the bunkhouse," she told Jerico defiantly. "I leased the ranch to you, not the house."

That was that. There was nothing that could be done about it. Whitaker finally walked out in disgust, Jerico followed him, with Pat at his heels. At the corral they stopped.

"I'd admire if you wouldn't say too much about this right now," Jerico told Whitaker. "We want to be kind of quiet for a while. There's one thing that I would like for you to do. Take care of any mail or any telegrams that come for Pat an' me, an' see that we get 'em out here. Will you do that?"

Whitaker nodded. He had a variety of things to do in Niroba and one thing more was not going to weigh him down. "Certainly," he agreed.

"Thanks," said Jerico. "Now I'll give you what we bargained for on the lease, an' I reckon you'll want to go on in to town."

He counted out bills to Whitaker, took a scrawled receipt, and watched while Lon Dennis and the lawyer got their horses from the corral. Dennis was to ride in with Whitaker, get his bedding, and return to the ranch. The lawyer and Jerico had a few final words, and then Whitaker mounted, joined the waiting Lon, and they rode off south, into the dusk.

When the two were gone, Jerico turned to Pat. "I'm goin' to camp, Pat," he informed. "I reckon we'll move in the mornin'. Mebbe you'd better stay here tonight an' hold down the place."

Jerico expected a refusal, but Pat, keeping his eyes carefully averted from Jerico's face, only nodded his agreement. Jerico waited a moment, and then went to the house. He found Polly Macklin in the kitchen busily

166

engaged in the preparation of a meal. Jerico noticed that there was enough meat cut to feed more than one hungry person.

"I'm goin' to ride to camp now, Miss Macklin," he said. "If it's all right with you, I'll leave Pat here to sort of hold down the place."

The girl looked up from her work, smiling. Her cheeks were flushed and her eyes bright. "I was getting supper for all of us," she said. "I wish you would stay."

Jerico shook his head. "I got to go," he answered. "You go ahead an' cook what you got. Pat'll eat it." He turned then and went back to the corral. The girl preparing supper and Pat making no objection to staying. Jerico grinned to himself.

"You go on up to the house, Pat," he directed the waiting Fallon. "There's some water to pump an' you better get some wood. I'm goin' along to camp." Chuckling to himself, Jerico went to the corral for his horse.

CHAPTER
FIVE

The Long L left their camp in the cottonwoods the next morning. With Doughgod driving his pack horses, Marty hazing the remuda along, and the others drifting the little bunch of steers that had been collected, they made the move. Without hurrying they were at the Seven M before noon. Polly Macklin had a meal ready.

When the men had finished eating and Doughgod had assumed charge of the dishes, Polly approached Jerico. She seemed different from the girl she had been the day before. Her eyes were brighter, and, while occasionally she stopped short in her talk and lapsed into a long silence, she was evidently recovering from the shock of her brother's death.

"I want to talk with you, Mister Jones," she said.

Jerico nodded. "Go ahead," he directed.

The girl hesitated for a moment. "We're in this together," she announced firmly. "I want to help. I don't want you to think that my staying here is a drag on you. There are Seven M horses in the pasture and I want you to use them. I can cook. I'd like to look after that. I want to help. You've been good to me. You . . ."

"That's fine," agreed Jerico. He knew just what this offer meant. It meant that Polly Macklin had banished any doubts concerning the Long L and Jerico Jones from her mind. He knew, too, that work would be good for the girl. It would give her something to think about besides her troubles. Another thing, and Jerico admitted it frankly, the release of Doughgod from kitchen duties would be a help. It would give him another man and Doughgod was a tough old warrior. Jerico held out his broad, calloused hand to the girl.

"Shake hands, pardner," he said. "You can help a heap."

That afternoon Lon Dennis came in, and with his advent Jerico set about the fulfilment of certain plans he had made. He sent Pat, Nig, and the Swede out with Lon to ride south and east. They were to learn the country as they rode, and incidentally throw what Long L steers they could toward the north. To Marty and Blake Wade, Jerico gave other orders. They were to throw the gathered Long L steers into a compact bunch and push them south along the road.

"Go about five miles," directed Jerico. "Drift 'em, an' then hold 'em. Don't let 'em work back north."

Marty grinned at the orders. "Just day-herd 'em in Sturgis's front yard," he interpreted. "Sure thing!"

Jerico's grin was sardonic. "You must think Sturgis has a hell of a big front yard," he said. "You start them steers!"

"What about tonight?" asked Marty.

"Come in about dark," directed Jerico. "If this bunch is scattered, we know where there's plenty more. You an' Blake stay close together an', if anybody comes ridin' up to you, stop him far enough off so that you can watch him."

"Hostile?" questioned Marty.

Jerico shook his head. "Not hostile," he answered, "just watchful."

Marty grunted, nodded his acknowledgment, and went to the corral.

Nebraska and Doughgod had already brought in a bunch of Seven M horses to add to the remuda that the Long L had brought from the camp. Jerico went out and looked the bunch over. He singled out the bay gelding that Bob Macklin had ridden the day he was killed. It would be fitting and proper to finish breaking that horse. Nebraska came over and joined Jerico.

"Get you a horse, Nebraska," directed Jerico. "You an' me are goin' visitin'."

"Sturgis?" questioned Nebraska.

Jerico shook his head. "Over west," he said. "We got some neighbors. We'll leave Doughgod here to hold down the place."

Nebraska nodded and Jerico went to the house to give Doughgod his orders. Polly Macklin was in the kitchen with the old cook. She listened while Jerico talked, and, when he left the room, she dried her hands and hurried out. Before Jerico and Nebraska had saddled, the girl appeared at the corral and stated her intention of going along.

"I know all the people west of us," she informed Jerico. "I'm going to ride with you."

Jerico, seeing the advantage that the girl's presence would give, nodded his head in agreement.

170

The three rode west. In the course of the afternoon they visited two ranches, Pedersen's Bar K Bar and Allen's Circle A. At Pedersen's they found the owner, Ales Pedersen, at home and visited for a time. At the Circle A they were informed that Allen, Sr. had gone in to town, but they talked with young Leonard Allen who was in the corral doctoring a horse.

When the three had ridden back into the Seven M yard, unsaddled, and turned their horses through the corral into the pasture, Jerico felt that the trip had definitely been worthwhile.

Pat, Nig, the Swede, and Lon Dennis came in shortly after Jerico and his companions arrived. They reported throwing quite a number of Long L steers toward the north, and both Nig and Swede seemed to have familiarized themselves fairly well with the country. Later, after the others had eaten supper, Marty Rafferty and Blake Wade arrived. They had seen no one, had not been molested, and they had left the gathered steers about five miles south. With horses penned in the corral for use should occasion arise, Jerico and his men repaired to the bunkhouse. Only Doughgod and Pat Fallon stayed at the house. Doughgod, unable to sever his connection with a cook stove, was washing dishes, and, wonder of wonders, Pat Fallon had stayed to help him. Jerico and the rest sat around the bunkhouse, smoking and talking. Presently Doughgod joined them, but they were all ready to turn in before Pat Fallon came down from the ranch house and opened his bed. When he had blown out the lamp and was ready to turn in on his borrowed bedding, Jerico grinned to himself. He knew sign, did Jerico Jones.

In the morning after breakfast, Jerico sent Blake and Nig to day-herd the gathered steers, and started Marty and Swede out to cover the country Swede had been over the day before. He himself, Nebraska, and Pat went with Lon Dennis to work on farther south. In that manner Jerico felt all the men could familiarize themselves with the country. Doughgod was left as a profane home guard and Polly Macklin busied herself in the kitchen, declaring that she was going to bake bread.

The day passed uneventfully, as did succeeding days. A sense of false security settled around the Long L lease. Pat Fallon was a frequent and apparently welcome visitor at the ranch house. The riders, in their work, encountered men from the Bar S, but these circled wide. Whitaker came out from town, remained for a meal, and went back again. Apparently everything was peaceful. Still Jerico kept his men riding in pairs and waited watchfully. The little bunch of Long L steers that had been gathered, augmented now by perhaps fifty head, were grazed farther and farther south. It was only a question of time, Jerico knew, and so he waited, content to let Sturgis make the next move.

That move came suddenly. At noon, a week after the lease had been signed, a little group of riders came from the west, rode into the Seven M yard, and, dismounting, walked toward the house. Jerico came from the bunkhouse to meet them.

There were four men: walrus-mustached Ales Pedersen and young Leonard Allen were in the group, together with two others Jerico did not know. It was Pedersen who did the talking, and with his first words Jerico saw that Sturgis had been at work.

"We come over to see what you figger to do, Jones," growled Pedersen.

"Do about what?" Jerico was calm.

"You know what!" Pedersen was angry. "You got a thousand head of steers in this country."

Jerico nodded. "That's the figure," he agreed.

"You ain't got enough grass leased to run 'em."

"I got two thousand acres leased an' the water controls about eight thousand more." Jerico spoke reasonably.

Pedersen shook his head. "We come over to warn you," he said bluntly. "Don't throw them steers on our grass."

"Who sent you over?" Jerico was equally blunt.

"Nobody sent us!" Pedersen's face was red. "We . . ."

"I don't bluff worth a cent, Pedersen," remarked Jerico. "My steers ain't been on your grass. They're east of here, an' you know it. I'll tell you somethin' . . . the Seven M has been runnin' a little bunch an' holdin' 'em close. You been usin' grass that belongs to the Seven M by custom, but that's all right. We ain't kickin'. All we want is our share."

"An' we come to tell you to stay off of ours." Pedersen was stubborn.

"An' we've stayed off," agreed Jerico. "Go talk to Sturgis. The Bar S owns five thousand acres an' runs ten thousand cows. If you're lookin' for a grass hog, go talk to Sturgis!"

One of the men that Jerico did not know spoke quietly. "There's been Long L steers usin' in my country," he said evenly.

Jerico looked at the speaker. "Whereabouts?" he demanded.

"I'm Allen of the Circle A, west of you," said the speaker. "My boy Leonard said you was over to our place, but I missed you."

"Throw 'em east when you find 'em," Jerico parried. "That's your riders' business."

Allen was adamant. "You got no business havin' cattle west," he said, shaking his head.

Jerico thought swiftly for a moment. He could readily see how there were Long L steers toward the west. Bar S riders had picked up little bunches and drifted them into Circle A and Bar K Bar range. Sturgis was smart.

"I'll put riders west," offered Jerico. "We can come to some agreement on a line an' I'll hold my stuff east of it."

"I hear you got more steers comin'," went on Pedersen, taking up the talk again. "We're servin' notice on you, Jones, not to hog our grass. Winter's comin' an' it'll be hard to carry our stuff through the way it is."

Jerico disregarded Pedersen and spoke to Allen again. "How about that proposition?" he queried.

Allen nodded thoughtfully. "I'll think it over," he answered.

Pedersen turned to his companion. "Think, hell!" he blared. "You know damn' good an' well, Allen, that you can't do it. You know . . ."

Jerico turned wearily. "I'll work with a man when I can, Pedersen," he said. "I ain't tryin' to stir up trouble. I've made Allen a fair offer. Suppose you keep your yap out of it."

Pedersen lost his head. "This is my business as much as anybody's!" he flared. "You keep your damn' cattle east of the railroad, or I'll . . ."

Jerico took a swift step. His eyes were glinting and he thrust his granite-hard face squarely into Pedersen's. Conciliation had failed; it was time to be salty. "You'll go back to Sturgis an' tell him I don't bluff!" he snapped. "You pore damn' fool, pullin' Sturgis's chestnuts out for him. This is open range. I'll follow custom as long as I'm let, but I won't scare. Git out, now!"

Pedersen backed up a step. The elder Allen was frowning. Jerico saw that he had lost ground. He turned to Allen. "You set the line," he said mildly. "I'll try to keep the Long L east of it. That all right?"

Allen pondered a moment. "I'll think it over," he said ungraciously. "Come on, Ales. You're gettin' mad."

Pedersen was fuming. Allen and young Leonard Allen pushed themselves between Pedersen and Jerico. Jerico waited a moment, and then turned and walked back toward the bunkhouse. By the time he had reached it, the four men had mounted and were riding west. Jerico shook his head. He was worried. He had known this was coming, but it bothered him nevertheless. Jerico was intrinsically fair. He wanted very much to hurt Sturgis, but he didn't want to harm the other ranchmen. He shook his head. You can't make an omelet without breaking eggs. Jerico knew that he was bound to encroach on grass that the Bar K Bar and the Circle A considered theirs. He was sitting on a bunk, thinking it over when Pat Fallon came in.

"What'd them fellows want?" demanded Pat.

Jerico told him. Pat thought it over a moment, and then shrugged. "Somebody'll get hurt," he prophesied. "It's tough, but in the long run it'll be better for them to have Frank Larey for a neighbor than Sturgis."

"Mebbe," Jerico said doubtfully.

"I'm goin' in to town," Pat announced. "We're about out of grub an' I want to see Whitaker. I got to wire Larey, too. We need some cash an' I want to know when them other steers are comin'."

"Hell!" Jerico got up, moved nervously, and wheeled on Pat. "This is a damned fool thing. I wish . . ."

"Are them fellows any worse off with us runnin' them Chihuahuas than they would've been with Sturgis buyin' 'em?" asked Pat.

Jerico's face brightened. "I reckon not," he agreed.

"You ride over east an' look things over." Pat put his hand on the older man's shoulder. "Quit worryin' about bein' fair. It'll all come out in the wash. I know Frank Larey. He'll do what's right."

"I reckon so," Jerico agreed grudgingly.

"Sturgis is just usin' them fellows." Pat removed his hand and turned toward the door. "Just keep rockin', Jerico."

176

Jerico nodded and Pat went on out.

Presently Jerico, too, left the bunkhouse. Pat's suggestion had been good. He would ride over and take a look at the country east. Pat was in the corral hitching a team. Polly Macklin, dressed and ready for the ride to town, was standing beside the corral watching Pat. Jerico's face lost its grim expression. He had noticed that Polly no longer called Pat "Mister Fallon". It was "Pat" now. A hopeful sign. Pat hooked the team to the wagon and helped the girl to the seat, then he climbed up beside her and took the lines. Polly waved to Doughgod who stood in the kitchen door. The wagon rattled out of the yard and Jerico went on to the corral for a mount.

The chunky bay horse that Bob Macklin had started was in the corral. Jerico roped the bay and saddled. The gelding was by way of making a fair horse. He rode east from the Seven M, not paying much attention to where he was going, just letting the bay get along. There were a number of things on Jerico's mind. He knew that the visit from Pedersen and Allen was a move on Sturgis's part. That was plain enough, and smart, too, Jerico could see that. He couldn't understand, however, why he had not had a warrant served on him for the killing of Bob Macklin. That should have been Sturgis's move. Sturgis evidently controlled the deputy sheriff and probably had plenty of drag with the sheriff's and prosecutor's offices. The fact that no warrant had been issued bothered Jerico.

Too, the continued close herding of the little bunch of steers on Sturgis's grass was not bringing the results that Jerico had counted on. He had thought that Sturgis would make some attempt to move those cattle. They were on Public Domain. Jerico had reasoned that, if Sturgis ran the bunch, or tried to intimidate the men holding them, the Long L could, with some lawfulness, protect themselves. Sturgis was clever. Too clever. There was something missing, some particular plan that Sturgis was formulating. Jerico wondered what it was. Sturgis had to make the first move; when he did, Jerico would go to bat. He knew that Sturgis was a crook and a killer. A man that would sit his horse beside a corral and talk to a boy while a killer lined rifle sights on the boy's head was too low a thing to be called a man. The very thought of Sturgis set the blood to ringing in Jerico's ears. The man needed killing. Jerico raised his head and saw that he was well away from the Seven M. He shrugged — better forget Sturgis for the present and attend to business. He was to look for Long L steers, not worry about Sturgis.

He proceeded about that business. Working west and south, he inspected bunch after bunch of cattle. Judging from the brand the cattle wore, he was on Bar K Bar range. There were not many of them and looking for Long L's was like searching for four-leaf clovers in a cow pasture. Jerico swung over the top of a ridge.

He paused a moment at the top, scanning the country. The ridge below him benched off and then dropped again. There were cedars on the bench and clusters of granite boulders. There was a movement in one of the boulder clumps. A horse was in there. Jerico leaned forward.

The horse moved again. Jerico dropped down from the bay as though he had been shot. He knew that horse in the boulder dump. It was Stranger, his own gray that had disappeared at the time the cattle were run off.

There was a clump of cedars perhaps twenty feet to Jerico's left. He pulled the reluctant bay to the shelter, tied it, and then, bending low, worked his way forward. At the front of the bunch of cedars he paused.

He could see Stranger well. The horse was saddled and tied. Jerico searched the country to right and left of the boulders. What was Stranger doing here? Where was Stranger's rider? Jerico wished that he knew. It was evident that he had not been seen when he came over the ridge. If he had, one of two things would have happened: either a shot would have whistled at him or Stranger's rider would have appeared. Who had the horse? Why? Jerico chose a knotted cedar tree and worked toward it.

From cover to cover, noiseless, careful, taking infinite pains, Jerico worked toward the gray horse. A rock tinkled under his foot and he crouched for five minutes, waiting to see what the sound brought. Nothing happened.

He reached the boulders where the horse was tied. Stranger, ears erect, watched nervously. Jerico dared not speak to quiet the horse. He worked through the boulders, slowly, patiently. Over to his right came the *clink* of metal. Jerico slid around a rock. Just below him, he could see a man sprawled at full length, a rifle extended between rocks, and down below, on the flat under the bench, a rider drove three cows toward a little pole corral. Jerico slid his gun from under his coat. The sprawling man with the rifle was Webb Greves.

He watched the rider on the flat pen the cows and dismount to close the corral gate. The rider was Ales Pedersen. Jerico recognized the sweeping mustache. Pedersen, the gate closed, paused to load and light a pipe. He stood by the corral, motionless, a perfect target. Greves was lifting the rifle, carefully lining the sights.

Jerico raised his own gun. "Hold it, Greves," he said gently. "You're covered."

Webb Greves turned his head. His light blue eyes blinked in his sunburned face.

Jerico read those eyes. "There's not a chance, Greves," he said. "Don't try it. Put your gun down."

Greves lowered the rifle and put his hands under him, ready to stand up.

Again Jerico issued orders. "Lay real still. Push your hands out ahead of you."

Greves obeyed.

Without taking his eyes from Greves, Jerico lifted his voice. "Pedersen, Pedersen, come up here!" he called.

There was a hoarse answer from below. Rocks clattered. A horse was coming up the hill. A bit of yellow paper, just the edge, showed from below Greves's leg. The approaching horse stopped, breathing heavily. Jerico risked a swift look. Ales Pedersen, atop his big black, was looking at Greves. Pedersen lifted his eyes and looked swiftly at Jerico.

"What the hell?" boomed Pedersen.

"Saw his horse," said Jerico swiftly. "I was lookin' for Long L stuff. Worked over here an' found him lyin' in the rocks. His sights was lined on you, Pedersen."

"You lie!" Greves cried, trying, hoarsely, to defend himself. "I was —"

"My horse is back by the ridge," interrupted Jerico. "You can see where I come down. His horse is in the rocks. Believe what you see, Pedersen?"

"You dirty killer!" Pedersen could scarcely speak.

"Stand up, Greves!" commanded Jerico. "Easy."

Greves got up, moving carefully. Jerico risked another glance at Pedersen. The big man had his gun out. It was pointing at Greves. The square of yellow paper that had been under Greves's leg was exposed. It looked like a telegram.

"Why?" blurted Pedersen. "Me an' the Bar S have always been friendly."

"Friends don't figure," answered Jerico. "Stand away, Greves. Watch him, Pedersen." Greves moved. Pedersen held his gun on the sunburned man.

Jerico took three swift steps, stooped, and picked up the paper. It was a telegram blank. The name, *Jerico Jones*, was on the address line. "Goin' to plant it on me," said Jerico in a monotone. "Here's why, Pedersen."

The hammer of Pedersen's big Colt clicked suddenly, three times, as Pedersen's big thumb brought it back. "Damn you, Greves!" shouted Pedersen.

"Hold it!" snapped Jerico. "Don't you, Pedersen!"

"He's a dirty killer!" A tinge of insanity was in Pedersen's voice. "I'm goin' to kill him! Lyin' there . . ."

"We'll tie him up," directed Jerico. "Get your rope."

Pedersen moved. Jerico went slowly toward Greves. The man was as dangerous as a mad rattlesnake. Jerico twitched Greves's Colt from its holster, dropped it, and stepped back. He was easier now. Pedersen had a length of short rope, a pigging string, in his left hand. He advanced toward Greves.

"You can't do this." Greves's voice was hoarse. "By God, Sturgis will —"

Pedersen's gun flashed up and then down. It thudded dully against Greves's hat. The man sprawled forward, falling. Pedersen's black horse snorted and jumped at the sudden movement. Pedersen, his gun raised, was stooping. He intended — movement and position showed it — to beat the life from Webb Greves.

"Stop it!" snapped Jerico.

Pedersen checked, stared at Jerico, madness in his eyes. Jerico's gun covered the big man.

"I want him alive," rasped Jerico. "Tie him!"

Sanity fought the madness in Pedersen's eyes, fought the battle, and won.

Jerico, watching, nodded his approbation. "That's it," he commended. "Put up your gun an' tie him."

As though in a daze Pedersen slowly holstered his gun, pulled Greves's arms behind his back, and began to work with the pigging string.

Jerico returned his own gun to the clip holster under his arm. He watched while Pedersen pulled the knots tight on the wrists and bound a loop about Greves's feet. Pedersen jerked viciously, pulling the knot tightly, looked at his handiwork a moment, and then stood up. He stared at Jerico who was reading the telegram. It was from Frank Larey at Marfa. Larey was getting a shipment of cattle ready.

Jerico lifted his eyes and looked at Pedersen. "You an' me talked this mornin'," he said gravely. "You might say we quarreled. If you was found dead down at that corral an' this telegram was found up here, what would've happened?"

Pedersen's eyes were completely sane now. "You'd've been hung," he said. "They'd've come in a bunch for you."

Jerico nodded. "That's what was planned," he agreed dryly. "No trial or nothin', just a hangin'. I'd've been out of the way an' there'd've been another place, your place, for Sturgis to gobble up."

Anger flashed across Pedersen's face. "What you goin' to do?" he demanded. "You goin' to let this feller go?"

"No." Jerico shook his head. "He's tried to bushwhack you. He's a killer. He's a damn' horse thief, too. That's my horse he's got in the rocks. What do you do to killers an' horse thieves up here?"

Greves was moving. He had recovered from the blow on the head. He stirred uneasily.

"Hang 'em," said Pedersen. "I'll go to Niroba an' get Touhy."

"No!" Jerico snarled the word. "Touhy is a Sturgis man."

"He ain't!" flared Pedersen. "Sturgis fired him."

"We don't want no deputies in this," said Jerico. "If you want to get somebody, get Allen an' your neighbors. We'll take this killer to the Seven M. I reckon you know what'll happen there."

Pedersen was reluctant to obey Jerico. He wanted to turn Greves over to the law. Jerico was obdurate. He knew that Webb Greves held the key to the killing of Bob Macklin. He planned to make Greves give up that key.

"Sturgis can have Greves out in an hour," he said contemptuously. "Help me load him on a horse. Is this country soft? Do you want to let Greves go? Can you fight Sturgis's money?"

Jerico had his way. He brought the gray Stranger from the boulder and together he and Pedersen heaved the bound man up on the horse and lashed him across the saddle. Jerico retrieved his bay and gave Pedersen orders.

"Get Allen," he directed. "Get as many more as you can. Bring 'em to the ranch. Hell, man! Bond Sturgis is behind this. Greves is just his killer. You think Sturgis is goin' to sit an' take it?"

Pedersen, unwillingly convinced, agreed. He mounted the black horse and for a long moment stared at the bound Greves, and then at Jerico. He was still a little suspicious of Jerico.

Jerico read that suspicion. "He'll be at the ranch when you get there, Pedersen," Jerico assured him. "I won't kill him an' I won't let him get away."

"I still think we ought to get the deputy," grumbled Pedersen.

"Get him then!" snapped Jerico. "Send word for him to come out. But you get Allen an' come to the ranch first. Go on!"

Pedersen, partially satisfied, turned the black and rode down the slope from the bench, looking back over his shoulder.

Jerico, starting Stranger ahead of him, rode east. The sun was just touching the tops of the hills in the west.

CHAPTER
SIX

At the Seven M the crew was in. Marty, Nig Bell, even Doughgod saw Jerico coming. They ran out to meet him. Jerico gave few explanations. Briefly he told what had happened. Marty and Nig pulled Greves from Stranger, hauled him to the bunkhouse. Pat Fallon pulled Jerico aside. Polly Macklin, face gray, was watching the men who dragged the inert figure.

"You can't do it, Jerico," said Pat. "Polly's here. You can't take Greves out an' hang him on this place. She'd never get over it."

"Hell!" rasped Jerico. "We ain't goin' to hang him. I want him to talk. He killed Bob Macklin. He's under Sturgis. Scare him enough an' he'll come across."

Pat's face was relieved. "I'll tell Polly," he said.

"What's the matter with your face?" rasped Jerico. "What happened to you?"

Pat's hand went up to a bruise on his cheek. "Sturgis," he said succinctly. "I seen him in town. I got to tell Polly, Jerico."

"Go tell her then!" barked Jerico. "Tell her that Pedersen an' Allen an' mebbe some more are comin'. Tell her we sent for Touhy. Then come back here. I want to talk to you."

186

Pat hurried over to the girl, and Jerico stalked to the bunkhouse. Marty Rafferty and Nig Bell had stretched Greves out on a bunk. The man was still tied, hard and fast. Nebraska, a coil of rope in his hands, was sitting where Greves's eyes could watch his fingers. Nebraska was looping the rope, taking turns about it. Lon Dennis stood in a corner of the room. Blake Wade, his face white, was watching Nebraska. Doughgod, standing beside the old cowpuncher, was giving advice.

"No need to take all that trouble, Nebraska," chided Doughgod. "This ain't no formal hangin'. Just tie a loop an' let him strangle."

Jerico stalked over and stood looking down at Greves. "Got anything to say?" he asked.

Greves shook his head. Jerico turned. "We'll wait for Pedersen an' Allen," he informed the men. Nebraska went on with his knot tying. Greves's eyes followed Nebraska's fingers, fascinated.

Doughgod cleared his throat. "I remember one time we hung a man," he recounted. "Took him damn' near thirty minutes to die. Look, Nebraska. If you tie that a little tighter, it'll slip down slow. Let him strangle a little at a time. Give it here . . . I'll show you."

Nebraska pushed Doughgod's hand aside. "Lemme alone," he snarled. "I know how to do this." He got up, stalked over, rope in hand, pulled Webb Greves's head up from the bed, and slid the looped rope around his neck.

At the touch of the rope Greves flinched away. His pale eyes filled suddenly with fright. His voice was a squawk. "My God, boys! Don't do that!"

Nebraska slid the rope down snugly on Greves's scrawny throat, twisted it until the knot was under Greves's ear.

"When in hell will those fellows be here?" demanded Nebraska.

Greves struggled against his bonds, threshed on the bunk. Horses tramped in the yard.

Pedersen's bull voice boomed. "Jones!"

Jerico hastened to the bunkhouse door. Pedersen, followed by Allen, appeared in the light of the doorway. It was almost full dark outside.

"In here," directed Jerico. "We're about ready to go ahead."

"We sent for . . ." began Pedersen.

Greves, nerve broken, babbled on the bunk. "Sturgis! It was Sturgis's . . ."

Jerico almost ran to the man's side. "Talk up," snapped Jerico. "Talk to save your life, man!"

Pedersen was behind Jerico now, peering over his shoulder. At the sight of the man, Greves broke completely. His fright was so great that his words were almost incoherent, but he told enough of a story so that the rest could be pieced out. Sturgis had ordered Greves to kill Pedersen. The telegram from Frank Larey had been filched from the depot office.

Jerico, grim-faced, turned to stare at Pedersen, and the big rancher nodded.

"What about Bob Macklin?" rasped Jerico. "You killed him. You was at the corner of the barn an' shot him with a rifle. Tell the truth, Greves."

188

Greves shook his head. His mouth settled into grim, stubborn lines.

Jerico whirled and grated a command. "Take him out, Nebraska!"

Nebraska Williams pulled on the rope about Greves's throat. It tightened perceptibly.

Greves struggled, gasped, and gave up. "I shot Macklin," he panted. "Sturgis . . ."

Nebraska let go the rope. Jerico straightened. "I reckon that'll do," announced Jerico. "Take off the rope, Nebraska. The sheriff'll be out here pretty quick. Take off the rope."

"You ain't goin' to hang him?" demanded the incredulous Nebraska.

"Not now," agreed Jerico.

Doughgod said — "Hell!" — disgustedly. Pat Fallon heaved a sigh of relief.

"He's worth more alive an' talkin' than he would be dead," Jerico said flatly. "Pull off that rope."

Unwillingly Nebraska jerked the rope from Greves's neck. He looked at the knot, grunted, and flipped the rope down to the floor.

"All that work!" remarked Nebraska, and spat at the rope.

"We'll go to the house," Jerico stated. "Lon, you an' Marty stay here an' watch this fellow. Come on."

Jerico turned and walked toward the door, Pat following him. Allen and Pedersen trailed out. Doughgod, Nig Bell, and Wade Blake followed Pedersen.

"You might make us some coffee, Doughgod," suggested Jerico over his shoulder. "Some of us ain't had supper."

"I'll be damned," grunted Doughgod, and broke into a trot toward the kitchen.

Pat came up and joined Jerico. They walked in silence for perhaps five steps. Behind them Allen and Pedersen were talking. Jerico heard Pedersen say — "Sturgis!" — and curse luridly.

"What happened in town, Pat?" asked Jerico.

"I seen him," growled Pat Fallon. "He made me a proposition."

"What was it, Pat?"

"Said that he wouldn't swear out a warrant for you on the Macklin killin' if we'd sell him the steers an' this lease we got."

"Huh," grunted Jerico.

"The nerve of that fellow," said Pat softly.

"Yeah?" encouraged Jerico.

"I told him to go to hell," Pat continued. "He got to talkin', hintin' around about Polly. I slapped his face an' he hit me. Then I knocked him down."

Jerico stared at his companion. They were in the light from the kitchen door. Pots and pans rattled inside the kitchen where Doughgod was busy. Pat flushed under Jerico's scrutiny. "Polly was with me or I'd've killed him," said Pat flatly.

Jerico nodded. "Like her, Pat?" he asked.

The dull red on Pat's cheeks deepened. Jerico had his answer.

"What did Whitaker say?" demanded Jerico.

190

"He's got 'em all tied up," answered Pat. "He's paid the interest on the mortgage an' he got an injunction against Sturgis. I don't know what all he ain't done. He wants you to come in an' see him."

Pedersen and Allen joined the two by the door.

Doughgod poked his head out. "I'm warmin' up some grub," offered Doughgod. "You all better come in an' eat a bite."

"Come in, men," invited Jerico.

They went into the kitchen. Polly Macklin, her face pale but her eyes alive and light, was at the table setting places. Jerico, Allen, and Pedersen went to the table. They sat down.

Allen leaned forward. "I sent Leonard for Touhy," he said. "He ought to be here any time now. What do you think, Jones?"

"I think that Sturgis is all through," answered Jerico thoughtfully. "With Greves testifyin' against him, Sturgis is done. Greves will tell aplenty. He's got to save his life."

"We ought to hung him." Doughgod set a platter of meat before Jerico.

Sharp and distinct, a shot roared in the night. The men at the table started up, exclamations on their lips. Nebraska and Nig Bell ran to the kitchen door, met in it, and wedged. There was confusion for a moment.

Nebraska got clear. He ran out. Nig almost fell down the steps. The men boiled out of the kitchen, running toward the bunkhouse. They thrust open the door, pushed inside, and stopped. Marty Rafferty, head bleeding from a long gash, lay on the floor unconscious, and on the bunk Webb Greves was stretched out, still bound, blood oozing out on his shirt.

It was Jerico who recovered first. He half turned and stared at Pat Fallon. "Dennis," said Jerico. "He was workin' for Sturgis all the time!"

The men filed out of the bunkhouse. Doughgod and Nebraska stayed to administer what aid they could to Rafferty. Greves was dead.

A search about the place revealed that there were no horses in the corral. Allen's horse and Pedersen's black also were gone, turned loose. When the men returned to the bunkhouse from their futile search, Marty Rafferty was conscious and talking. He had been watching Greves. He had heard Dennis move behind him, had turned to speak to him, and that was all he remembered.

Jerico swore softly at Marty's report. "Hit Marty," he said. "Went an' turned loose the horses. Got himself a mount, an' then come back here an' killed Greves. Damn me, I should've knowed."

"It ain't your fault, Jerico," Pat said. "We'll light out an' . . ."

"We're afoot," said Jerico bluntly. "He's headed for Sturgis on a run. Sturgis will know all about what's happened. Damn it!"

"But what can Sturgis do?" questioned Allen. "Pedersen an' me heard what Greves said. We know who's behind the trouble."

"Sturgis has got mebbe twenty-five men," interrupted Jerico. "He can do aplenty."

"What's goin' on here?" demanded a voice. The men in the bunkhouse turned to see Lance Touhy in the doorway with Leonard Allen looking in over his shoulder. The deputy sheriff strode on into the room.

"What's goin' on?" he demanded again.

There was a babble of voices as all the men tried to talk at once. Gradually out of the turmoil, order was restored. Pedersen and Allen, now separately, now talking together, told Touhy what had happened. The deputy asked questions. He examined Greves and heard Marty Rafferty's story. He listened, learned, and, when he had the facts, faced Jerico.

"It's damn' lucky for you that some of this happened, Jones," said Touhy bluntly. "I got a warrant in my coat for you, accusin' you of killin' Bob Macklin."

"Goin' to serve it?" Jerico grinned wryly.

Touhy shook his head. "What do you want to do?" he demanded.

Jerico looked around the room. The temper of the men was in their eyes. Again Jerico stared at the deputy. "You might get a posse here," he said slowly.

"Well?" questioned Touhy.

"Mebbe you want to arrest Dennis for killin' Webb Greves." Jerico's voice was casual. "Mebbe you want Sturgis in the Macklin killin'."

"Of course, I want 'em." Touhy's voice was brusque. "I ain't goin' to go up against an army, though. Sturgis will have all his 'punchers."

Jerico interrupted. "Me," he drawled, "I been plannin' to ride in to Niroba an' talk to Sturgis. So, Pat?"

Pat Fallon's hazel eyes were bright. "Sure," he agreed.

Over by Webb Greves's body, Marty Rafferty voiced the opinion of the Texas men. "Gun talk!" grunted Marty.

"You're crazy!" snapped Touhy. "Sturgis will be waitin' for you. You think he's goin' to be sittin' back holdin' his hands? There's half a dozen places between here an' town where he can lay for you an' blast you to hell. The thing for us to do is get hold of the sheriff. Get him over here with a bunch of deputies an' . . ."

"Go kiss Sturgis?" completed Pat Fallon.

"Hell!" Touhy lost his temper.

Jerico took charge. "We're goin' to town, Touhy," he said. "Either we'll go as your deputies or we'll go without that, but we're goin'. We'll leave here by daybreak. Nobody's goin' to waylay us or dry-gulch us. Not this bunch. We'll arrest Sturgis. Mebbe we'll take a few more into camp. What in hell do you want to do, Touhy? Call out the cavalry?"

Touhy gave up. He snorted disgustedly, glanced around, and spat on the floor. "Raise your right hands," he ordered. "I'll swear you in."

The men in the bunkhouse mumbled words after the deputy, lowered their hands, and instinctively looked to Jerico for orders. Jerico would have deferred to Touhy, but the deputy sheriff would have none of that.

"You're the boss," he said to Jerico. "You can ramrod this madhouse."

Accordingly Jerico issued orders. There was no use in moving before daylight. Young Leonard Allen and Touhy were to run in a bunch of horses before daybreak. They were the only mounted men in the bunch. Guards were posted, Jerico wisely taking precautions against a surprise blow by Sturgis. This was war, range war, and Jerico realized it. Doughgod he dispatched to the kitchen to reheat the meal. Pat Fallon he sent to the house to reassure Polly Macklin. Jerico was worried about the girl; he would have to leave someone at the place to look after her, lose a man from his fighting force. Greves was carried outside and deposited in a root cellar. Jerico ordered the rest to bed.

That was one order that was not well obeyed. The men were excited. They wanted to talk, did talk. Allen and Pedersen, catching the spirit of the Long L men, wanted to get horses and ride to outlying ranches for recruits. This Jerico forbade.

"No use gettin' the whole country into this," he said. "Besides, we only got two horses up on the place. It'ud take a couple of hours to find the remuda tonight. Better turn in."

Gradually the Seven M quieted down. Nig Bell and Swede Hanson, weary and taking Jerico at his word, stretched out on bunks. The lamp in the bunkhouse was blown out. Doughgod, having fed Jerico, Allen, and Pedersen, put his kitchen to rights and turned in. Standing by the bunkhouse door, Jerico could see Pat Fallon's cigarette glow on the porch of the ranch house.

195

Pat was talking to Polly Macklin. Jerico grinned grimly. He could just about guess what Pat was saying. He would have to look out for Pat tomorrow, keep him back. Jerico squatted by the bunkhouse wall, waiting, waiting. *Maybe tomorrow* — Jerico pushed the thought away. There had been more than one night such as this in his life. A man can't spend eight years in the Ranger force without having trouble. Still — Jerico shrugged and fumbled in his vest for papers and tobacco. He heard Pat Fallon's feet as the lad came to the bunkhouse. A good boy, Pat Fallon.

CHAPTER
SEVEN

Morning broke. The sleepless Jerico wakened Leonard Allen and Nig Bell, sent them out after the horses. Doughgod's alarm clock went off with a bang and rattle. The old cook stifled it, stretched, yawned, and got up. Smoke came from the chimney of the ranch kitchen. Men began to stir. The guards came in, Marty and Nebraska.

Breakfast was ready before the horses were run in. The men ate silently. Leonard Allen and Nig came up from the corral and announced that the horses were penned.

Touhy came to Jerico. "You still bent on this, Jones?" he asked.

"Might as well get it over with," assented Jerico. "Mebbe Sturgis will just come along peaceful."

"You don't know Sturgis," grated Touhy.

"I aim to know him better," drawled Jerico.

Touhy walked away. His load was heavy on his shoulders. He was responsible even though Jerico was the boss. Jerico liked the deputy. Touhy was a good man. He wanted to do what was right. His trouble was that he couldn't decide what was right and what was wrong. Jerico shrugged. He walked over to the corral, spoke to Allen.

"Better leave your kid here," suggested Jerico.

Allen looked relieved.

"You can stay with him if you want to," Jerico told him.

Allen shook his head, his face darkening. "I'm goin'," he stated.

"Tell your boy." Jerico turned away. "I got to leave somebody else here, too. Somebody older. They might break back on us an' come down on this place."

"Leave your cook," suggested Allen.

"Doughgod?" Jerico grinned. "That old heller will be right up in front. We'd have to fight to get away, if we tried to leave him."

Pat Fallon, a rope in his hand, came from the bunkhouse toward the corral.

Jerico hastened his stride and intercepted Pat before the hazel-eyed boy reached his goal. "Better put your rope up, Pat," said Jerico. "I'm goin' to leave you here with Polly."

Pat shook his head. "You don't leave me," he snapped. "Send Polly over to Allen's with the kid."

It was an idea. Jerico nodded slowly. "I'll do that," he said. "You go tell her. We'll see her start."

Pat, rope in hand, hastened toward the house.

The Long L men were in the corral roping out their mounts. There was no laughter and very little talk. This was a roundup day, all right, but it was a grim, forbidding roundup. Pat came back to the corral, went through the gate, and, selecting a horse, roped the

198

animal. Jerico watched while Pat put Polly Macklin's saddle on the horse. Young Leonard Allen, tears that he tried to keep back in his eyes, came to Jerico and pleaded to be taken along. Jerico was adamant. Pat roped out a horse for himself and another for Jerico. Jerico left the disappointed Leonard Allen and got his own saddle. Polly Macklin, dressed and ready, came from the house. The Long L men stopped their preparations long enough to see her ride away, westward, with Leonard Allen, then, when the two were gone, Jerico finished his saddling and looked about him. The men were ready. Jerico mounted.

The little body of horsemen rode south. Ahead of them Nig Bell and Marty Rafferty rode the ridges. Behind them smoke rose from the chimney of the deserted Seven M.

Pat Fallon, riding beside Jerico, looked back over his shoulder.

"Look ahead, Pat," ordered Jerico gruffly. "You'll see the place when you ride in this evenin'."

Pat grunted.

They circled wide of the Bar S buildings. The place looked deserted. There was no smoke and no movement. The Bar S was not at home.

Near the outskirts of Niroba, Jerico, watching Marty Rafferty, saw the Long L man rein in. Jerico, Pat beside him, spurred ahead. The others spread out in a thin line. Nig Bell was riding toward Rafferty. Another man appeared, riding out from the direction of town. It was Whitaker, the lawyer. The five — Bell, Marty, Jerico, Pat, and the lawyer — met, reined in, and stopped.

Whitaker looked at the men he confronted. He glanced past them and saw the others coming on: Allen, Nebraska, Doughgod, Pedersen, Blake Wade, and Touhy. Whitaker's mouth was a thin, hard line.

"So you come to town?" he said between his tight lips. "Well, they're waiting for you."

"Where?" demanded Pat.

"In the Stag," answered Whitaker. "Sturgis and every man he could muster."

"It's good they're all together," drawled Jerico.

"He's had men watching you," warned Whitaker. "Dennis came in last night with word of what had happened. He said that you killed Webb Greves."

The other men of the posse had ridden up and were grouped about Jerico and Whitaker.

Jerico moved his arm in warning. "Scatter out," he commanded. "Don't bunch up like this." Then to the lawyer: "You seem to know a heap about it, Whitaker."

"I do." Whitaker nodded as the posse men moved to obey Jerico's order. "I've been paying a bartender in the Stag, waiting for a time like this to come."

"An' what else do you know?" queried Jerico.

"I know that two men rode into town ahead of you," answered Whitaker. "They know you are coming."

Pat Fallon spoke nervously. "Do you reckon they watched the ranch?"

"I know they did," Whitaker answered Pat.

"What about Polly, Jerico?" Pat voiced the reason for his nervousness. "You don't reckon . . . ?"

"We'll ride ahead," said Jerico. "Whitaker, I thank you kindly."

Whitaker turned his horse. The butt of a rifle peeped over the top of his saddle. "I'm going with you," he said precisely. "There are times when the legal profession is not entirely satisfactory."

Jerico suddenly laughed aloud. "Good man," he commended. "Let's pull out. Start ahead, Nig, you an' Marty."

The two point men spurred off. The others rode on at a slower gait. There was no particular hurry. They were expected. Sturgis was waiting. Something inexorable in the steady jog of the horses, Jerico turned in his saddle, looking at Whitaker.

"Dennis killed Webb Greves," he said. "Lemme tell you."

Whitaker listened while Jerico related the happenings of the previous day. From time to time the lawyer nodded.

"And you are all deputies?" he asked, when Jerico finished.

"Yeah," said Jerico.

"What do you plan to do?"

"Arrest Sturgis."

Whitaker sniffed. "Easier said than done. He will fight."

"An' so will we."

Whitaker held out his hand. "Give me your tobacco," he requested. "I think I'll smoke a cigarette."

Jerico brought out the makings. The lawyer's thin fingers curled paper about tobacco. "Any plans?" he asked.

"None to speak of." Jerico was frank.

They were at the outskirts of Niroba. The sun had risen over the Rock Ribs, was sending long slants of light down into the valley. The town stood stark and deserted, heavy shadows on the western sides of the buildings. The men closed in on Jerico, the point riders falling back.

Jerico spoke to Touhy. "Want to take it from here?" he asked, tendering command.

Touhy shook his head.

"We'll ride in," Jerico spoke slowly. "I'm goin' to ride ahead. You all keep back. Watch the houses. Whitaker says they're in the Stag. I don't want nobody to get hurt. Keep covered. Don't shoot unless you have to. I reckon you know when."

He moved his horse ahead, advancing down the street. The others waited until an interval of perhaps 100 feet intervened, and then they, too, rode ahead. They moved slowly, keeping their horses down to a walk. The houses on either side were dead, deserted apparently. It might have been a ghost town they entered.

Turning left, Jerico swung into the main street. Down at the end of the street was the depot. The stores were closed. The trough in front of the blacksmith shop, where Jerico had watered Stranger when he first came to town, was just to Jerico's right. He reined in and moved his right arm wide. Behind him the others, interpreting his gesture, stopped. Men slid down from horses, leading their mounts into the recesses between buildings. Jerico looked back, saw that his forces were disposing themselves, and then, looking forward again, sat waiting. From the Stag Saloon, farther down the street, a man emerged, walked out on the board sidewalk, and stood leaning against a pillar that supported the porch roof in front of the saloon. It was Sturgis.

Jerico put a little pressure on his spurs. His horse moved forward. Solitary, Jerico rode toward the waiting Sturgis. Fifty feet from the man, he halted.

"We come for you, Sturgis," he said. "You're wanted for murder. Greves talked last night before Lon Dennis killed him."

Sturgis's face was flushed. He stared at Jerico. "Why damn you, Jones," he said flatly, "you won't take me!"

"I think I will, Sturgis." Jerico was calm.

Sturgis moved his hand toward the Stag. "I've got the Macklin girl in there," he said. "We were watchin' when you left the Seven M."

There was truth in the man's voice. Jerico's eyes shifted from Sturgis's face. For an instant he was nonplussed. Then he spoke, his voice strong. "Give up, Sturgis," he said. "We've got you. If you hurt that girl . . ."

From the Stag a gun crashed. Jerico's sentence was left unfinished. He went down from his horse, falling limp, like a sack of meal sliding from the tailgate of a wagon. The frightened horse reared high. Sturgis, running like a frightened rabbit, leaped for the door of the Stag. From up the street guns answered the shot from the Stag, and Jerico Jones, sprawled on his belly, lay inert in front of the saloon.

He lay motionless. He dared not move. From the corner of his eyes he had sighted a telltale movement in the saloon door an instant before the shot. He had thrown himself sideward and let his body go limp. The lead had breathed against his cheek but had done no harm. The horse was gone. Jerico lay there, right arm under his body, eyes opened a crack, watching the front of the Stag.

He heard Pat Fallon call to him. Dared not answer. He knew that, if he moved, a second and better placed shot would come to finish him. The men in the saloon were keeping up a constant firing. From the outside, the posse men answered that fire. A ring of steel and lead surrounded the Stag Saloon.

Save only in front. Jerico suddenly realized that there was no lead going over him. There was, he remembered, a vacant lot directly opposite the Stag. No place for a man to take cover. The attackers were firing at the Stag's front from an angle.

From up the street, in the direction from which they had come, Jerico heard the pound of hoofs. He widened his eyes, risked turning his head a fraction. There was a horse coming down the street, running full out, belly to the ground. Pat Fallon was astride that horse, bent low, crouched in the saddle. Jerico realized what Pat was doing. The Texas boy was taking an awful chance, bent on rescuing Jerico if a spark of life was still in Jerico's body. And Jerico didn't want to be rescued. From where he lay he commanded the front entrance of the Stag. There was no other way to do it. Jerico alone, of the attackers, knew that Polly Macklin was in the saloon. The firing grew hot from the posse men. They were shielding Pat Fallon as best they could. From the saloon the fire increased in volume. Pat Fallon, riding like an Indian, swept down on Jerico, swung down from his saddle to catch an arm and drag a wounded man out of range. His hand clutched Jerico's left arm. To an onlooker it would have seemed that the speed was too great, that Pat had lost his grip. Actually Jerico Jones jerked his arm from Pat's hand, rolling inertly in the street.

The horse swept on, staggered, and went down. Pat threw himself clear and at a faltering run, sought shelter around the corner of the store adjoining the Stag. Still Jerico lay inertly. A bullet plucked dust from the street beside him. Another tugged at his coat.

Gradually the firing lessened in volume. It was a stalemate. No chance for either side.

Touhy called from the store where Pat had taken refuge, called to Sturgis. Apparently Touhy had taken over the command. "We got you, Sturgis. Give up an' come out!"

A wild, high yell answered from the saloon. That was all.

Now the shots were spasmodic. The men in the Stag were shooting only when they saw a target. The attackers were planning some move; Jerico could not imagine what it might be. The Stag would be a hard nut to crack. From somewhere out of town a train whistled, a long, wailing blast. It seemed to Jerico that he could lie still no longer, that he must move to ease his cramped muscles, but he dared not. The train whistled again.

There was a yelp from inside the Stag. Something had happened that Jerico could not see. He heard Marty Rafferty call tauntingly, could not understand the words. As he lay there in the dust, he heard a sound foreign to the fight, a crackling sound. He saw smoke seep from a shattered window in the Stag. Touhy and the Long L men had succeeded in firing the saloon. They didn't know that Polly Macklin was inside. Jerico gathered himself, bunching his muscles. He would have to make a run for it. He had to tell Touhy and Pat where Polly was. Even as he gathered himself, he saw the front door of the Stag open a crack. A dirty bartender's apron tied to a broom handle was shoved out. The posse men ceased their fire.

Sturgis called from inside the Stag. "Touhy!"

From the left the deputy answered. "Give up, Sturgis!"

Sturgis's voice was high and shrill. "The hell I give up! We've got that Macklin girl in here. We're comin' out with her in front of us. If you shoot, you'll kill her."

The announcement must have caused consternation. Jerico could guess how Pat felt, could imagine Touhy's reaction to the information. He waited now.

Sturgis called again. "Get horses out in front for us! Get 'em out!"

Pat Fallon called to Sturgis. "If we turn you loose, will you let the girl go?"

The answer was a taunting: "Maybe!"

"How many horses?" called Pat.

"Three," Sturgis answered. "Hurry. If you want to see that girl alive . . ."

Apparently there was dissension inside the Stag. Yells went up. There were angry shouts. The Bar S men did not take kindly to being deserted by their leader. The flames were crackling louder. Evidently the fire was growing.

Suddenly, as though thrown by a gust of wind, the door of the Stag was flung open. Polly Macklin appeared in the doorway. The girl was limp, supported by an arm around her waist. Behind her was Sturgis, holding her up with one arm. The other hand clutched a gun. Man and girl were on the sidewalk. Lon Dennis, gun in hand, backed out of the door, menacing the men inside, holding them back. Sturgis took a step. If a man fired from either side, he might hit Polly Macklin. Sturgis and the girl were clear. Dennis was out of the door. They were perhaps fifteen feet from Jerico Jones, sprawled in the dust, his right arm still beneath his body.

"Get them horses!" yelled Sturgis, and took a step.

As he moved, Jerico came up from the street. His gun was in his hand. Sturgis saw that movement, tried to turn, tried to throw the girl in front of him. Too late. Jerico's Colt spoke imperatively. Sturgis reeled back, releasing his grasp on the girl. Polly Macklin pitched forward. Lon Dennis had wheeled, gun rising to level at Jerico. Again the Colt in Jerico's hand bounced up, roaring. Dennis fell back, the second slug striking him even as he fell. His head struck the threshold of the Stag's doorway. He lay still.

Jerico, on his feet, ran toward Polly Macklin, bent to lift her and carry her to a place of safety. There was no need. A man, his hands shoulder high, stepped from the saloon, lifting his feet to clear Lon Dennis's head. He was followed by others. The Bar S was through, finished.

Pat Fallon ran from the corner of the store toward Jerico. Suddenly the street seemed filled with men. It was all over.

Jerico looked about him. Pat Fallon had Polly Macklin in his arms, was cradling the girl against his chest. Jerico could see Polly's eyes open and stare wonderingly up into Pat's face. The girl's arm stole up to encircle Pat Fallon's neck. Allen of the Circle A was close to Jerico. He had his arm thrown across young Leonard's shoulders. The boy was white-faced; there was blood on his shirt and an arm was bandaged. Touhy was at Jerico's side. Whitaker came running from a building, trailing a rifle.

Touhy's voice rasped in Jerico's ear. "I thought you was dead, Jones."

"So did I," answered Jerico. "Let's get these fellows lined up. What will we do with 'em, Touhy?"

The Long L men, reinforced by Pedersen, had the beaten Bar S fighters lined up on the walk in front of the vacant lot. There were fourteen Bar S men. The Stag Saloon was burning fiercely. Townspeople, wide-eyed, were gathering about. Whitaker joined them. He gave orders; men ran for buckets. They must fight the fire to keep the town from burning.

Touhy looked at Jerico. He looked at the men held prisoner. He shoved back his hat. Two townsmen passed carrying Sturgis's limp body. Others were picking up Lon Dennis, carrying him away. Men were crawling out on the roof of the store nearest the burning Stag. They were not attempting to save the saloon, but were trying to keep the fire from spreading. A line of men was passing filled buckets.

Touhy said: "Hell."

"Goin' to hold 'em?" asked Jerico.

"I got to," answered Touhy.

"Give 'em ten minutes to get out of town. Tell 'em to leave the country. Shucks, Touhy, they was just workin' for Sturgis. They ain't bad."

Touhy grunted, looked at Jerico, and turned away. Jerico watched a man quench a flying ember on the store's roof. His eyes searched for Pat Fallon, failed to find him. Nig Bell was at Jerico's side. So was Marty Rafferty.

"We goin' to let them sons go?" shrilled Marty. "We goin' to turn 'em loose?"

"I reckon," agreed Jerico. "Where's Pat?" He stopped short. Searching for Pat, his eyes had encountered an unexpected sight.

There was a train in at the depot, a stock train. Smoke trailed up from the engine. Striding up the street from the station was a giant of a man, two men flanking him on either side. Frank Larey.

Jerico took a step forward and waited. He hardly heard Marty Rafferty's disgusted: "Shucks!"

Larey came on. He glanced at the burning Stag, waited until a bucket had passed, and stepped through the line. He halted in front of Jerico Jones. Mustache bristling, blue eyes filled with questions, Frank Larey confronted his man.

"What the hell does this mean, Jerico?" demanded Larey. "What's happenin' here? Where's Pat? What sort of rawhidin' do you call this?"

Jerico felt strangely weak. It was all over. Done. He looked up at Frank Larey's questioning eyes and made answer. "Why, Frank," said Jerico Jones, "we just come to town to receive them steers."

Nine Coffins for Bellaire

Thirteen years elapsed between the appearance of "$teers", featuring Jerico Jones, and the third and final story about him, "Nine Coffins for Bellaire", published in *Star Western* (3/48), a Popular Publications pulp magazine. Some character names were altered by the magazine prior to publication. These have been restored, based on the author's original manuscript.

CHAPTER
ONE

Jerico Jones spread his legs against the swaying of the caboose and scowled at the stock car. The first section of Freight Thirty-Two was roaring along like a bat out of hell on the grade below Hidry, and Jerico was unhappy. The stock car trailing the caboose contained his horses and, for Jerico's money, should have been up ahead, just behind the engine. A pulled drawbar and much switching at Hidry accounted for its presence in the rear.

"Wheelin' 'em, ain't he?" Unobserved, the rear brakeman joined Jerico on the platform and shouted his comment above the roar of the train. "Got to make the siding at Bellaire for second Thirty-Two." The brakeman was a grinning oaf, Jerico decided, and scowled at the pleasant young face framed by light from the door of the reeling caboose.

"Them horses" — Jerico raised his voice to combat the noise — "are goin' to be skinned from their ankles up, that's what's goin' to happen. I'm goin' to sue this tin-pot outfit for every dime they got."

He meant this at the moment. He was displeased with the whole El Paso and Kansas Railroad, from general freight agent on down. He wished the officials

213

were taking this ride, yes, and in his horse car, too. He wished . . . Air sighed through the train line and wheels shot sparks. Up ahead, the engineer made a second reduction. Speed diminished and with it the noise of passage. Curiosity, always a governing factor with Jerico Jones, dulled the edge of anger.

"We got to wait here for a train?" he demanded.

"Second Thirty-Two," the brakeman agreed. "We lost time at Hidry when we switched your car behind. Second Thirty-Two is carryin' a car of silk, an' they're on time. They'll go into Vuelta ahead of us. Goin' to feed your horses at Vuelta?"

"If I ever get there," Jerico growled.

The train stopped. Now a growing rumble told of slack coming out. Jerico braced himself, accepted the jerk, and they were in motion again. The brakeman, lantern hooked over his arm, was on the platform step. A switch light swung past in the night and the brakeman dropped off. Jerico also went down the steps, peering back through the moonlight. He saw the brakeman move by the switch, saw the switch light change from red to green, saw the lantern swing a signal. First Thirty-Two stopped with a *clank* of couplings. From the front of the caboose the conductor and the flat-faced man who had boarded the train at Hidry descended, the conductor carrying a lantern. Jerico alighted with a grunt. He had no light, but the moon was bright enough for him to see how many horses had been knocked down during that wild ride off the hill.

214

There were, as nearly as he could tell, no horses off their feet. He scrambled up the side of the car seeking a vantage point for better observation. From the west a wailing whistle sounded. A headlight — a bare pinpoint — showed on the grade. Staring into the car, Jerico spotted the Bar T dun after looking around a bit.

"Hi, you," Jerico greeted.

The Bar T dun was — well, not a friend, exactly, but he and Jerico were intimately acquainted. Nobody, including Jerico Jones, had ridden the Bar T dun for a long time. At the moment the Bar T dun, in company with other outlaws and a bunch of mustangs right off the Ocate flats, was *en route* to Kansas City where, so Jerico fondly hoped, he would be sold.

In horses Jones had no ethics, none whatever. The Bar T dun lifted a defiant head. Jerico climbed down. On the main line the rails began to sing and the growing beat of an engine came faintly from the west. Jerico skirted the end of the stock car, scowled at the spot the drawbar should have occupied, and reached the other side of the car. His right boot struck soft dirt. He lurched, fought for balance, lost it, and fell, rolling through the weeds of the embankment. At the bottom he stopped and started to his feet, looking up the slope. For an instant he saw his horse car, plain in the headlight of the onrushing engine. Then there was a crash — a mighty rending of wood and metal — and the headlight went out. Something hurtled past Jerico's head. Something else knocked him sprawling. Steam hissed. He heard horses screaming in pain and terror. A brilliant red flashed before his eyes and was gone.

Jerico Jones lay very quietly in the ditch.

The coroner, the coroner's jury, the witnesses, and the spectators eyed Jerico Jones. He sat, his head bandaged, beside a table, and answered questions as best he might. It was the afternoon following the wreck at Bellaire siding.

"I seen him turn the switch," Jerico stated stubbornly. "I was on the step of the caboose an' I seen him turn it."

"But it was at night," the coroner said gently.

Everything was moving gently, subdued and quiet. The coroner and his jury had viewed five bodies: the engineer, fireman, and head brakeman, the remains of a tramp who had apparently been riding the blind on second Thirty-Two's car of silk, and the body of first Thirty-Two's rear brakeman. Such things are oppressive sights. The coroner was handling his witnesses with care. He was checking everything, double.

"It was moonlight," Jerico stated, "and anyhow I seen the lamp turn. It was red, and then it was green. I got down an' looked at my horses. I walked around the end of the car an' the switch light was still green. That's how it was." He stared at the coroner and jurymen.

There were railroaders on the jury, three of them. There was a farmer, also, if Jerico knew anything about bib overalls, and there were two men from town.

"That's all," the coroner said wearily. "Any other witnesses? No? You're excused." He waved his hand at the men and women in the little room. "The jury will retire to bring in a verdict."

216

Everybody went out, the jury one way, witnesses and spectators the other. Jerico found himself in step with Albe Sothron, claim agent for the El Paso and Kansas.

"You'll want to file a claim for the horses you lost," Sothron said, his voice weary. "Come down to the office and I'll give you what blanks you need."

"Right now," Jerico replied, "I'm goin' to the hotel an' sleep. My head hurts . . . an' I can still hear them horses screamin'." He shivered slightly, parting company with Mr. Sothron.

He had reached the hotel when Webb Gushard, the flat-faced man of the caboose and of Hidry, caught up with him.

Gushard had killed the horses. He was a special agent — a railroad bull if that sounds better — and, when Jerico had come to and scrambled up the embankment, Gushard was the first man he saw. It was light by that time, faint morning spreading over the scene of the wreck, and Gushard had confronted Jerico, gun in hand, demanding who, what and where? Only Jerico's bill of lading on the horses had satisfied Gushard's questions.

Jerico had been out of the picture a long time. Second Thirty-Two plowed into the first section about 4:00 a.m., and here it was almost six o'clock. At Jerico's plea, Gushard had ended the agony of the injured animals. He seemed to enjoy doing it, bending down, putting the muzzle of his .38 close to a twitching ear, squeezing the trigger, and watching the last convulsive threshing. Gushard had done that fourteen times. Now

217

he hailed Jerico at the entrance of Vuelta's Commercial House.

"Jones!"

Jerico halted.

"I got a room here," Jerico announced. "Come on up if you want." He stumped across the hotel lobby, a tired man, a weary man, a man who wanted to take off his boots. Gushard followed.

In Jerico's room he stood by while the boots came off. "Did that hind brakeman talk to you before the wreck?" Gushard demanded abruptly.

"He told me we was goin' to wait at Bellaire for the other train." Jerico spread out on the bed. "He said it would pass us an' go on to Vuelta, an' that it was carryin' a car of silk. That's all he told me."

"Nothin' else?"

"Not a thing. Why?" Jerico's head ached. He wished the flat-faced man would leave.

"Funny that you got off," Gushard said. "Sure he didn't tell you to get off?"

"I told you what he told me." Jerico's voice turned a little hard. "I got off under my own steam. It was my idea. I wanted to look at my horses."

Gushard said — "*Hmm*" — grudgingly. "Well, then, if that's the way it was, that's the way it was."

"You're proddin' into somethin'," Jerico observed. "What?"

The special agent favored Jerico with a fishy stare. "None of your business," he stated, and walked out, closing the door firmly.

"To hell with you then," Jerico told the closed door. "All right. Now I sleep."

That was optimism. He dozed, but when he dozed, he heard the horses, heard their agony. He heard, too, the flat shots of Gushard's gun. He woke up sweating, and still tired. He wished, he really wished, that he didn't like horses so much. He wished, too, that he knew where the live horses were. Damn it! Seven horses alive out of a carload, and he didn't know where they had gone. He tried to sleep again. A quick knocking on the door forestalled the effort.

"Come in!" Jerico ordered.

A woman obeyed the command. She was young, full-bodied, with dark hair framing her oval face. Her lips were pale and her eyes reddened by tears, but her small round chin was determined. She closed the door gently and put her back against it. Jerico remembered his bootless feet and tried to hide them.

"You're Mister Jones," the girl said.

"Jerico Jones," Jerico agreed. "What is it, ma'am?"

"My name," the girl said, "is Fay Eden." Her lips trembled. "I am . . . I was Tom Baldwin's girl. We were going to be married."

Tom Baldwin. That was the name of the rear brakeman on first Thirty-Two, the boy who had gone back to close the switch, the boy whose body lay in an undertaking parlor. "Yes?" Jerico prompted.

"I came . . . I wanted to ask you . . ."

"Sit down," Jerico invited, forgetting his lack of boots. "What is it, Miss Eden?"

"They're saying," the girl blurted, "that Tom didn't close that switch. They say the wreck was his fault."

"That ain't so." Jerico shook his head gently. "I seen him close the switch."

Fay Eden, in the hotel's frowsy rocking chair, bent her head and hid her face in her hands. Her shoulders shook.

Jerico, half panic-stricken, got off the bed with haste.

"They say he was one of the gang." The girl's words were muffled by her hands and her tears. "They say he opened the switch on purpose."

Jerico's fingers closed on the girl's shoulder, clamping much harder than he intended. This was the first he had heard of anything like a gang, or a wreck, caused intentionally. The girl winced under the grip, but it stopped her crying. She straightened.

"Gang?" Jerico said thinly. "What's this about a gang?"

"The gang that's been stealing from the railroad." Fay Eden met Jerico's eyes fairly. "Didn't you know? While they were trying to get the men out of the engine, someone broke into the silk car and stole thirty thousand dollars' worth of raw silk."

Jerico retreated to the bed and sat down. "You an' me had better talk," he said. "I'll tell you this. Your boy went back an' closed the switch. I seen him do it. Now . . . how do you know about a gang an' how do you know what they're sayin'? An' who are 'they'?"

The girl hesitated. Jerico's yellow eyes were hard; his square jaw, beard stubbled; his nose, broken at some prior time, pugnacious. His was a face unmarred by beauty, yet . . . "I work in Mister Canfield's office," Fay Eden said. "He's the division superintendent and I'm his secretary. That's how I know about the stealing. And Mister Canfield and Mister Sothron and Mister Gushard were talking. They said that Tom left the switch open."

"They didn't say why he got himself killed, did they?" Jerico rasped. "They . . ." He had said the wrong thing. The girl was on the verge of breaking down again. "Easy now," Jerico warned. "Look. You tell me where you live. I'll come around an' see you. You don't want to talk now."

"I don't know why I came!" she blurted. "Only . . . I was at the inquest and I heard what you said. You were the last one to see Tom, and, when I heard Mister Canfield and those others . . ."

"Sure now," Jerico comforted, "you go ahead an' cry if you want. You loved your boy, an', when they took to tannin' him down, you couldn't stand it. I *sabe*."

"And Tom didn't belong to any gang!" The words came between sobs. "He didn't. He didn't . . . He was honest and brave and honorable and . . ."

"Sure he was," Jerico comforted. He locked his hands between his knees and stared at the girl. She had lost her man, the boy she loved, and she was all broken up. Jerico could understand that.

He teetered gently on the edge of the bed. His eyes and thoughts were far away. There was the Bar T dun and all those other horses. The mustangs had run on Ocate flat, free and untrammeled. Most of them were dead. The outlaws of the bunch, the buckers, the toughs — most of them were dead, too. And there was, particularly, the Bar T dun. The dun horse that had never given in to man, that, both forelegs broken, belly ripped open by a jagged beam, had still looked at Jerico Jones and defied him until the shot ended misery. Maybe Jerico owed the horses something. Maybe he owed the Bar T dun something.

"I'll put on my boots," said Jerico Jones, "an' then I'll take you home."

CHAPTER
TWO

Jerico stood on a slope and looked off across level land to where men from the work train still labored at Bellaire siding. This, be it understood, was later — two nights and three full days later. Behind Jerico a roan horse rested on three legs, head low as he dozed. The horse was from the livery barn at Vuelta, as was the saddle. On the saddle, bulging the left fender slightly, was Jerico's most recent purchase, a Winchester .30-30 with an eighteen-inch barrel. Jerico Jones was not a gunman, at least not a six-shooter man, but he held a profound respect for his hide and also for the things 170 grains of soft-nosed lead could do when traveling at 1,800 feet a second. Hence the .30-30.

In the time that had elapsed since the wreck, Jerico had been busy. Beginning with the visit of Fay Eden to his hotel room, Jerico had been a veritable bee for activity. His brain rolled the results of that activity around in his head a good deal like a puppy playing with a bone, and also like the puppy, the brain arrived nowhere.

To begin with, Jerico had taken Fay Eden home from the hotel and met her father and mother. Mrs. Eden was motherly and matronly. Steve Eden was a spare, hard-bitten man, an engineer in passenger service on the second district east of Vuelta. Jerico had liked Steve Eden at sight, which feeling was apparently returned. Fay, Steve Eden had said, was all broken up about Tom Baldwin. He was pretty well broken up himself. He had listened to Jerico's story of the wreck and grunted over the matter of the switch. Switch lamps, Steve Eden had said, could be removed from the standards. It was entirely possible for a lamp to be turned one way when the switch was turned the other. Jerico had listened with respect, absorbing information. Leaving the Eden cottage, he had returned to the hotel and supper.

After supper, prompted by curiosity, he had visited the undertaking parlor where the bodies of the dead men reposed. The night man on duty there was lonely. The night man also liked a drink. Halfway down a pint of good liquor, the night man had invited Jerico in.

"Want to look at 'em?" he had asked.

Jerico had been just reluctant enough and the night man had urged him. "Nothin' to be scared of. Come on, I'll show you." He led the way.

The trainmen brought out of second Thirty-Two's wrecked engine were mangled and had been burned by live steam, but the body of Tom Baldwin was singularly unmarked. Death had been caused by a fractured skull.

"Somethin' must have fallen off the engine and hit him," the night man had said. "Look here. Here's a queer one." He pulled back the sheet covering the body of the tramp. "A piece of three-eighths steel rod went right through his heart." The night man had pointed to

224

a small hole in the tramp's chest. "I saw Doc take it out."

"Looks like a bullet hole," Jerico had observed.

"It ain't, though," the night man had said, replacing the sheet. "Let's finish that bottle."

Next morning Jerico had visited the division offices hard by the depot. In Sothron's office, after some discussion, he had filed a claim against the El Paso and Kansas Railroad for his lost horses. Sothron was a tall man, thin, gray-faced and apparently perpetually tired. There was a telltale bulge under his left armpit and his mouth twisted nervously. Claim agents, Jerico believed, did not generally go armed, but Sothron was surely packing a gun and he was surely jumpy. Jerico had made out his claim for $1,500 — reasonable enough. From the claim agent's office he had returned to town.

There he had fallen in with Vuelta's police force, such as were on duty, and noticed with pleasure that both officers wore high-heeled boots. There is a bond of fellowship among the wearers of such boots, and Jerico had talked, given out some information, and asked some questions. He wanted, he had said, to recover such horses as still lived. The police force had seen the point and made suggestions. There were three ranches in the vicinity of Bellaire siding. Doubtless the riders of those ranches would do all that they could to help Jerico in his desire, particularly if he made it worthwhile. Jerico had agreed to that and asked directions. He also gratuitously had acquired the information that Vuelta's police force — chief, day man, night man, and jailor — were at odds with the sheriff's office. The chief also knew where a man could get a good rifle, cheap. So the second day had passed.

On the third day, riding a roan horse from the livery barn, Jerico had left Vuelta and visited the T Tumbling T and the Box Dot headquarters. At each place he had left a list of his horses, brands, and descriptions, and the information that he would pay $5 a head for their recapture.

Now, on the fourth day, he was *en route* to the Cross L, located to the south and west of the Bellaire siding.

Bellaire siding was west of a long stretch of marsh country, flooded by the river. The railroad, coming down a long grade from Hidry, entered low country at Bellaire. From just beyond the siding, an embankment stretched toward the east and on the north side of this railroad fill was a semi-dry lakebed, overgrown with tules. Jerico watched the big hook lift a car truck and deposit it on a flat car. He saw, too, three big white cranes fly up from the tules. Turning his head, he observed the wagon road, bearing off north into the hills.

"Hell!" said Mr. Jones.

Vuelta's police force was fully aware of the stealing by which the El Paso and Kansas suffered. As two cowpunchers to another cowpuncher, the police force had commented and advanced ideas. Theft, the police force said, did not occur in the Vuelta yards. The yards swarmed with special agents, and, besides, the night patrolman cast an occasional eye over them, and the night patrolman was a tough jigger. No, sir. Where the El Paso and Kansas lost stuff was from trains *en route* to Vuelta or from Vuelta. Cars were broken into and goods dumped out — things that wouldn't be damaged: shoes, drygoods, such truck. The stuff was thrown off along the right of way to be picked up. It was home talent, the police force said, strictly home talent. Railroaders did the stealing — train crews, for the police force's money — and there were confederates working with the crews. Things didn't just walk off from the right of way and neither did they fly. Somebody with a wagon removed the purloined articles. Weights, the police force pointed out, were moved on wheels. If the sheriff's office and the railroad special agents were worth a damn, they would think of these things. The police force nodded its collective heads. Turn *them* loose, the police force said, and there would be arrests!

But they were not turned loose. Their province was to contend with crime in Vuelta, not in the county, and the sheriff was just no damned good. Neither was this chief special agent, Webb Gushard.

Jerico, to some extent, agreed with the police force. Their premise was correct, he thought. But he did not think that a duly elected sheriff would overlook such simple reasoning, nor did he think Webb Gushard just dumb. Those flat, fishy eyes were not the eyes of a dumb man.

The big hook dangled another car truck in the air and Jerico mounted his roan horse and rode on down. The section foreman, engaged in bossing his crew as it repaired track, came down the fill to meet him.

"You're the man that had the horses," the section boss said. "I saw you the day of the wreck. Remember? Before you went to town."

"That's right," Jerico agreed.

"We buried the horses," the foreman said.

Jerico dismounted, tied his horse to a convenient bush, and accompanied the section boss back up the embankment. From its top he could look south where, spreading away for miles, were tules. A glint of water showed.

"There's the river," the section man said. "One of these days there'll be a flood. Then they'll have to move this track north on the hills. Too expensive to do it now, but every spring we keep flat cars loaded with rock, on all the side-tracks. Have to use 'em, too. The Río's a heller when it's up." He paused to shout directions in Spanish to his crew.

"How far to the river?" Jerico asked.

"Two, three miles."

"And where is the Cross L headquarters?"

The section boss pointed south and west. "Up there. 'Bout ten miles."

"Thanks," said Jerico.

Feet crunched on gravel. Jerico turned. The section boss moved off.

Webb Gushard, face flat and expressionless, said: "Hello, Jones. Lookin' things over?"

"Lookin' for what horses I've got left," Jerico corrected. "No need to lose 'em. I've been over to the T Tumbling T and to the Box Dot. Told the boys I'd pay 'em five dollars a head for any they caught. I thought I'd go over to the Cross L, too."

"Might be a good idea," Gushard said absently. "I wired back to Ocate an' got a report on you, Jones. Sheriff back there says you're a troublemaker."

Jerico flushed darkly. "So?" he drawled.

"That's what he said." Gushard surveyed Jerico with flat, fishy eyes. "Goin' back to town?"

"I thought I'd go over to the Cross L," Jerico answered. "I want to tell them about the horses."

"Do it tomorrow," Gushard said. "Your horse is beat out." He looked at the roan. "I'll give you a train ride back to town if you want. Think he'll ride on a flat car?"

Jerico made instant decision. There was a reason for the offer. He didn't know what it was. "We can try an' see," he said cheerfully.

"Work train's about ready to go in," Gushard said. "Get your horse."

The roan rode in a boxcar, not on a flat. Jerico and Webb rode with the roan, Gushard smoking a cigar as he loafed by the door, Jerico studying the special agent. He wondered how he would feel in Gushard's shoes. He would, Jerico decided, be worried. Somebody had stolen $30,000 worth of silk while Gushard was present and supposedly on the job. Of course, the special agent had been busy helping to get men from beneath a wrecked engine, but, just the same, he was around when the theft was committed. That didn't look too good.

Another idea popped into Jones's mind. Maybe Gushard wasn't worried about his job. Perhaps he had no reason to worry. Suppose, just suppose, Gushard knew all about that silk, who got it and where it was. Suppose Gushard had a cut coming. Whoever stole from the El Paso and Kansas was a railroad man and in a position to know when valuable shipments would go through. Gushard fit that description. Also, the thief would have to have accomplices. Gushard, as chief special agent, could pick and choose, promising immunity to his confederates. Jerico squinted his eyes thoughtfully. It seemed that Webb Gushard might fit.

The work train pulled into Vuelta and Jerico unloaded the roan horse. He thanked Gushard for the ride and went uptown. At the livery barn he left the roan; at the hotel he ate supper. After supper he walked over to Steve Eden's cottage.

Fay was in the living room with her father and mother. Jerico sat down. Talk was desultory for a while until Jerico spoke of his recent activities. "I ought to get 'em back," he said. "Tomorrow I'll rent another horse an' go out to the Cross L. I'll tell 'em about makin' five dollars a head and that ought to do it. I'll get my horses back."

Fay lifted a wan face. "I went to the office this morning," she announced. "Your claim is on Mister Canfield's desk. Three thousand dollars. I think he approved it."

"Three thousand dollars?" Jerico said. "Why, I —"

The girl broke in. "Mister Sothron brought it in," she said. "I wish . . . I wish other things were as easy. I wish . . ." She broke off and left the room, her mother hastening after her.

230

"They're going to bury Tom tomorrow," Steve Eden said. "Poor kid. She can't hardly take it. I'd like to get hold of the man who is responsible for this . . ."

"An' so would I," Jerico grated. "I'll go 'long, Mister Eden. Good night."

CHAPTER
THREE

In the morning Jerico secured another horse from the livery barn, a bay this time, and rode west. He might, he thought, have stayed for Baldwin's funeral, but he disliked funerals. And he had more pressing business. Not just the business of advertising his strayed horses and offering a reward. No, this business was more urgent than that. Jerico frowned as he considered his work so far.

There were no surplus wagons at either Box Dot or T Tumbling T, but that meant nothing. There is a wagon or two on every ranch, and the ranches he had visited were no exceptions. More important was the fact that there were no telltale wagon tracks around the scene of the wreck, nothing to show how the stolen silk had been moved. Maybe he was wasting his time. He wondered. He took the wagon road west from Vuelta and climbed into the hills. Where the road came down, close to the track again, he paused. This was Bellaire siding again, just as yesterday, only now the work train was gone.

Jerico spent a good two hours working around Bellaire siding, scouting it out, reading what sign he

232

could find. At the end of those two wasted hours he rode on southwest.

Twilight was coming when he reached Cross L headquarters in the foothills just above the river. Riders were unsaddling weary horses, and, as Jerico rode up, a long-legged man, who said his name was McAles, came out to meet him, invite him to turn his horse loose, and eat. Jerico said that he would be glad of a meal and a bed, and that he would buy a feed of grain for the bay.

There were, Jerico noted as he unsaddled, no undue number of wagons around Cross L headquarters, either — in fact there was nothing out of line at all. At the supper table he met the rest of the crew, McAles, the foreman, mentioning Curly, Bert, Custer, and Ed. They were a hard-faced bunch, as was the cook, and McAles was no pilgrim. The meal was taciturn, food taking precedence over conversation, and halfway through Webb Gushard arrived. They heard his horse and stopped their eating while McAles went out. He returned with the special agent in tow and bade him sit down and fall to.

"Got another visitor," McAles said. "This here is Mister Jones, Webb."

"I've met Jones," Gushard said, and loaded his plate.

When supper was done, talk followed. Cigarettes curled smoke ceilingward and McAles asked questions about the wreck. It was apparent to Jerico that Gushard was well acquainted here. McAles called him by his first name, and Gushard called McAles by his first name, Ray. Gushard discussed the wreck briefly and answered questions. Jerico, alert, could not quite get the drift of things. All was friendly, and yet he had a feeling of tension, not so much toward himself as between McAles and Gushard. There was no break, no apparent rift; still, to the listening Jerico, it seemed that an undercurrent, some taunting thing, was beneath the spoken words.

"Why don't you ask Jones about it?" Gushard said presently. "He was there."

Attention was focused on Jerico. He was pleased to a degree. He mentioned his mission concerning the missing horses, and went on from there, being led by questions, interpreting those questions as best suited him. Presently he was describing the bodies.

"The undertaker invited me in," Jerico said. "I didn't much want to go, an' still I did. You know how it is?"

Nods answered the question.

"Well" — Jerico re-lit his smoke and puffed thoughtfully — "I tell you, those railroad men were all beat up, all but one. The hind brakeman . . . on the train I was ridin' . . . had his head smashed. The undertaker said that somethin' fell off the engine and hit him, an' I guess that's right. But I've seen several dead men, and, if it hadn't been for the wreck, I'd've said that man had his head beat in with an iron pipe. It was just that way. The hobo was queerer yet. There was just one hole in him, where a three-eighths-inch steel rod had gone through his heart. The undertaker said he saw the doctor take it out."

Again Jerico fussed with his smoke, licking down the flap. He had told this story at the Box Dot and the T Tumbling T. Now, again, he watched the faces about him. "It looked just like a bullet hole," Jerico drawled, his cigarette mended, "just exactly. It kind of gave me an idea. If I ever have to shoot a man an' don't want anybody to know what killed him, I'm goin' to stick a piece of iron rod in the hole. That is, if there's a wreck handy to account for the rod bein' there." He grinned at his joke.

No one else seemed to think it funny. McAles, Curly, Ed, Bert, Custer, and Webb Gushard stared at him.

"Damn this smoke," said Jerico. "Anybody got a match?"

Shortly thereafter the conversation ceased. McAles, escorting Jerico and Webb Gushard to the bunkhouse, bemoaned the shortage of beds. "I got just one extra," he said. "Plenty of blankets, but no extra bedstead. If you don't mind sleepin' together . . ."

"I just never could sleep with anybody," Jerico interposed. "Tell you what . . . give me a couple of soogans an' I'll sleep in the barn on your hay. I'm used to it, an' Gushard, here, is a town man, so he ain't."

Gushard said nothing. McAles said: "Well, if you don't mind. But you an' Gushard could sleep together. Or else I'll sleep with him an' you take my bed."

"I wouldn't put you out," Jerico answered. "Just let me have them soogans an' I'll head for the barn."

He had his way. McAles produced two old quilts and a blanket. These Jerico bore barnward. He spread his bed down and sat on it, tugging off his boots. McAles walked back through the moonlight to the bunkhouse. No sooner had he departed than Jerico was up. Briefly he visited the saddle shed, returning with the short-barreled .30-30. Then he rolled the blanket into a long cylinder and placed it on one quilt. He kinked the blanket in the center so that, in the dimness of the barn, it resembled a man sleeping with his knees doubled up, put his hat nearby the end of the blanket, and, with the second quilt, went farther back into the barn.

Here he bestowed himself, stretching out on the quilt, the rifle convenient to his hand. He did not mean to sleep, he meant to watch.

Time dawdled along as always under such circumstances. Despite his good intentions, Jerico dozed. Nor was he awakened. Morning light, filtering into the barn, roused him, and he sat up, mentally berating himself. He visited his trap. It had not been molested. Yawning and stretching, Jerico left the barn, his bedding over his arm.

There was no talk at breakfast. The men left the table and went to the corral. The horses were already in. Saddles were laced on; McAles laid out the riding. Men departed.

"The closest way to town," McAles told Jerico, "is to hit for the railroad and ride down the track. That way you can go across the tules an' not around 'em."

Jerico spoke his thanks and twisted out a stirrup.

"I wish," McAles said, "that you'd give me the dope on them horses again. I want to write it down." He produced a brand book and a stub of pencil.

Jerico gave information, and McAles painfully and slowly put it down. Webb Gushard had already departed, riding off to the west.

"That's got it," McAles said. "Now cut right back the way you came and go along the railroad till you're past the tules. Saves about six miles. So long."

"Thanks," Jerico said, "I'll do that. So long."

He let the bay horse take an easy gait. Vuelta was thirty-eight miles away, six miles saved cut it to thirty-two. Almost two hours after leaving the Cross L, Jerico reached Bellaire siding and turned east to follow the railroad fill. He kept to the path beside the tracks, noting the tules, brown now in the fall, the small birds flying, the few ducks in the occasional pools that showed between the rushes. Ahead, a cloud of birds flew up and Jerico marked them.

"Somethin' . . . " he said.

From the rushes a shot cracked, flat, hard, sending the marsh into a panic. Ducks flew, as did the smaller birds. Two great whooping cranes floundered into the air. These things Jerico Jones did not see. The bay horse ran riderless down the north slope of the fill, entered the marsh, and stopped, bogged to the knees. Jerico Jones, hatless, rifle in hand, lay prone between the rails and searched the tules with his eyes.

There was movement in the tules, just a stirring of the tall cat-tails. Jerico waited. The furtive movement stopped, and then resumed. Something pushed through the tules — the rounded prow of a flat-bottomed boat. It emerged, and stopped. Jerico lay still. Then a hat lifted above the brown growth.

Now from the barrel of the Winchester came a stream of fire as Jerico's hand raced on lever and trigger. Seven shots he fired, one hard on the heels of its fellow, into the tules above the boat. The hat went out of sight. Rushes bent and swayed convulsively, and then were still. Jerico shoved shells through the loading gate, raised, and, at a crouching, weaving run, went up the track. Then, stopping, he straightened and looked down. The boat was there, and in the boat the body of a man was sprawled. Cautiously, the rifle ready, Jerico went down the slope and reached the boat. The man's face, what was left of it, was upturned.

Ed, I guess, thought Jerico. *Yes. It looks like the one he called Ed.*

He sat down on the embankment, absently counting the shells in his pocket. Twenty shells to a box. Seven fired, seven in the gun, six in his pocket.

Of course, Jerico reflected. *That's why there never was any wagon tracks. That's sure the reason.* He stood up, still fingering the shells. Seven and six made thirteen and there was another box in his saddle pocket. He had to get the bay horse out of the bog and send it along. The bay would go back to the livery barn, to oats and good sweet hay.

"And then," Jerico Jones said, thinking out loud, "I'll take a boat ride. Now, why didn't I figure it was the river? Why didn't I think of that?"

238

CHAPTER
FOUR

The bay horse was not badly bogged. Jerico stripped off boots and trousers and retrieved the bay. He put the extra box of .30-30 shells in his coat pocket, looped the reins over the saddle horn, and slapped the horse with his hat. The animal started for home, and Jerico returned to the boat.

Examination failed to disclose Ed's weapon. Probably it had dropped overside into the tules. Jerico hauled Ed out and put him close by the track, not on it. The engine man of the first train would find Ed. This done, Jerico scanned the sky, saw that it was noon — for the sun stood at the top of its arc — and then he returned to the boat. He put on his trousers and boots, settled his hat firmly, and shoved off.

The boat was a flat-bottomed skiff, such as duck hunters use. It slipped readily over the shallow water. There were both a pole and oars, and Jerico used the pole. No boatman, he had plenty of trouble. He pushed the pole into the mud and almost lost it. He tried the oars and they didn't work, being hampered by the tules. Also, Jerico did not know the marsh. Waterways he followed ended in masses of growth through which he could not go. But he kept the sun ahead and to his right, and battled along, doing it the hard way. Finally he reached the river.

"Up or down?" Jerico asked himself, mopping away sweat. For all the winter season, he was really hot. "It's the Cross L doin' business but . . ." He scratched his head, scowling. A grin replaced the scowl as an idea formed. He put the oars in the oarlocks and shoved out into the stream, turning the boat's bow against the current. Jerico had never rowed before but he had seen pictures of men rowing. He turned his back to the current and pulled lustily. Despite his efforts, the current carried him.

"That's the answer," Jerico said finally. "Them fellows are riders . . . they ain't a lot better rowers than I am, and it's a mortal cinch they never took any heavy loads upriver. They went downstream." He stopped rowing and the boat drifted. The current ran about five miles an hour and the tule-lined banks slipped past.

"But where downriver?" Jerico soliloquized. "How am I goin' to know when I reach where I'm goin'? Damn my time! I got to have a lot of luck this time." He pulled briefly on the right oar, straightening out the boat. The river flowed, placid and undisturbed.

An hour crept past, and then another, and still a third. Jerico had drifted perhaps fifteen miles. He was out of the tules; there were willows along the banks now, and these lifted sharply above the stream. The sun was low, dark coming early. Jerico squirmed uneasily on the thwart.

I'd better get to the bank before dark, he told himself. *I won't be able to see a thing in another thirty*

240

minutes. Once more he shipped the oars in their locks and made ready to pull. Then he saw what he was looking for. From among the willows a wharf projected, a crude affair of planks, low and close to the water. Jerico pulled lustily.

He missed the wharf by twenty feet. Standing in the bow, he pulled on willows, hauling his craft back upstream. Reaching the wharf, he tied the boat, and then, carrying his rifle, stepped nimbly to the planks.

This here is below Vuelta, he thought. *Maybe this is the right place . . . maybe it ain't. Anyhow, I know how they do it. I know where the stuff goes after it's thrown off the cars.* He left the wharf and climbed the bank above it. The sun was low; it was nearing twilight. Wheel tracks led from the wharf; a sort of road wound through the bosk of the river bottom. Jerico followed the road.

Boots are not built for walking, and Jerico was pleased when the road entered a little natural clearing. On the clearing's far side stood an adobe house. He scouted the house carefully. It was deserted, but the wheel tracks went to the door, and there were three empty wagons parked nearby.

A straggling fence, running from tree to tree, bespoke a horse pasture. The house door was fastened with a padlock, the windows covered with heavy planks. Entrance was refused. Jerico swore feelingly. He wanted in. He needed to know for a certainty what was behind the padlocked door and shuttered windows. He went to the wagons and, working now by the moonlight that filtered into the clearing, took a tie rod from an end-gate. With this he pried away at the hasp. Nails and screws resisted, then creaked protest as they came clear. Jerico pushed open the door and walked in. A match flamed in his hand and he looked about. Here, piled ceiling high, were boxes and crates, some broken, others intact, some showing marks of immersion, others clean. Something gleamed in one corner. Jerico struck another match and went to it. The match died; his hand touched paper. A third match spurted into life, and Jerico looked down. Here was raw silk, one thin bale opened.

"An' that's the payoff," Jerico muttered grimly. Rifle in hand, he moved back to the dim light of the door.

He had closed the door and pushed back the screws and nails of the hasp when he heard voices. At a crouching run Jerico made for the bosk that bordered the clearing. He crouched there as men rode into the moonlight in front of the house. They dismounted as McAles rasped: "Damn Ed, anyhow! He should've got back before we left. Curly, you an' Bert get the horses up. The rest of us will mule a wagon to the door an' start loadin'."

Five men — and Ed was missing. That meant that the cook had come along. Two riders made for the gate in the fence. Three men went to a wagon. McAles took the tongue, hauling it around. The others pushed and the wagon was rolled up in front of the door.

Jerico, squatting in his hiding place, watched the proceedings. The three men carried goods from the house and loaded the wagon. They had it filled, when the horses arrived. Curly and Bert drove animals into

242

the clearing, caught the horses expertly, and harness was brought out and put on. A team was hitched to each wagon, a heavy wagon sheet was thrown over the load, and that wagon was pulled away from the door. Now all five men labored at loading the second wagon.

Jerico moved stealthily, rising, stretching his cramped muscles until no stiffness remained, and then worked around the clearing. He reached a point nearest the loaded wagon, dropped down, and, like a big snake, crawled forward. Shadows favored him. The men, intent on their occupation, were not alert. Jerico gained the loaded wagon, lifted the heavy tarpaulin, and slipped under it. A wooden case thrust a corner into his ribs as he squirmed down; a protruding nail made its presence known. Jerico pushed the nail back with his rifle butt and adjusted himself to the box corner. He waited.

Sounds informed him of the progress of the loading. There was not a great deal of talk. Occasionally McAles gave an order. Once or twice a man cursed when a sliver tore his hand or a box caught a finger. The second wagon was moved from the door, the third replacing it. Then McAles said: "That's a load. Let's go. Custer, you and me will take the saddle horses."

Jerico's conveyance swayed as the driver climbed to the seat. The box prodded Jerico unmercifully as the team moved into their collars.

"Geddup!" the driver ordered. "Git on now."

The road beyond the clearing was rough. There were chuckholes and rocks. Jerico fought the box with both hands and wished he had not been so impetuous. He wished somebody had paved the road. He wished the damned box would stay put and that he was home in bed.

The road improved as the wagon assumed a slanting angle. They were leaving the river bottom. Jerico braced his feet against the end gate and his shoulders against the box to keep it from sliding down on him.

The trip was better after the river bottom had been cleared, that is, there were not so many rocks or chuckholes. Jerico stayed still as possible. His muscles cramped and ached and perforce he changed position but he did so cautiously, a little at a time. The rasp of the wheels drowned other sounds and occasionally they went up or down a hill.

Then, abruptly, the journey ended. The wheels were still, and directly to Jerico's right someone spoke.

"Get unloaded as soon as you can. Boylan's on first Thirty-Two and he'll pick up the car."

The voice was familiar, but Jerico could not be quite certain of the owner for the heavy tarp muffled his hearing. He braced himself, gripping the Winchester, ready to come out shooting if he had to — when the tarp was thrown back. But the tarp was not thrown back. Instead, the wagon lurched as the driver descended from the seat. Jerico waited. He heard wheels move, heard a man say — "Whoa!" — heard other voices. Lifting the edge of the tarp, he peered out cautiously.

The moon was still high enough to give light. Shielded by the tarpaulin, Jerico looked the length of the wagon. A boxcar loomed ahead and a wagon was drawn into place before its opened door. Between the door and wagon men toiled feverishly, unloading, carrying goods into the car. A man stood on the ground, looking up.

Jerico lifted the tarp and slid down out of the wagon. He crouched in the shadow beneath.

The first wagon was empty and was drawn away. A second took its place. Men climbed up on it, and, from the shadows beyond Jerico and to his left, a flat voice issued a command.

"Hold it! Hands up! You're surrounded."

Webb Gushard!

Under the wagon Jerico grinned and his thumb pulled back the hammer of the Winchester. He was not surprised.

That flat command had halted the men by the boxcar. They stood for just an instant. Then the tableau broke into swift, vicious action. The tall man on the ground dropped down, flame blossomed in flickering ring, and a gun crashed. That was the signal.

The shot was answered from the shadow. Men dived for shelter, under the boxcar, into the boxcar, and, from those vantage points, began to fire. Horses stampeded. The wagon above Jerico lurched away, and he felt naked, flat on the ground.

A single gun answered the fire. *Gushard had lied a little*, Jerico thought, grinning. *He didn't have this bunch surrounded. He was all alone. Well, maybe not entirely alone.* Jerico shifted position slightly, looked along the Winchester barrel, and squeezed the trigger. Sights were no good in light like this. A man fired by instinct, more or less. Jerico's instinct was good. A man flopped out from the corner of the boxcar and sprawled in the moonlight. Thoughtful of his own hide, Jerico changed position swiftly. His second shot screamed off a car wheel.

To the right front of the car, Webb Gushard said — "What the hell?" — incredulously.

"Ain't it the truth?" Jerico answered, and changed position.

Conversation ceased. The firing checked. Men were seeking targets and not finding them. Jerico believed he saw movement, sighted, then held his fire.

"Look," he called. "You stay put, Gushard! Let me do the movin'."

"To hell with that," Gushard answered. "Think I want to get downed?"

Jerico had shifted as he spoke; fortunately, too, for three chunks of lead plowed into his recently occupied position. Gushard also fired from another spot. The answering shots gave Jerico a target. He fired three times and was rewarded by a scream.

"Two down!" Jerico called cheerfully. "Four to go." He thumbed shells through the loading gate.

"Three! I got one," Gushard answered. "Think I can't shoot? You . . ." He broke off to fire twice. A man pitchpoled down from the car door and crawled toward the shadows, almost reached them, and then dropped prone.

"Two to go!" There was triumph in Gushard's voice. "Give it up, Sothron. You're done."

246

"The hell I'm done." The defiant answer was flung from the boxcar. "Come and get me!"

Jerico, at the instant, was engaged in just that task. He had reached the corner of the car and now moved along it in the shadow. Two men were left. Sothron, in the car, and the other outside, probably sheltered by the front truck. Jerico was taking chances. Two men and Webb Gushard. Gushard would surely fire if he saw movement. It was a fool thing to do, but Jerico was angry and inclined to foolhardiness. Sudden activity at the car end told him that foolishness had paid off, and that another fool was at work. Shots smashed into the night from under the car. Gushard evidently had worked in, just as had Jerico. He did not pause to learn the outcome of the special agent's work but, having reached the car door, boosted himself up and over the edge of the floor, rolling into the gloom. The car reverberated with shots that should have stopped him. The echoes died. Jerico crouched, motionless.

"Jones!" That was Gushard, outside. "Jones!"

If Gushard tried to come into the car, he'd come shooting. Jerico couldn't chance that. "In the car!" he yelled, backing his words with a shot. Instantly he changed position.

"You damned fool," Gushard said.

Now there was silence, broken only by heavy breathing in the car. Jerico tried to determine the point from which that breathing sounded, but could not.

Outside, Gushard said: "You're through, Sothron. All done. You've stolen your last and killed your last man.

Did you know that Baldwin was my sister's boy, Sothron? Did you know that?"

No answer came. Away to the east a whistle sounded faintly.

"Thirty-Two's comin'!" Gushard called. "She'll stop to pick up this car, won't she? Boylan is the conductor. He'll stop her. But he won't pick up the car. Not this time."

Gushard was trying to taunt Sothron into movement, trying to madden him into some attempt. The whistle sounded again, nearer now. The main line rails hummed. The whistle blew two sharp blasts, almost at hand, and then light began to grow in the car, sharp, yellow, increasing in brilliance. For an instant a man, almost at the car door, showed, sharp and distinct. The Winchester's crash was drowned by the blast of noise that beat into the car. The light was gone. Jerico, leaping forward, gun ready, caught his foot against soft flesh and fell. He pushed out a cautious hand.

"Sothron!" Jerico rasped.

The crashing noise of Thirty-Two had died. He heard steam sighing gently, feet crunching on gravel.

"Jones!" Gushard shouted.

Jerico said wearily: "I'm all right, Gushard."

A lantern was raised by the car door, lighting the interior. Jerico sat up. Sothron, the El Paso and Kansas claim agent, did not move from where he lay across a torn bale of raw silk.

The three of them, Jerico Jones, Webb Gushard, and Canfield, the division superintendent, sat in Canfield's office. Outside, a switch engine pushed cars along a track; downstairs a battery of telegraph sounders *clicked*. Canfield knocked the ash from his cigar. This was the morning after Jerico's boat ride. The time was almost noon.

"So Sothron was behind it," Canfield said. "I never thought . . . I didn't believe . . ."

"Neither did I," Jerico said. "For quite a while I thought it was Gushard." He grinned at the flat-faced special agent.

Gushard grunted. His eyes were expressionless but they didn't seem to be fishy. At least, not to Jerico.

"When did you think it wasn't me?" Gushard asked.

"When Fay Eden told me that my claim for three thousand dollars was on Canfield's desk," Jerico answered promptly. "I'd put in a claim for fifteen hundred. Sothron raised it on his own hook. He was goin' to keep the difference. A man that will high-grade one way will high-grade another. What were you followin' me around for, Gushard? What was the idea? The sheriff at Ocate wired you that I was a troublemaker."

A faint grin flickered on Gushard's face. "An' he told me you were a damned good man to have along, too," the special agent said. "I didn't tell you all that was in that wire. What was the idea of sleepin' in the barn up at the Cross L, and then not stayin' in bed? I came out to the barn an' couldn't find you. I wanted to talk to you that night."

Jerico laughed. "I thought somebody would want to see me," he answered, "but I didn't think it would be a friend. I set out to watch, an' then I went to sleep."

"Might have saved a lot of trouble," Gushard grumbled. "If we'd got together, I mean. I knew it was the Cross L an' Sothron. I didn't know how they moved what they stole. That river business was smart. Throw stuff off in the tules where it wouldn't break, pick it up, take it downstream, and then, by God, load it right back on the railroad in a car that Sothron ordered. They were smart."

The men mused a moment after Gushard's outburst. Then Canfield said: "You know how Thirty-Two was wrecked? You know who did that?"

"McAles told us," Gushard answered. "Sothron was on first Thirty-Two, ridin' the engine. He dropped off when the head man opened the switch. Said that he was goin' to ride the caboose to Vuelta. He slipped back along the train, smashed in Baldwin's head, opened the switch, an' changed the lamp. Then he ducked. It was him that killed the hobo, too, an' stuck that rod in the bullet hole. You were pretty cute to figure that out, Jones, but what was the idea of needlin' that bunch at the Cross L with it? You might have got killed."

"Not if I could help it," Jerico answered. "That's why I made the dummy for my bed an' why I was goin' to stay awake. If somebody called, I'd know it was that Cross L bunch that moved the goods."

"Three train crews," Canfield said. "Three crooked crews on the division. I'm glad there weren't any engine men mixed into it."

250

"They didn't need engine men," Gushard stated. "Sothron didn't want any more than he had. The more men to split with, the less he got."

Jerico stared at the special agent. "What beat me," he announced, "was when I found out you was by yourself. That fixed me for a minute. I thought you had an army with you when you called for them to put up their hands."

Gushard laughed awkwardly. "I laid out above the Cross L and watched 'em through field glasses," he said. "When they pulled out, I followed, but they didn't come through town. I was afraid if I left 'em to get my boys, I'd lose 'em, so I just stuck along . . . just for the hell of it!"

"An' then called 'em single-handed." There was respect in Jerico's voice. "You had your nerve with you, Gushard."

Again there was an awkward pause. Then Canfield said: "Nine men killed. The engineer and fireman of second Thirty-Two, the head brakeman, Tom Baldwin, that tramp, Sothron, the man you killed up at Bellaire siding, and two more last night. There are three in the hospital . . . maybe they'll live, maybe they won't. Lord! Think of it! What started it all anyhow?"

"A greedy man," Jerico said gravely. "One greedy man . . . Sothron."

"And what dragged you in?" The superintendent stared at Jerico Jones. "Why did you take a hand?"

"Because of them horses," Jerico answered, after a pause. "I guess that was it. I kept hearin' them horses scream. I couldn't sleep. I guess it was the horses, one horse in particular. An' then Fay Eden come to me. I . . ." He broke off, staring thoughtfully at the wall.

"Speaking of your horses," Canfield said, "I had a wire yesterday. Your claim has been allowed. For three thousand dollars, too. I want you to take it."

"I've got fifteen hundred comin'," Jerico said quietly. "That's all. An' word's come in from the Box Dot. They got the seven head that lived. I'll take them and fifteen hundred dollars."

Canfield shuffled papers on his desk. "If you'll sign a release, I'll have a check made out," he said. "You can pick it up this afternoon." He shoved a blank across to Jerico.

Jerico, dipping a pen, wrote on the paper. "There," he said, "that does it." He waved the paper in the air, then put it down. "An' now," he continued, "I'm goin' uptown. I guess I'll have to stick around for a day or two. I'll have to testify for the coroner, an' there'll be some other stuff to clean up. An' I got a dinner invitation." He grinned at Canfield and Gushard.

"So have I," Gushard said, "but not till tonight."

"That's when mine is. At Steve Eden's?"

"At Steve Eden's."

The two men faced each other, Gushard expressionless, Jerico grinning. "We might as well go together then," said Jerico. "You goin' to side me?"

"Turn about," Gushard stated. "You sided me last night. Let's go. So long, Canfield."

"So long," said Jerico.

He and Webb Gushard went out together.

252

Canfield, division superintendent for the El Paso and Kansas Railroad, picked up the release blank Jerico had signed. He heard footsteps receding on the stairs, the *thump* of Jerico's boot heels, the flat pad of Gushard's shoes. He looked at the release. Across the bottom was written:

Payment in full for one dun horse, branded Bar T.
                                                    J. J. Jones.

Pot Luck Pardners

At the same time that the Gila City stories were appearing in magazines published by Popular Publications and Jerico Jones took his last bow in "Nine Coffins for Bellaire", Bennett Foster introduced a new series character, Jiggs Maunday, in Street & Smith's *Western Story*. "Pot Luck Pardners" in *Western Story* (6/47) was the first of these Jiggs Maunday stories. The character proved so popular with readers that a continuing series of stories followed, three more of which will be published in *Jiggs Maunday* (Five Star Westerns, 2007).

CHAPTER
ONE

Jiggs Maunday met the boy and the dog a mile or so north of the rimrock. The lead cattle stopped and Jiggs, spurring Quién Sabe around the little bunch, found the cause of the delay in a ditch beside the road. The ditch was not very deep and the boy was visible from the waist up. Beside the youngster was a dog, dull blue, the color of a cedar berry, and, like the boy, the dog had blue eyes. Jiggs, Quién Sabe, and four old cows all eyed the couple in the ditch.

After a moment Jiggs spoke gravely. "Good evenin'."

"Good evenin'. The boy's response was equally grave. He paused a moment, then nodded his towhead toward the cows. "I thought mebbe I could hide in the ditch an' they'd go by. They smelled me, I guess." He was apologetic.

"Likely," Jiggs agreed. "They ain't used to a man on foot."

Again the hatless towhead nodded. "I'm goin' to cut across to the store," the boy said. Then, blue eyes fixed earnestly on Jiggs: "Do you want to hire a hand? I'm kind of lookin' for a job."

Intuitively Jiggs sensed that the youngster was serious. He was perhaps ten years old and dressed in a torn, faded blue shirt and tattered denim overalls.

"I reckon not," Jiggs answered. "I ain't got many cattle."

"Well" — a bare foot scuffed the brown grass of the ditch bank — "I thought I'd ask."

"I'm sorry I can't take you on," Jiggs told him gravely. "But I'll keep you in mind if I need a hand."

"Thanks." Again the boy's blue eyes met Jiggs's own. "Come on, Tige."

Boy and dog struck off across country. Jiggs grinned. A nester kid and his dog, asking for a job. The grin faded. October weather in this high mesa country was cold and Jiggs was willing to bet that the boy didn't have anything on under the thin shirt and worn overalls. Barefooted, too. It was tough, being a lad in a poor country. Thinking back to his own childhood, Jiggs knew just how tough it was. Then his grin returned. Now that he was a man, he remembered the hard spots, but when he was a kid, he hadn't thought them hard. Jiggs trotted back to join Ceferino.

Ceferino Trujillo, one-eyed and pockmarked, accepted all things with equanimity except the absence of coffee or tobacco. Jiggs, having spent a profitable ten days among the natives below the mesa, had hired Ceferino to help him move the cattle he had bought. The pockmarked man grunted as Jiggs joined him.

"Pretty soon she's fin' a place for stop?" he suggested.

"Yeah." Jiggs glanced at the lowering sun. "Soon as we find water."

"Theese place" — Ceferino waved a broad hand — "w'at you call the ol' Espuela line camp, she's *dos* miles *más allá*. She's got water."

Part of Ceferino's value — and Jiggs was beginning to think it was the major part — was that he knew the country.

"All right," Jiggs agreed. "You point 'em, I'll sack 'em up, an' we'll go there."

They traveled over sparse, brown grass across a fenceless land. Ceferino, once the direction was set, dropped back and, sensing water ahead, even the old bulls in the bunch hurried their pace. They came up a long swell of ground, and, reaching its top, Jiggs saw in the valley below a broken windmill, a dilapidated corral, a dirt tank, and a sod hut set into the hillside. Beyond these, winter wheat glinted bright green behind a tight three-wire fence.

"*¿Bien no?*" Ceferino questioned.

"Good enough," conceded Jiggs.

Cattle and horses watered at the tank. Jiggs, letting Quién Sabe drink, looked over his outfit with a proprietary eye. It was good to own cattle, even a bunch of culls like these. From the time he had started, a wet-eared, gangling kid back in Texas, owning cattle had been Jiggs Maunday's ultimate goal. And now, by Jiminy, he had reached it.

Here in this dry farmer country atop the mesa, he would buy more cattle. Nesters always had stock to sell: old bulls and cows, dairy calves, odds and ends. When

Jiggs had two loads, he would ship and, with the money he made, buy again.

After a while he would have a bunch of cows and a lease to run them on. Then he would own the lease. In twenty or twenty-five years, say by the time he was fifty or thereabouts, he'd go rolling into Kansas City, or maybe Denver, with a whole trainload of cattle wearing a big JM on their ribs. The prospect was pleasant and Jiggs felt as virtuous as though it had already come to pass. It was time he settled down and quit juning around the country, he told himself as he helped Ceferino hobble the loose horses.

When Ceferino unpacked the cooking outfit, he held up the empty coffee sack and looked reproachfully at Jiggs.

"No hay más café," Ceferino announced. "Mira, Meester Jeegs."

Jiggs, rolling a cigarette, glanced at the limp sack in his hand. "We're out of tobacco, too," he answered. "Whereabouts is a store, Ceferino?"

"Yo sé." Ceferino's pockmarked face brightened. "I go to theese store an' —"

"You stay here an' build a fire an' get chuck ready," Jiggs interrupted. "Tell me where the store is an' I'll go."

Sulky at being deprived of a trip, Ceferino gave grudging directions and Jiggs shifted his saddle from Quién Sabe's grulla back to that of a dun horse he called Placer. The store, according to Ceferino, was up the road. Jiggs loped off on his fresh horse.

260

He struck the road where the fence cornered and, following the curve of the highway, saw a collection of buildings perhaps a mile away. Distance slid by under Placer's black hoofs and a few minutes later Jiggs stopped in front of the buildings.

There were five horses at the hitch rail, and at the end of the store's porch was a barrel lying on its side. Jiggs tied Placer and, as he passed the barrel, read the sign tacked on the post above it: **$5.00 for the dog that brings the badger out**. A chain ran from the post into the barrel, and the animal inside snarled warily as Jiggs walked by.

Inside the store a pot-bellied stove gave off pleasant warmth. On one side of the room was a counter, shelves behind it filled with merchandise. On the other side was a plank bar.

Six men were in the room and all turned to look at Jiggs. He returned their stares. Four of the men he classified instantly. Unshaven, hair too long, clothes too dirty — grangers. One, a hawk-faced man, sat on the counter; two others lounged in chairs by the stove; the fourth was at the bar. The other two men required longer consideration. One was at the bar, the other behind the counter. The man at the bar was young, dressed, like the first four, in bib overalls and work shirt, but there the resemblance ceased. He was clean-cut and stood out like a thoroughbred in a herd of Indian ponies. Plainly he did not belong.

The man behind the counter, Jiggs knew, was the proprietor. He wore long black sleeve guards and his vest was open. A neat bow tie decorated his white shirt, and above the bow tie was a blank, expressionless face, its only unusual feature a pair of blank, lead-colored eyes. The man wore a small mustache, and his hair, black and parted exactly in the middle, was smoothed down on his head like a shining cap. Somehow that cap of black hair seemed oddly incongruous. Jiggs barely repressed his grin. The merchant was wearing a wig.

"Somethin' for you, mister?" the man behind the counter said.

Jiggs advanced. "I want five pounds of coffee," he answered, "an' six sacks of Durham. Grind the coffee, will you?"

The storekeeper nodded and, taking a sack from the shelf, opened it and dumped the contents into the red coffee mill.

"Have another drink, Charlie?" one of the men at the bar said.

The hawk-faced man on the counter lifted his voice in order to be heard above the racket of the mill. "Charlie don't dare take another drink. He's goin' callin', ain't you, Charlie? Old Man Pruitt would throw him off the place if he smelled whiskey on him."

One of the loafers beside the stove chuckled. "What Charlie needs is a mouthful of cloves," he said. "Better fix him up, Tanner."

Jiggs saw the young farmer's face grow red as he half turned. He moved his arm in a gesture, just a little too wide, just a little uncertain.

"Tha's a lie!" Charlie's voice was thick. "Ol' Man Pruitt won't throw me off the place. I'm goin to have

262

another drink. I'm goin' to have as many drinks as I want. Fill 'em up, Tanner."

"In a minute." The gray-eyed man kept the coffee grinder turning. "Soon as I get through here."

Jiggs's eyes narrowed. He had, although he would not have admitted it, something of the contempt of the horseman for those who work on foot, but that was not what caused the narrowing of his eyes. This bunch of would-be toughs was getting the kid drunk. And the kid ought to have his pants kicked.

Tanner emptied the ground coffee back into the sack and tied it. He put six sacks of Bull Durham on the counter and said that Jiggs owed him a $1.30 for the supplies.

"Mister Tanner?" a voice said eagerly as Jiggs paid the bill.

The towheaded boy was in the doorway, the blue roan dog beside him.

"Yeah?" Tanner paused halfway between counter and bar.

"Is that right about the five dollars? You'll give it to me if my dog gets the badger out of the barrel?"

Jiggs, watching Tanner, saw the man's lips curve into the semblance of a smile, but the leaden eyes did not change.

"Sure," Tanner said. "That's what's on the sign."

"Badger fight, boys." The hawk-faced man slid down from the counter. "Goin' to sic your dog on the badger, kid?"

"Tige can whip any ol' badger!" The boy nodded violently.

Jiggs, looking at the dog, was dubious. He knew how badgers fought and he doubted that Tige would make the grade. "You'll get your pup cut up," he cautioned. "Badgers are tough."

Scowls from every man in the room were turned on Jiggs. The boy considered him gravely. "You don't know Tige," he observed. "An' I need the five dollars."

"Come on outside," Tanner commanded. "Let's go see a badger fight, boys."

Jiggs put the tobacco in his pockets, picked up the coffee, and followed the others. The seven men formed a semicircle in front of the barrel from which now came a high-pitched snarling. The boy, kneeling beside his dog, hissed softly. "Sic 'im! Go git 'im!" The dog's hackles stiffened and he answered the snarl with a deep growl.

"Sic 'im." The boy let Tige go, and the dog dived for the barrel, head and forequarters disappearing.

Momentarily Jiggs expected to see the dog emerge, cut and yelping. Badgers are equipped with strong, sharp teeth, a hide so loose that it almost defies a grip, long, coarse hair, a rank smell, and a set of scythes on each front foot. As a fighting machine, a badger is formidable.

Beside Jiggs, the hawk-faced man rasped: "Bet five dollars on the badger."

Antagonism welled from the hawk-faced man and an answering pugnacity arose in Jiggs. He was about to take the bet when a shout went up. Tige was backing from the barrel, the badger clamped in his jaws.

264

"He brought him out," the boy shrilled. "Gimme five dollars!"

"The kid's won the money," said Jiggs.

"No, he ain't!" Hawk-Face flared. "Let 'em fight."

Tige shook his victim savagely, but, unhampered by the barrel, the badger was getting organized. It squirmed, half turning within its own hide. The hissing, spitting snarl increased in volume and one set of razor-sharp claws raked the dog's shoulder.

"You won the money, kid," Jiggs said. "Call your dog. No use gettin' him cut up."

The boy seized the dog's collar. "Drop it!" he commanded. "Drop it, Tige!"

Squirming badger and pulling boy were too much for Tige. He tried for a new hold, lost his grip, and was hauled away. The badger, at the end of the chain, flattened to the ground and lay, hissing and snarling, ready for what came next.

Jiggs, watching boy and dog, sensed, rather than saw, the blow coming. He shifted instinctively and the hawk-faced man's fist struck his shoulder. The coffee sack hit the ground and burst as Jiggs dodged a second blow.

"Keep your blasted nose out of things!" Hawk-Face snarled. "Damn' cowpuncher! I'll teach you to butt in."

Behind Hawk-Face, the others crowded forward, intent on a fight. Jiggs took a step back, shifted his weight, and, as Hawk-Face tried again, uncocked a lethal left hand. Hawk-Face paused as though rammed by an iron bar and staggered back a step. Jiggs, gray eyes slitted, followed his advantage, striking twice more.

The second blow exploded against Hawk-Face's throat; the man's head snapped back and his eyes rolled in pain as he went down. The others were advancing belligerently, fanning out to take Jiggs from all sides. He backed from them, reached the hitch rail, and, dropping his hand, pulled his gun, fully intending to use it.

At sight of the weapon the advance stopped. Jiggs's voice rasped in his throat. "I'm too old a head to let a bunch like you gang up on me. Where's the kid?"

"Right here, mister," the boy's voice piped.

"Pay him!" Jiggs commanded, his eyes singling out the storekeeper. "He won the money."

Hard eyes and leveled gun enforced the command. Tanner, cursing, fumbled in his pocket and money clinked as he tossed it to the boy.

"Get it, kid," Jiggs ordered, not taking his eyes from the men.

"I got it!" the boy called after a moment.

"Now scat." Jiggs backed toward the hitch rail, grinning faintly at the curses that showered upon him. "Coward" was the least thing he was called. His groping left hand touched leather, and, one by one, he freed the horses until only Placer was left. Placer, too, he untied and led out, keeping the horse between himself and the men as he mounted. Secure in the saddle, Jiggs spoke again.

"Just to teach you." He put spurs to Placer and the dun horse jumped his full length. Jiggs yelled, shrill and high. The gun in his hand exploded twice, lead smacking into the roof of the store's porch.

266

The freed horses stampeded, and, as Jiggs bore down on them, Tanner and his men scattered like quail. Placer, indignant at his treatment, pounded down the road. Jiggs fired one more exultant shot, slid his gun into its holster, and began to laugh.

CHAPTER
TWO

Night came before Jiggs reached camp. Ceferino's expectancy changed into a bad case of sulks when he learned that Jiggs had not brought coffee. Nor did the account of the business at Tanner's store better matters. Supper was cooked, but without coffee. Ceferino said he didn't feel like eating. He would hardly answer Jiggs's questions. The hawk-faced man, Ceferino said, was named Crown, and he was *muy malo*. The others Ceferino didn't know, or claimed not to know. He made an announcement when Jiggs had loaded his plate and begun to eat.

"*Mañana* I'm theenk I go home. My wife, she's want me."

This development did not suit Jiggs at all. He had counted on Ceferino to stay with him until he got his cattle located behind a fence. He tried to talk Ceferino out of the idea but had no luck.

"*Mañana*," Ceferino said firmly, "I'm go home. *Voy a mi casa.*"

That was that. Jiggs swore and, opening a can of peaches, loaded his plate again, putting half the can fully on another plate in an attempt to tempt Ceferino. It didn't work. Jiggs threw away the can and sat down.

He had a big, smooth bite of peach in his mouth when something cold touched his neck. He jumped a foot.

Out beyond the firelight the towheaded kid said: "Don't do that, Tige." The blue roan dog, ears erect and head cocked, was beside Jiggs.

"Come into camp, kid," Jiggs ordered.

The boy advanced into the firelight, tentatively offering the remnants of the five-pound sack of coffee. Ceferino took it.

"You walked from the store out here?" Jiggs demanded.

"Yes, sir. I waited till Tanner an' them went inside, then I scraped up the coffee an' followed along the road till I seen your fire."

"*Mmm*," said Jiggs. Ceferino was putting coffee into the pot. "What's your name?"

"Beau . . . Beauford Jackson Wright."

"Had your supper?"

"No, sir."

Jiggs got a plate, loaded it, and handed it to the boy. Beauford Jackson Wright was plenty hungry. So was the dog, who nudged Jiggs's leg. Jiggs cleaned the Dutch oven of bread, mopped the frying pan, and fed the dog.

"Won't your folks be worryin' about you?" he asked the boy.

"I ain't got no folks." Beau looked up briefly. "They're dead."

"Don't you live with somebody?"

"I used to. I don't now."

"Can you ride a horse?"

The boy looked at Jiggs, just the beginnings of hope flickering in his eyes. "I can ride some. We used to have milk cows an' I herded 'em."

Jiggs thought a while. "You asked me for a job this afternoon," he said suddenly. "Still want one?"

"Yes, sir!" Beau's voice trembled.

"Then," said Jiggs, "you're hired. Ten dollars a month an' I'll furnish your outfit." He had never seen eyes like the boy's. There was a flame in them and they were filled with longing. Jiggs did not dare to keep on looking at Beau. If he did, he would walk over, pick up the kid, and hug him, and this had to be man's business. "Suit you?"

"*Yes, sir!*" The answer fairly exploded from the eager-faced Beau.

"Then you're workin' for me. Beginnin' right now."

The blue roan dog nudged Jiggs's arm. Jiggs turned his head. "Ain't you satisfied?" he began. "I done fed you an' . . . Well, shucks! He's brought me a present."

The bright tin can that had contained the peaches lay between the dog's paws. He pushed it toward Jiggs with his nose.

"Tige always does that when he likes you," explained Beau. "He wants to shake hands now."

Sure enough, the dog was holding out a paw. Jiggs took the paw and shook it gravely.

Ceferino, his ruffled feelings soothed by coffee and what food Beau had left, made an overture. "Meester Jeegs, I'm theenk mebbe my wife don' want me now. I'm theenk I stay."

"An' I think" — Jiggs got up — "that one cowhand an' a boss is all this outfit can stand. Tomorrow you roll your bed an' cut your string, Ceferino. No man quits me twice."

Jiggs began to pull soogans from his bedroll. "You can make your bed by the fire," he told Beau. "As soon as we get these cattle located, we'll see what we can do about an outfit for you."

When Jiggs awakened next morning, Beau was out wrangling wood for the fire. Immediately after breakfast Jiggs paid Ceferino and sent that worthy on his way. Then, with Beau mounted bareback on sedate Chub, the cattle were bunched.

There were twenty-two head, four old bulls, ten cows, and eight drafty, rangy steers. Jiggs explained to Beau what was to be done. Until a pasture was acquired, it was Beau's business to herd parada.

"Just watch 'em," Jiggs told the boy. "Go around 'em if they start to scatter, but don't try to hold 'em close."

Beau nodded his understanding and pointed past Jiggs. "There's somebody comin'."

Reining Placer around, Jiggs saw a horseman coming from the west.

The newcomer, when he arrived, proved to be small and grizzled with cowman stamped on him in letters a foot tall. He rode around the loosely bunched cattle, scanning them with sharp eyes, reined in, produced the makings, and began to roll a cigarette.

"Campin' here or figurin' to stay?" he inquired after he had licked the flap.

"We camped here last night," Jiggs answered. "The place seemed to be deserted."

"It is." The newcomer scratched a match. "Old Spur line camp. There ain't no more Spur. This is government land. Aim to homestead?"

"No." Jiggs grinned. "I'm buyin' cattle. I want to get a place to hold these an' put some more with 'em. I ain't a nester. My name's Maunday."

"Rodrick." The small man nudged his horse forward and held out his hand for Jiggs to shake. "I run the Two X down under the mesa."

"You're ridin' early," Jiggs ventured.

"I ride early every mornin'." Rodrick's black eyes were keen. "I make a pretty wide circle. That's the only way to do when you got some folks for neighbors. That your kid?"

"He's workin' for me."

Rodrick removed his cigarette and eyed it. "An' you want a place to hold your cattle while you try to buy more?" he drawled. "Why don't you get a winter wheat pasture?"

"I hadn't thought of it."

"Good for the cattle an' don't hurt the wheat," Rodrick told him. "Old Man Pruitt is just north of you. That's his fence. Why don't you go and see him?"

"Thanks. I will."

Rodrick took two more drags on his smoke, then ground it out against his saddle horn. "I'll see you," he announced. "I live just about halfway down Oso Cañon. Maybe I've got some old cows that you'd want."

"I'll be over," Jiggs promised. "Thanks, Mister Rodrick."

Rodrick lifted his hand and his bay moved off. The horse was a good one, Jiggs could see. Nothing unusual in that. A man like Rodrick would ride good horses.

"You stay with these cattle, Beau," Jiggs directed. "I'm goin' down to see Pruitt."

Pruitt's house was a tar-paper shack, and the farmer was in the yard tinkering with a wagon. He came to the gate, a tall, stooped, white-haired man, and looked up at Jiggs. Dismounting, Jiggs gave his name and stated his business, mentioning that Rodrick had sent him.

Old Man Pruitt thought about Jiggs's request, his faded blue eyes scanning the cowboy's face. "Rodrick is a pretty fair neighbor," Pruitt said at last. "How much would you pay for the pasture?"

"Two bits a head a month," answered Jiggs.

"Come on to the house," Pruitt said. "I want to see what Freeda thinks about it."

The tar-paper shack was glitteringly clean inside and there was a wonderful scent of baking cinnamon rolls, but Jiggs hardly noted the cleanliness or the odor. Thirty seconds after he had stepped in the door and heard Old Man Pruitt say, "This is Mister Maunday, Freeda," Jiggs could not have told whether he was leasing wheat pasture or walking on a cloud.

Freeda Pruitt was not tall nor was she short, but just right. Her eyes were blue, her cheeks were flushed with her baking, her lips were rose-red, her hair, in two neat braids around her head, glistened like a brand-new $20 gold piece. She was something to see and Jiggs looked as hard as he could while Pruitt explained what was wanted.

Freeda thought it would be all right to lease the winter wheat for pasture. She asked questions that Jiggs somehow managed to answer, and she came up with a practical suggestion. The old Espuela line camp could be made habitable, and Jiggs could stay there where he could look after his cattle.

Jiggs thought that was wonderful, and not on account of the camp's being close to the pasture, either. He paid Pruitt $5.50, a month's pasturage in advance, and he ate two cinnamon rolls and drank two cups of coffee. What happened between then and the time he found himself on Placer, riding back to camp, he didn't really know. From the minute Jiggs stepped into Pruitt's house, he was hooked and his bobber sunk. By the time he got back to the camp, he had recovered a little. Freeda Pruitt was just a mighty pretty nester girl, Jiggs kept telling himself, but she wasn't anything special. He knew that he was lying.

Beau and Tige and the cattle were all accounted for when Jiggs returned. The three of them drove the herd to a gate and pushed the cattle and loose horses through. Jiggs thought that he would get Pruitt to sell him some feed so that he could grain his horses every morning. They watched the cattle spread out and begin to graze on the dark green growth, then, side-by-side, boy and man rode back to the windmill.

274

The inside of the soddy was littered and filled with dirt. Jiggs and Beau set about cleaning it. They worked hard, Beau thinking about his job, Jiggs about Freeda.

Beau spoke first. "Mebbe you won't need me, now that you got a pasture for the cows."

"Huh?" Jiggs said. "What's that?"

Beau repeated his statement, and Jiggs, coming back to the present, scowled portentously. "You tryin' to quit?" he demanded.

"No. Only —"

"I need you to stay right here an' look after them cattle," Jiggs interrupted. "Come on. Let's get the outfit in here. It's clean enough."

Beds and packs were carried in. Beau built a fire in the fireplace at the end of the soddy. After they had eaten, while the boy washed the dishes, Jiggs dug out some spare clothes. They didn't come anywhere near fitting Beau.

"We got to get you some clothes an' some shoes," Jiggs stated. "I got a piece of buckskin that might make moccasins for you. Let's see."

The buckskin, produced from Jiggs's bedroll, appeared to be big enough. Jiggs was working on it, sewing a pair of clumsy moccasins, when someone called outside. Boy and man went to the door. Freeda Pruitt and her father, mounted on two work horses, were in front of the soddy.

At Jiggs's invitation they got down and came in, examining the housekeeping arrangements. Freeda had brought a pan of cinnamon rolls. Beau ate three. It was a nice, friendly visit. Pruitt and Jiggs went out to look at the corral and the windmill while Freeda took over the shoemaking. At the corral Pruitt told Jiggs about his hired hand.

Beau, Pruitt said, was an orphan. His father and mother had died in a diphtheria epidemic a year before. Since then the boy had lived with various families on the mesa.

"He won't stay with you," Pruitt warned. "There's been five different people tried to keep him. Him an' that dog always run off."

"I think he'll stay with me," Jiggs answered quietly. "An' I want to get him some clothes an' beddin'. Next time you go to town, I wish you'd take him with you an' buy him an outfit. I'll give you the money."

"Freeda's goin' in to town pretty soon," Pruitt said. "But why don't you go down to Tanner's store? He might have what you want."

Jiggs, liking the old man, informed him of his reasons for not going to Tanner's.

Pruitt frowned. "The bunch that hangs out at Tanner's is tough," he warned. "I've told 'em to stay off the place. You might have some trouble with 'em."

Jiggs shook his head. He thought that the men at Tanner's were four-flushers. Mean and troublemakers, yes, if they thought they could get away with it, but not really tough. Dismissing the difficulty at the store, he asked Pruitt about cattle on the mesa. Pruitt thought that Jiggs could buy quite a bunch. He gave directions and Jiggs put down the names in his dog-eared brand book.

276

"You an' the boy come over to supper tonight," Pruitt invited. "Me an' Freeda want you."

When the Pruitts left, Beau had on a brand-new pair of moccasins, made a lot better than Jiggs could have made them. Freeda echoed her father's invitation and Jiggs and Beau promised to come. After the Pruitts were gone, Jiggs shaved. Then he took an old blanket and, by trimming it and cutting a slit in the middle, made a serape for Beau.

"The Mexicans down in old Mexico wear 'em," Jiggs told the boy. "It'll keep you warm, anyhow."

Jiggs and Beau cut across the wheat field when they went to the Pruitts'. They came down the long slope to the house, went through a gate, and, reaching the yard, ran squarely into trouble. Pruitt at the gate to the road, his back turned, was laying down the law to a man on horseback.

"I've told you to stay off this place, Benton," Pruitt rasped. "An' I meant it. Freeda don't want to see you. Now git out!"

Jiggs rode over. The man facing Pruitt was Charlie, the young fellow who Jiggs had seen at Tanner's store. Charlie's face was red.

"I want Freeda to tell me that herself," he said doggedly. "The last time I saw her she didn't tell me not to come again. An' you were friendly enough."

"That was before I found out you hung around Tanner's drinkin' an' raisin' sand. You'll get in trouble with that bunch, Benton."

"What I do is my business," Charlie Benton said.

"Not if you want to come here, it ain't. You come botherin' around Freeda an' I'll run you off with a shotgun."

For the first time Benton saw Jiggs. His face grew even redder. "You damned old coyote!" he snarled at Pruitt, and, jerking his horse around, he pounded off down the road.

Pruitt stepped back, almost bumping into Jiggs's horse. "I ain't goin' to have any of that bunch on the place," he growled. "Charlie Benton used to be a pretty good boy. His daddy an' his mother were fine people, an' he's got a good place. But he won't have it long."

"He looks like a good kind of fellow," Jiggs said.

"He was all right till his folks died." Pruitt started back toward the house. "Since then, Charlie's gone clear bad. Put your horses in the pen, Maunday, an' come on in."

When Jiggs and Beau entered the house, Freeda was not in evidence. She came out of her bedroom presently, her face fixed in a smile of welcome. Jiggs could see, however, that the girl had been crying. Supper was not a talkative meal, and, shortly after it was over, Jiggs and Beau left. Jiggs surmised that Pruitt and his daughter had some talking to do.

CHAPTER
THREE

For the next five days Jiggs kept busy. Using the names Pruitt had given him, he traveled over the mesa and bought some cattle. At the end of the five days he had thirty-six head, and during those five days he had also seen Freeda Pruitt seven times. On the sixth day he started early, taking Beau and Tige with him, and headed for Rodrick's place.

The 2X, when Jiggs reached it, made him feel homesick. Rodrick had a real outfit down in Oso Cañon. The long, low house, the tight barn, the good sheds and pens, were just what a cowman would want. Jiggs had worked on many such a layout.

Rodrick was at home. He and two *vaqueros* were working cattle in the corral. The cowman made Jiggs and Beau welcome and promised to be with them as soon as he was through.

"We're cuttin' a little bunch," he explained, "an' there's some of them old cows I mentioned in it."

"I'll lend you a hand," Jiggs announced, and climbed down from Quién Sabe.

When the cattle were shaped up according to Rodrick's fancy, the men went to the house. Dinner was ready, and, when the meal was over, Jiggs and

Rodrick smoked. Tige, admitted with the others, sat at Rodrick's feet. After a time the dog walked over, picked up Jiggs's hat, and carried it to the ranchman.

"Bringin' you a present," Jiggs said, and explained Tige's habit of bringing a gift to those he liked.

Rodrick went through the handshaking ritual and said that he would get Tige something in return.

While the ranchman was in the kitchen, Beau spoke his thoughts. "Gee, but this is a swell place."

Jiggs felt a twinge of envy. There was a lot of difference between a place like the 2X and Jiggs's little greasy-sack outfit.

"Would you like to stay here?" he asked.

Beau didn't think when he answered. "Gee! I sure would."

Rodrick came back with a bone for Tige. The dog gnawed on it and Beau hovered by Rodrick's chair. After a time they went out to the corrals. Beau climbed up on the fence while Jiggs and Rodrick entered the pen.

"How did you an' the boy tie up?" Rodrick asked.

Jiggs related as much as he knew of Beau's story. "He's a good kid," Jiggs completed. "Funny, ain't it? If he'd been a calf, there'd be twenty men wantin' to put their brand on him. A dogie kid ain't got much chance."

Rodrick's eyes were sharp. "I'll take him," he offered. "It would be kind of good to have a kid around, an' I've got none of my own. Never got married. Never had time for it."

"The kid likes it here," Jiggs said. Then, ignoring Rodrick's offer: "What cows did you have in mind to sell?"

Rodrick showed Jiggs the cows and they bargained over the price.

When an agreement was reached, Jiggs had what he wanted, two carloads of cattle. Also, he had just enough money to ship them and to last until he received his check.

"Stay tonight," Rodrick invited. "I'll give you a hand up the hill with 'em tomorrow."

Jiggs agreed.

After supper that night, while Tige dozed over a second bone, Rodrick produced a pair of his boots. His feet were small and, by putting on three pairs of sox, the boots were a perfect fit for Beau.

"He'll outgrow 'em," Rodrick predicted. "That boy's goin' to have feet when he grows up."

Again, as he listened to Beau thank the ranchman for the boots, Jiggs felt a pang of envy. A pair of shop-made boots, almost new, was a far cry from homemade moccasins and a blanket serape.

The following morning Rodrick rode with Jiggs and Beau all the way to the wheat pasture. Freeda saw them as they put the cattle in and she came to the fence. When the men rode over, she told Jiggs that she was going to town the next day.

"I've got to go to Cantando myself," Jiggs told her. "I want to order some cars so I can ship. I wish you'd take Beau with you. It's pretty far for a bareback ride."

Freeda said that she would be glad to do so, and returned to the house.

Rodrick grinned at Jiggs. "Kind of like your neighbors, don't you?" he said.

"They're good people," agreed Jiggs.

Rodrick declined Jiggs's invitation to stay, and, as he rode off, Jiggs, Beau, and Tige went back to the old Espuela camp.

In the morning, early, Jiggs took Beau down to the Pruitts'. He saw the boy and Freeda load into a light spring wagon and start for town. Pruitt was not going. His back was bothering him and he said that he didn't want to jolt for fifteen miles in a wagon, then stay overnight in Cantando.

Jiggs took Chub back to the pasture and turned him out, then started for town himself. He passed Tanner's store, seeing no one, and, half a mile beyond, overtook Freeda and Beau. Charlie Benton was riding alongside the wagon when Jiggs came up.

Jiggs didn't say much to Freeda, simply that he would go on to town and meet her there. The girl's cheeks were flushed and her eyes bright. Jiggs rode on, sore at the whole world. He had gone about a mile when Charlie caught up with him.

"My name's Benton," the young farmer announced as he reined in beside Jiggs. "Freeda says your name's Maunday."

"That's right."

"I was in Tanner's the other evenin'." Charlie Benton did not look directly at Jiggs. "I'd been drinkin'. I want

282

to apologize, Maunday. I don't generally mix up in a thing like that, particularly in tryin' to cheat a kid."

Jiggs tried hard not to like Charlie Benton. He didn't want to like anybody who could make Freeda blush and her eyes sparkle like that. "That's all right," he said ungraciously.

"You heard Old Man Pruitt cuss me out," Benton went on. "I'm goin' to square things with him."

"You better leave him alone," Jiggs warned.

"I want to square up with him." Charlie disregarded the warning. "Well . . . I just wanted to tell you, Maunday. So long."

He loped away and Jiggs went on toward town.

The town of Cantando was just a single street with a railroad depot and two grain elevators at one end of it. There were a few houses scattered out behind the street. Jiggs completed his business with the agent, ordering two cars for his cattle. The agent said that before evening he should have word as to when the cars would arrive. Jiggs went back uptown. He visited the pool hall, passed up a saloon, and was loafing in front of a store when Freeda and Beau arrived.

Freeda left the boy with Jiggs while she drove on to her friend's house. Jiggs and Beau went to the general store. When Freeda returned, accompanied by her friend, Jiggs had almost completed Beau's outfitting.

The four ate dinner together at Cantando's small restaurant. Freeda's friend insisted that there was plenty of room at her home for Beau, and it was evident that the boy wanted to stay in town and show off his new finery. With the girls chattering to each other and Beau absorbed in his new outfit, Jiggs felt like a fifth wheel. He wished that there was some place in town where he could take Freeda, but Cantando had nothing to offer. After the meal the girls went home, taking Beau with them. Jiggs loafed at the depot until seven o'clock when the agent finally received an answer on the request for stock cars. Then Jiggs got on Quién Sabe and started for camp.

It was already dark when he left the town. By eight, halfway along the road, the moon came up. At nine o'clock Jiggs passed the Pruitts'. The house was dark and Jiggs surmised that the old man had gone to bed.

When he reached the Espuela camp, Jiggs let out Tige who had been left in the soddy with food and water. The dog was glad to see Jiggs and couldn't do enough to show it. Jiggs turned Quién Sabe into the wheat pasture and went to bed. He was lonesome and so was Tige, who curled up at his feet.

With no reason to get up early next morning, Jiggs loafed. When he did arise, he cooked and ate a leisurely breakfast, then went out to feed his horses. Only Quién Sabe was at the fence. Jiggs hung a gunny-sack feedbag on Quién Sabe's grulla head and stared at the pasture.

There was not an animal in sight. Usually cattle grazed along the fence, but not this morning. Jiggs waited until Quién Sabe had finished eating, then led the horse back to the soddy and saddled. With Tige trotting along beside him, he entered the wheat field.

There were no cattle at all grazing on the wheat. Jiggs found the gate to the road open and there the sign

284

was plain. Horse tracks, overlaying the cow tracks, showed where the stock had been driven through. Jiggs put Quién Sabe to a lope and headed toward the Pruitts'.

CHAPTER
FOUR

No one answered his knock. Jiggs beat on the door again and still no one came. The latch string was not dangling from its hole in the door. Tige began to bark excitedly, pointing his nose at the house and exhibiting all the symptoms of knowing that something was wrong. Jiggs rammed his shoulder against the door and heaved. Nothing gave. He tried again, and then again, and the door broke. Jiggs tumbled inside, propelled by his own thrust. Scrambling to his feet, he stared at the room.

Pruitt lay under the overturned table; blood pooled around his body. Kneeling, Jiggs saw that the old man had been shot twice, once in the body, once through the head. The farmer's shotgun lay near his lifeless, outstretched hand, the stock broken. Jiggs, examining it, saw that the gun had not been fired. Tige had come in and was sniffing at Pruitt's feet. Sternly Jiggs ordered the dog outside.

The room was a wreck. Chairs had been broken, the cupboard pulled down, and the stove overturned. Stepping back from Pruitt, Jiggs saw a shoe projecting from beneath the cupboard. He heaved the cupboard up, shoving it against the wall. There, where the cupboard had covered him, was Charlie Benton, and beside Benton, half concealed by his arm, was a Colt .45.

Again Jiggs knelt. Pruitt's body had been stiff with *rigor mortis*, but Benton's body was limp. His eyes were rolled back until only the whites showed, and, when Jiggs lifted him, Benton groaned faintly. Jiggs let the body slump back to the floor.

Outside, Tige was barking furiously. Stepping to the door, Jiggs saw the cause of the alarm. Rodrick, with one of his *vaqueros*, was riding down from the wheat field. Jiggs remembered what Rodrick had said: *I ride early every mornin'. I make a pretty wide circle.* He was mighty glad that the cowman had spoken truth. The two men pulled up in front of the Pruitts' house.

Rodrick was scowling. "I'm lookin' for ten head of steers," he announced crisply. "They were in the horse pasture above my place last night. This mornin' they're gone. We saw the tracks where they were drove into Pruitt's field."

"Did you see the tracks where they come out, along with my cattle?" Jiggs asked quietly. "Get down an' come in here, Rodrick. Pruitt's been killed."

Rodrick and the *vaquero* dismounted and followed Jiggs into the house.

"Great Scott!" Rodrick exclaimed. "Pruitt's dead?"

"As a last year's bird's nest," Jiggs said grimly. "Benton's alive. I don't know if he'll make it, though. His head's laid open."

They knelt beside Charlie Benton. He was breathing shallowly, and the gash in his head, laid open by the shotgun stock, was bleeding a little.

"Better get him out where we can look after him," Jiggs said. "I expect his skull's broke."

Lifting Benton, they carried him outside. While Jiggs brought water to wash Benton's wound, and found a clean dishtowel in the disordered house, Rodrick gave swift directions to his *vaquero*, bidding him ride to Cantando and bring out the deputy sheriff and the doctor. The rider departed at a long lope and Rodrick came back to help Jiggs.

"What do you think happened?" he asked.

"I don't know," answered Jiggs grimly. "But I do know this . . . Pruitt ran Benton off the place. Yesterday I saw Benton on the way to town. He kind of halfway apologized to me for somethin' that had happened, an' he told me that he was goin' to square things up with Pruitt."

"It looks like he done it. Has that Colt been shot?"

"I don't know," Jiggs said again. "I didn't look. The way Benton talked yesterday, he didn't mean nothin' like this. I thought he was goin' to try to fix things up with Pruitt."

"Maybe that's what he meant when he talked to you," Rodrick suggested. "Then, when him an' Pruitt got to talkin', trouble started. Benton's been drinkin' a lot lately."

Jiggs nodded soberly. "We might as well look around an' see what we can," he said. "We've got a long wait ahead."

Rodrick agreed. Tige was not in evidence when Jiggs and Rodrick went into the house. They examined it thoroughly, not moving anything, but looking carefully.

288

The two bedrooms were undisturbed; only the kitchen had been upset.

"This is goin' to be mighty tough on Freeda," Jiggs said.

"Yeah." Rodrick was thoughtful. "You kind of like her, don't you?"

"I do. So does Benton."

Their examination finished, the two men went outside and sat down beside Benton. He lay on blankets brought from the house, and two other blankets covered him. His appearance had not changed except that his eyes were closed.

"They'll pin it on him," Rodrick prophesied moodily. "With what you know, an' the way things were inside, they're bound to. That gun's been shot twice, too?"

Jiggs nodded. "Do you think this ties in with stealin' the cattle?" he asked.

"I don't see how," said the cowman.

"Who do you think got your steers an' my stuff?"

Rodrick looked at Jiggs narrowly. "You think the same as I do," he observed. "Tanner's bunch. But you'll never prove it. I've missed stock before an' thought they had 'em, but I couldn't prove they did."

"I'd like to do some lookin'," Jiggs said. "If it wasn't for this" — he gestured toward the house — "I would."

Tige came around the corner of the house, carrying something in his mouth. He lay down and chewed contentedly on it. Neither man paid any attention to the dog.

Three hours after the departure of Rodrick's *vaquero*, Price Logan, Cantando's deputy sheriff, arrived at Pruitt's house. Thirty minutes after Logan, Dr. Spruel drove up in his buggy. With the doctor was Freeda Pruitt. In the interim Logan had seen the body, examined the house, and heard from Jiggs and Rodrick concerning the missing cattle and the discovery of the tragedy. It was Freeda who gave Logan the first intimation of difficulties between her father and the injured man. She broke down when she saw her father's body, and, when she saw Benton lying inert under the blankets, she almost fainted.

"Why did you come, Charlie?" she wailed. "Why did you do it?"

Logan was an alert officer. Freeda's outburst gave him an inkling that there had been previous trouble. Questioning the girl was useless, so Logan went to work on Jiggs. Reluctantly Jiggs told of meeting Charlie Benton on the road. That was enough.

"I figure that Benton came over here to see Pruitt an' they fought," Logan said. "It's the only way you can figure it. Pruitt hit Benton with the shotgun an' Benton shot him."

Jiggs offered objections. How, he inquired, could a man who had been hit like Charlie Benton had been hit, do any shooting? And, conversely, how could a man shot through the head like Pruitt was, hit a man with a shotgun?

"I don't know," Logan answered honestly, "but it happened somethin' like that. Benton killed him, an' I'm goin' to arrest Benton for murder. How is he, Doc?"

Spruel, not sure whether Benton's skull was fractured, insisted that the injured man could not be moved, but must be put to bed.

290

Freeda had lapsed into an almost trance-like state and the doctor was worried. He wanted her taken to a neighbor's, but the girl, rousing, refused to go. After Benton had been carried in and placed on a bed, Rodrick rode off for help. He returned in less than an hour, accompanied by a raw-boned, competent-looking woman driving a wagon. Mrs. Thompson, the neighbor woman, took charge of Freeda, coaxing the girl to lie down in her bedroom and rest. Spruel stayed in the house where he could look after both Benton and the girl while Jiggs, Rodrick, and Logan squatted outside the door and smoked.

"What are you goin' to do now?" Jiggs asked the deputy quietly.

"I telegraphed the sheriff before I left," answered Logan. "He'll get here sometime tonight. I reckon we've got to hold an inquest. Tanner's the JP in this district. I expect I'd better tell him about it an' have things ready for the sheriff when he gets here."

Rodrick and Jiggs exchanged glances. "We'd ought to see if we can find them cattle," Rodrick said.

"I want you to stay here," Logan vetoed the rancher's suggestion. "Old Man Pruitt was pretty popular. When folks find out he's been killed, they're goin' to be stirred up. You can't tell what they'll do, an' I might need help. Here comes somebody now."

Indeed, a wagon was coming along the road. Jiggs stood up so that he could see, and then sat down again. "It's Beau," he explained. "Bringin' the Pruitt wagon out from town." Jiggs felt a thrill of pride. Beau was taking hold like a top hand.

Beau pulled into the yard and stopped the team. He was white-faced as he climbed down from the wagon. Tige, in ecstasy because his master had come, frisked around the boy. But Beau pushed him away and came straight to Jiggs who put an arm around the lad's sturdy shoulders.

Then others began to arrive. Word had spread to the neighbors, carried no doubt from the Thompsons'. Hard-faced men wearing bib overalls and brogans rode up on work horses, tied their mounts to the fence, questioned Logan, peered into the disorder of the Pruitt kitchen, and then stood around, their talk low-voiced and indistinct, but carrying an ominous growl.

Logan went into the house, returned, and addressed Jiggs and Rodrick. "You two are deputized," he said. "If I need help, I'm goin' to call on you."

Jiggs grunted. He was worried not so much about the forming crowd and what it might do, but about Beau. The boy was sticking close to him.

"You'd better go up to camp, Beau," Jiggs said.

Beau shook his head. "I'm goin' to stay with you," he answered.

Jiggs had no time to argue with the boy for Rodrick said sharply: "Here comes Tanner."

CHAPTER
FIVE

The storekeeper, accompanied by the hawk-faced
Crown and two other men, rode into the yard. They
came directly to Logan, dismounted, and formed a
group around him. Crown, glancing toward Jiggs,
scowled darkly.

The group broke up and Logan came back to
Rodrick and Jiggs. "I don't like this a little bit," he
announced. "Tanner says there's no need of an inquest,
and him and Crown are talkin' pretty tough about
takin' Benton in."

Dr. Spruel came out of the house and the men eyed
him questioningly. Spruel shrugged. "Just the same," he
said. "His pulse is a little better. I doubt that there's a
fracture. Freeda and Missus Thompson are sitting with
him."

"Freeda?"

"She says she knows Charlie didn't kill her father."

"An' I think she's right," declared Jiggs, his voice
firm and emphatic.

"Here they come," Logan growled.

The men in the yard, perhaps fifteen, all told, were
advancing toward the house, Tanner and Crown in the
lead. Jiggs, Rodrick, Logan, and the doctor formed an

irregular line in front of the door, Jiggs in the center and Beau just back of him.

The advancing men stopped, also forming a sort of line, and Tanner spoke levelly. "We want Benton."

Jiggs waited for the deputy sheriff to reply. When Logan didn't speak, Jiggs answered the storekeeper. "You can't have him."

Attention was focused on Jiggs. Crown was still scowling, but Tanner's face was impassive. The men with them stirred restlessly, and then came a diversion.

Tige had been trying in every way he knew to get his master's attention, but the boy was frightened and preoccupied. Now, resorting to an old trick that always worked, the dog brought Beau a present. Dangling from Tige's mouth was a mat of black hair, chewed and scuffed and dirty. Beau was behind Jiggs, and Tige laid his gift at Jiggs's feet, barking once sharply. Jiggs, watching Tanner narrowly, saw the man's lead-gray eyes change color. Glancing down, he saw Tige's gift and recognized it for what it was.

"A wig!" Jiggs exclaimed. "Tanner . . ."

There was no time for more. Tanner broke from immobility into action. His hand went into his pocket, and, jerking it up with a swift motion, he fired twice through his coat.

Jiggs had moved with Tanner. He thrust Beau down to the ground and went for his own gun.

Tanner's first shot cut Jiggs's holster from his belt just as the gun cleared. His second shot missed by inches. The big Colt kicked sharply into the fork of Jiggs's hand, once, twice, three times, as he thumbed hammer and fingered trigger. Tanner seemed to fold by sections, bending forward first, and then his knees giving way. As he fell, his hat rolled off and the man's bald head glistened.

In his concentration on Tanner, Jiggs had not noticed the action beside him. Now, with Tanner down, he saw that another man had fallen. Crown lay writhing on the ground, and from the corner of his eye Jiggs could see that both Rodrick and Logan held weapons. The crowd surged forward, breaking the spell in which sudden violence had held them, then, menaced by three leveled guns, the motion was checked.

"It was Tanner," Jiggs said hoarsely. "He killed Pruitt an' tried to kill Benton. Can't you see? He lost his wig in the fight an' the dog found it."

That did it. At the end of the line two men broke away and ran toward the horses. Pursuit was instantaneous. The two were brought back, struggling and fighting. The flight and capture relieved the tension, gave the crowd something to do, and momentarily distracted attention from Jiggs. He had, he knew, been lucky. If Tanner had pulled his gun and taken time to aim, instead of firing through his coat pocket, the results might well have been entirely different.

Dr. Spruel knelt beside Crown, working swiftly and deftly to check the man's bleeding. There was no use in working over Tanner. Jiggs had shot for keeps, and, while both Logan and Rodrick had fired on Crown, they had not been as accurate as their companion.

Jiggs, looking down at Tanner, felt a little sick. Then, remembering Beau, he went to the boy.

Beau was frightened. The swift, deadly action, the angry turmoil that followed, the dead man and the wounded man on the ground, had been entirely too much for him. Beau clung to Jiggs, hiding his face against Jiggs's chest as the man knelt and put his arms around the boy.

"It's all right, Beau," Jiggs reassured him. "It's all over now, kid."

Gradually Beau's shaking stopped. Jiggs was possessed of a happy thought. "Go in an' tell Freeda it's all right," he ordered. "Tell her that Benton's in the clear." He carried the boy to the door of the shack, set him down, and, putting his hand on Beau's back, gave a little shove.

Out in the yard Logan lifted his voice. "Crown's tryin' to say somethin'! Shut up!"

That brought comparative quiet. Logan's yell centered attention and brought a semblance of order. The men crowded around Crown, Logan, and the doctor.

Crown, afraid that he was dying, pleaded for mercy and sought to win help by telling the truth. With Tanner and two others, Crown had stolen Jiggs's cattle and Rodrick's steers. While in the wheat field, they had been discovered by Benton and Pruitt, who had come out of the house into the moonlit night. Tanner and Crown had ridden down from the field, answering Pruitt's challenge. It had been Tanner who shot Pruitt while Crown struck Benton down.

Pruitt and Benton had been carried into the house. There Tanner had hit Benton again, using Pruitt's shotgun. Afterward Tanner and Crown had broken up the furniture in the kitchen, making it appear that a fight had taken place, and had fired two shots from Benton's gun and put it beside his body.

"We thought Benton was dead," Crown said. "He wasn't breathin'. So we put the gun under him an' dumped the cupboard on top of him."

While Crown talked, the man made way for a white-faced girl. Freeda listened briefly, then, glory in her eyes, went running back to the house.

Crown's story was corroborated by the men who had tried to escape. They had stayed in the wheat field while Tanner and Crown went to the house, and they had heard the shots. They talked willingly enough, and in that talk disclosed the location of Rodrick's steers and Jiggs's cattle. They had had a lot of trouble moving Jiggs's bunch, the men said. The old bulls and cows were slow. They were not far away, hidden in a cañon on the eastern breaks of the mesa.

"Can he be moved, Doc?" Logan asked, when Crown had told his story.

Spruel nodded. "Crown's not hurt as badly as he thinks. You can move him."

"Then," Logan announced, "I'm goin' to take him an' them other two into town an' lock 'em up." He looked at the faces around him, daring anyone to object. No one did.

"Somebody can hitch up a team," Logan directed. "I want to get started. You come along, Maunday. You an' Rodrick."

Six hectic days followed for Jiggs Maunday. There were preliminary hearings to attend, and testimony to be given. Jiggs heard the Justice of the Peace in Cantando declare that Tanner had been killed in self-defense and that Jiggs Maunday was to be congratulated on good, straight shooting. He heard the JP bind Crown and his two companions over to a grand jury and set $10,000 bail for each. He went to Old Man Pruitt's funeral, standing beside the grave, with Beau's hand in his and his eyes fixed on Freeda's tear-stained face. There was another funeral that no one except two gravediggers attended. Tanner was buried by the county, and his store locked up and sealed, awaiting the action of the probate court.

Besides the legal business and the funeral, there was work to be done. Cattle and Jiggs's horses were brought from the hidden cañon and driven to the stockyards. Brands were inspected, and finally the cattle were loaded into cars.

At two o'clock in the afternoon of the sixth day, Jiggs Maunday stood beside Rodrick and watched a freight train pull away from the Cantando depot, heading east. On the rear step of the caboose the conductor waved a highball, and away ahead the whistle sounded twice.

"There they go," Rodrick said.

There, indeed, they went, two full carloads of cull cattle consigned to a commission house in Kansas City.

298

"I'm sure obliged for your help," Jiggs said.

"That's all right." Rodrick didn't look at Jiggs. "What are you goin' to do now, Maunday?"

"Wait for my check from the commission man," answered Jiggs.

"I mean, after that."

"I don't know."

Rodrick looked up, meeting Jiggs's eyes steadily. "Freeda will marry Charlie Benton as soon as he's well enough," he said.

"I know that."

"An' it kind of jolts you." Rodrick's black eyes were friendly and wise. "You're sweet on her. But it wouldn't work, Jiggs. They'll farm Charlie's place an' the Pruitt place. You'd never get a pair of two-buckle shoes on them feet of yours."

Involuntarily Jiggs glanced down at his feet, encased in tightly fitting, shop-made boots.

"You don't ride a gang plow in a pair of boots," Rodrick stated. "An' you sure don't need spurs to milk cows."

"No," agreed Jiggs.

"So," Rodrick continued, "you're better off. It hurts you now, but you'll get over it. What are you goin' to do about Beau?"

"Take him with me."

"No." Rodrick refuted the idea. "You can't. Beau's just a kid. He needs a home an' schoolin'. Somethin' he can tie to. I want to take Beau."

"The kid will want to go with me." Jiggs's voice was harsh.

"Sure, he'll want to," Rodrick agreed. "He's a loyal little cuss an' you're kind of his hero. He'll always remember you. But you can't take him, Jiggs."

"I guess you're right," admitted Jiggs. "I can't give him what you can, Rodrick."

"But you will be givin' it to him," Rodrick objected. "Don't you see that?"

In a way, Jiggs could see what Rodrick meant. By leaving Beau with the cowman, Jiggs would insure the boy's future.

Beau and Tige came out of the depot where they had been watching the telegraph operator. With the dog frisking about him, the boy came up to the men.

"Are we goin' pretty soon?" he asked.

"Back to the ranch," Rodrick said. "You go around an' get the horses, Beau."

Obeying Rodrick unquestioningly, Beau and Tige started off. That was the way it would be, Jiggs thought. By the time he had his check and was ready to pull out, Beau would be established at the 2X, settled on the place. It would hurt both of them when Jiggs left, but the hurt would heal. And it was the right thing to do.

"It looks like I got what the little boy shot at," commented Jiggs. "Nothin'."

"No," Rodrick disagreed. "That's not so. You see them hills away out there?"

Away beyond the smoke of the crawling freight train Jiggs could see the dim blue lines of mountains against the sky.

"That's what you get," Rodrick continued. "There's them hills . . . an' there's a lot more. You're young,

Jiggs. Someday you'll set down an' stay in a place. Someday you'll find what you want. But not here, an' not yet. Before you do that, you'll look at the other side of a heap of mountains."

Looking at the line of hills away off in the distance, Jiggs Maunday's eyes lost their somberness. He stirred a restless foot.

"An' I can always come back," he said almost absently.

Beau and Tige came around the end of the depot, the boy leading three horses.

"Sure," Rodrick agreed, "you can always come back." He started toward the horses and his words were pitched so low Jiggs could not hear them. "But you won't."

About the Author

Bennett Foster was born in Omaha, Nebraska, and came to live in New Mexico in 1916 to attend the State Agricultural College and remained there the rest of his life. He served in the U.S. Navy during the Great War and was stationed in the Far East during the Second World War, where he attained the rank of captain in the U.S. Air Corps. He was working as the principal of the high school in Springer, New Mexico, when he sold his first short story, "Brockleface", to *West Magazine* in 1930 and proceeded to produce hundreds of short stories and short novels for pulp magazines as well as *The Country Gentleman* and *Cosmopolitan* over the next three decades. In the 1950s his stories regularly appeared in *Collier's*. In the late 1930s and early 1940s Foster wrote a consistently fine and critically praised series of Western novels, serialized in *Argosy* and Street & Smith's *Western Story Magazine*, that were subsequently issued in hardcover book editions by William Morrow and Company and Doubleday, Doran and Company in the Double D series. It is worth noting that Foster's early Double D Westerns were published under the pseudonym John Trace, although some time later these same titles, such as *Trigger Vengeance* and *Range of Golden Hoofs*, appeared in the British market under his own name. Foster knew the terrain and the people of the West first-hand from a lifetime of living there. His stories are invariably authentic in detail and color, from the region of fabulous mesas, jagged peaks, and sun-scorched deserts. Among the most outstanding of his sixteen previously published Western novels are *Badlands* (1938), *Rider of the Rifle Rock* (1939), and *Winter Quarters* (1942), this last a murder mystery within the setting of a Wild West show touring the western United States. As a storyteller he was always a master of suspenseful and unusual narratives.

ISIS publish a wide range of books in large print, from fiction to biography. Any suggestions for books you would like to see in large print or audio are always welcome. Please send to the Editorial Department at:

ISIS Publishing Limited
7 Centremead
Osney Mead
Oxford OX2 0ES

A full list of titles is available free of charge from:

Ulverscroft Large Print Books Limited

(UK)
The Green
Bradgate Road, Anstey
Leicester LE7 7FU
Tel: (0116) 236 4325

(Australia)
P.O. Box 314
St Leonards
NSW 1590
Tel: (02) 9436 2622

(USA)
P.O. Box 1230
West Seneca
N.Y. 14224-1230
Tel: (716) 674 4270

(Canada)
P.O. Box 80038
Burlington
Ontario L7L 6B1
Tel: (905) 637 8734

(New Zealand)
P.O. Box 456
Feilding
Tel: (06) 323 6828

Details of **ISIS** complete and unabridged audio books are also available from these offices. Alternatively, contact your local library for details of their collection of **ISIS** large print and unabridged audio books.